FINDING HOPE

Berkshire, England

by
K. M. Buckland

For Carrie,

Welcome to the World of Hope.

Enjoy.

Katy xxx

Strategic Book Publishing and Rights Co.

Strategic Book Publishing and Rights Co.
12620 FM 1960, Suite A4-507
Houston TX 77065
www.sbpra.com

ISBN: 978-1-62212-007-9

To my darling daughter, Kaye.

You are the piece of Hope I was looking for.

xxx

Acknowledgements

A massive and great big thank you to my wonderful husband, who has shared me with my writing for many years and only complained a couple of times.

A big squeeze for the 'real' Ali, who very kindly approved of this book before anyone else.

And huge hugs to my wonderful friends and family who have supported me, with a special and extra large hug for the 'other' K.M.B., who has been the best at encouraging me. Love ya, Mrs.

xxx

Contents

PREFACE

In the darkest depths of my mind, my memory sees a light in the distance, flickering like the flame of a candle. The light draws closer to me as a velvet voice follows its path.

"The speck of light that brightens the dark." Its presence is calming even though it doesn't seem human.

"She is a warrior of magic," the man says, "a creature of the ancient ways and a guide to the modern world. She has fought for the acceptance of a united magic and a form of balance. Her immortal soul has continued in this quest for many lifetimes, seeking a family of love, blood, and magic." The explanation is true, but my heart yearns for more—a yearning that causes my body to ache.

The man takes my hand and I feel his fear for the future. I feel his pain as I look into his brown eyes. I couldn't give him what he wanted—not all of it, at least—and for that I was truly sorry.

"She seeks an alternative peace. That is why she is still alive."

Another man says, "She seeks a time of acceptance: a time when what is old and what is new can co-exist."

"She has no fight left in her," a familiar voice says, taking my other hand. "Peace has become impossible and without her I fear the scales will tip forever. Without her we have no hope of gaining any form of balance. Is there nothing that can be done?"

A thoughtful silence hangs in the air for a long moment. With each heartbeat, the individual sighs grow less hopeful, and despair fills the air.

A new voice interrupts the silence. "She is the key to our future because she is a part of all our pasts. Her blood is what will save us, but she must give it willingly."

"But she has no incentive to stay or to fight again. She does not love as we do. She does not feel the need for another. She is alone and she is tired." A young woman's voice pleads as I continue to lie still.

The velvet, inhuman voice whispers to my mind. *Child, could you open your heart to a greater power? Could you accept your true self as you evolve into the unique creature that you shall become?* I cannot move my lips to speak; the only movement is a single tear that rolls down my cheek as my pain reaches deep within me. A greater power seems such a burden to carry, and a burden I fear I no longer have the strength for.

You are blessed with a heart of such strength and power that your kindness has been misunderstood. You have wept for those that have gone but have continued to fight for the balance that our world needs. Another tear rolls down my cheek as I feel the bitterness of my lonely existence. Although I had chosen it, it still hurts. *If you open your heart to love in all ways, your burden will become light. Your kindness will be reciprocated with friendship and family, and even a true love.* I cannot even frown at the comment. I am a warrior; I cannot love, and I cannot have friends or family. A warrior's life is a lonely one. *Accept what has already begun to evolve within you. You are no longer a warrior. You will always be a creature made by the ancients, but let yourself be filled with a power that is older than time itself. The decision will always be yours, but you will not die on this night.*

The velvet voice speaks aloud so that those surrounding my body can hear. "Her soul must rest until a time comes that her heart can be calmed. We must each sacrifice a piece of ourselves to ensure a balanced future. Only once she has willingly given her blood will those pieces be returned. She will need our guidance and our protection until that time comes." All those surrounding me agree willingly, each of them placing a hand on my body. "When her decision is made, she shall make her final journey and fulfil her purpose. Peace will follow when the balance is restored."

Together, the voices surrounding me chorus in their spell. "We return hope to the earth's plane. Let her soul rest until a time of acceptance is upon us. Only when her heart is calmed with the love of a soul mate will she restore the balance. As we command it, so shall it be." With their spell complete my soul heals my body, and with a sigh of relief, I fall into a deep sleep.

***

"Awake dear, one," a voice whispers. This voice is sweeter than any other, and yet familiar from so many previous dreams.

"Who are you," said the caterpillar. This was not an encouraging opening for a conversation. Alice replied, rather shyly, "I—I hardly know, Sir, just at present—at least I know who I was when I got up this morning, but I think I must have changed several times since then." – Lewis Carroll, Alice in Wonderland.

1: FAMILY & PRESENTS

Beep, beep, beep, beep.

Saturday, 6:30 a.m. Time to get up. Today's going to be a long day.

I reel through my list of things to do for the day while I dress in jeans and a t-shirt. Breakfast, to the yard, muck out the horses, take Bee out, check on the foals, and then to Nicky's to have my hair done, meet up with Ali, and then home for our final preparations for tonight's party.

Goodness—definitely a long day.

Tonight's party is a gift from my Aunt Dion (D for short), because from next week I'm on my trip of a lifetime, apparently: an alleged journey around the globe, which my family (although none of us are related by blood) had organized. They had scheduled all flights, train rides, visits—the lot—right up until New Year, when I'm *allowed* to wander alone.

I know I should be grateful for their concern, and to be fair, I am. I know full well I wouldn't have been able to organize flights and places to stay for the next six months without making a real "pig's ear" of it. But somehow my decision to take a gap year has been taken as a time for a long line of lessons. Although I'm excited about travelling, even if it is with various chaperones, I'm a little sad to be leaving—my aunt, my home, Mister Bee, and best friend, Ali.

Ali has been my best friend since her first day at secondary school. We have laughed and suffered all trials that we have faced together: from periods and boyfriends to A-levels and exams. Now we'll be going our separate ways for the first time. Ali starts at Winchester University in September, doing a degree in Art History, and is working all of the summer to save some money for her beer fund. She's taking a few days out from her "slave labour" to join me in London before I meet up with my first chaperones, Uncle Kirk (Professor Kirk Dobie) and my Aunt Louise.

***

As I come down the stairs into the kitchen, D is already up making toast and pouring tea.

"Good Morning, Hope" she says cheerily. It was amazing to me that even after all these years the woman is still chirpy in the morning, knowing full well she sleeps less than I do.

"Morning," I reply, still feeling sleepy. I sit down at the table and start sipping at the tea, trying to coax my brain into gear.

"So the caterers will be here around four to set up the hog roast. The marquee is on its way now, so that will be up by lunchtime, and then Emma and Sophie will be here to sort out the decorations. So I guess you and Ali just need to be down here on the dance floor by eight looking absolutely stunning." Again, amazing—if you had seen us three months ago, you wouldn't think it was the same people here now. Ever since my 18th birthday it's like a huge weight has been lifted off her shoulders. I don't know if it's because I'm now legally an adult and that her ties to me are no longer necessary, but as the weight has lifted off her shoulders, I feel an immense increase in mine.

***

Aunt D has been my guardian since I was born. My mother passed away a few days after my birth. The memories I have of her are my aunt's: the stories of the two of them climbing trees to pick apples, or walking through the woods collecting wild flowers is a connection. I adore these second-hand memories, but wish I had some of my own.

My father, labelled a coward by D, has not been seen since my mother was pregnant with me. I have not once received a birthday card or even a letter to say that he still exists. Or cares. Hence, D doesn't talk about him.

My 18th birthday had been agreed to be a family affair, as I would have a party after my exams. The day was much the same as any other. Although as the day went on, it gradually became crowded with my unrelated family. My aunt, the chef of the family, cooked a mass of food and it was like a normal family dinner.

My gifts, however, were not.

A long purple coat from Peter and Sarah; it's like satin only thicker, and it sparkles, not like glitter, but as if tiny diamonds were embedded within its weave.

Kirk and Louise had given me a new set of paints and several large canvases, no doubt for my visit with them. Kirk is more of an artist than a professor of its history. Olly (Oliver the adventurer) had given me a hat. It's just like Crocodile Dundee's, but without the teeth.

Simon and Joanna had given me a beautiful silver-handled dagger. Its blade was an intense midnight blue with shots of purple, just like how I'd imagined the northern lights to be—swirling through the blues and purples as it moves in the sky.

Terry had given me two sets of walking boots—one pair is ankle boots and the other pair is knee high and fleece lined.

My Aunt D gave me a simple silver bracelet with two charms hanging from it: an apple and a forget-me-not.

All of the gifts had a tag that read: "For your journey."

This is a journey that apparently involves lots of walking, a need for sparkling coats, and a dagger, and somewhere in between there'll be time for painting.

My aunt had decided that I was at the age that I could inherit my mother's things, after all my years of begging and her refusing, saying, "You're too young for such things." Eventually, she gave in and presented me with my mother's wooden box.

The box is made of rosewood and is engraved on all sides with pictures of animals, flowers, people, the moon and the stars, and the sun and the sea. I've admired the box all my life. My Aunt insisted that I had to wait until I was at the proper age before I could open it. When I finally opened it, I found myself disappointed. Within the box was a leather-bound book with a plaque on the front. The plaque was blank, as were the pages inside the book. My heart sunk as I flipped through the pages, finding nothing. The one thing I had wanted for so long had proven to be empty. Not just of words, but of my mother.

***

I walk into the hall, finishing my toast as I grab my bag and pull on a pair of wellies.

"Don't forget I'm going to Nicky's for 12 o'clock and then I'm meeting up with Ali. So I'll see you this afternoon," I shout. D appears around the corner, clipboard in hand. *Oh hell. Sergeant Major D is in control today. Get out while you still can.*

"Okay, are you and Ali having some lunch while you're out?"

"I think so." I hesitate. "Unless you want us here to help?" *Please say no. Please say no. The crazy woman's got her clipboard. This can only end in bloodshed.* Although I do love my aunt, she's very controlling and can get quite stressed, and I would rather be out of the way even if I don't have a say in my own party. I don't want to fall out with her just before I leave over something trivial, like the color of the balloons or the shapes of confetti. It's just not worth it.

She smiles. "No. You and Ali have fun. I'm sure I'll be fine without you." And then she whispers, "Especially with Sergeant Major D in charge!" *No way.* I didn't say that out loud. Maybe we've talked about it before—her and her clipboard. I can't remember. I look back at her, trying not to look shocked and confused.

"Well, with the Sergeant Major in charge, the party will go off without a hitch." I give her a gentle hug. I grab my keys and head out the door.

I'm just about to start the car when I hear a knock at the window. I wind down the window. It's the postman. "This is for you, Love. I need a signature." He passes me a large envelope and I sign the slip.

"Thanks," I say, and toss the envelope into the glove box, knowing that I don't have time to open it; I'm going to be late.

2: LAST RIDE OUT WITH MISTER BEE

I park the Land Rover under the trees and leave the windows open. I can't believe how hot it is. I walk over to the stables, bracing myself for my last dose of mucking the horses out. I find Bee tied up and tacked with a big red bow on the saddle and a note tucked under the stirrup leathers.

> Everything's done. Just go out for a long ride with Bee. Don't forget he's an old man now. Take it steady. Let him out with the others when you're back.
>
> See you later,
>
> Jen
>
> xxxx

Bless her—my last ride with Bee and no mucking out. Yippee! I get my hat and lead him out into the yard. Not wanting to waste any time, I mount up and grab the reigns. "So, where shall we go?" I ask out loud. Knowing full well I wasn't going to get a reply, I say, "Well, seeing as it's our last ride, I think we'll go up to the Brail." We cross the road and walk gently onto the bridal way.

The Brail is a large wood between the two Bedwyns. There are many trails that entwine in and around the wood, with one long, wide track that runs down the middle like a main road. There is an old, tired cottage at the far end; it was probably pretty once, but is long forgotten now.

Bee and I have been coming here since he first came home with me nearly ten years ago. My Aunt and I bought him after seeing him at a show. The previous owner had said that he was past his "sell by date" because of his age and would be no good for further eventing.

That was fine, as I didn't want a horse for that; I merely wanted a companion when I went out painting or drawing, so he came home with us and began a life away from the show ground.

***

Mister Bee is a seventeen hand, absolutely handsome Connemara. He's a deep chestnut color except for a small white star on his forehead. His temperament is quite surprising for a horse of his age (nearly 25 human years). He gets enormous bouts of energy and needs to run or gallop. One time, we were out on the Gibbet at Coombe, and he suddenly bolted. By the time we had stopped we were in Oxenwood, nearly five miles away from the Gibbet.

I remember telling my aunt and her flying off the handle. "Why didn't you try and stop him? What if you'd fallen off and hurt yourself?"

"Well, maybe he needed a good run as much as I did." I'd never felt unsafe with Bee, even with his occasional bolting, but after that time at the Gibbet I didn't tell my aunt about Bee's bolting again.

It was a need to release—stresses, troubles, everything—and let the air rush around us as we galloped along the fields and meadows.

***

As the bridleway begins to open out into the Denford meadows, Bee begins dancing and getting ready to go flat out across the lush, green meadow.

"Are you sure?" I ask with concern and a bit of excitement. Jen would kill me if he had a heart attack or something, but I know how much we both love to go fast. "I know it's our last time out, but are you sure you don't want to take it steady?" Bee whinnies loudly in reply, almost as if he was saying, "Come on. Just let yourself go." I let the reigns go and hold onto the buckle. And we're off, flat out, faster than ever before.

The greens and golds of the meadow become a blur as we gallop along and enter the woods. Bee doesn't slow down as we weave through the trees, causing me to duck around branches and young trees. He's never gone this fast through the wood before. I begin to get concerned as the weaving becomes narrower and the trees are bashing my knees. I lift up my head to take hold of the reigns and

16

bang headfirst into a thick low branch. I fly through the air, and land on the ground with a heavy thud.

My head feels fuzzy as I try to open my eyes. I can't. Then suddenly, I feel this overwhelming warmth—not as in physically warm, but in that warm, fuzzy feeling of love—like a glowing sensation. I can feel someone crouching next to me, and I hear the sound of fabric moving in the breeze, yet I can't move. I make myself open my eyes and I'm faced with a woman wearing a hooded velvet robe, the folds of which showed different shades of violet. She seems so familiar, but I can't place her.

Who is she? Her hair frames her face; it's a subtle brown with sun-kissed streaks, like mine. Her eyes are a deep brown with hints of purple, also like mine. Her heart-shaped face with rosy cheeks has a subtle bronze tone, like mine.

Oh God, I'm dead. Hit my head and bam—I'm dead. No trip around the world, no handsome boyfriend. No nothing. No wonderful, amazing life to leave behind. The woman shakes her head.

"I'm not dead?" I ask, shocked.

"In fact, I'd say you're just about to start living," the woman says in reply.

"But . . ." I'm too confused to understand.

"You're at an age that you can now embrace your gifts."

"Huh?"

She looks up as a small ball of light floats toward us. I start to panic. *She was lying. I'm definitely dead. Glowing light, can't feel my body, definitely dead.*

"No, my sweet, really—you're not dead." I look at her, trying to find some truth in her eyes, as the ball of light floats in the air before us. "Hope. The world you've grown up in is about to change."

"Why?" I ask.

"The answers will come. Just follow your heart." She leans forward and kisses my forehead, and then she's gone, as is the ball of light.

I hear Bee nibbling grass near me. I open my eyes and struggle to my feet. I look at the low branch and I can see where I hit it; the moss from the tree is smeared into my clothes. I take off my hat, which is covered in moss too. *Wow. I must have blacked out.* I touch my head, waiting to feel the tenderness of cuts and bruises, and think that today was maybe not the best day to be going quickly through the woods, but there's nothing. I breathe a deep sigh of relief. I stretch out my arms and legs, letting the bones and muscles crack back together. I'd actually say I'm feeling pretty good considering I just clouted into a tree. I look at Bee, who's still happily nibbling.

"I don't know," I say with my hands on my hips. "So much for being an old man." I cross my stirrups over the saddle and take the reigns over Bee's head. "Maybe we'll just walk for a bit, alright?"

I stroll along through the wood, with Bee's nose gently nudging me now and then. As we break through into the clearing I get the feeling that I'm being watched. I scan the clearing and see nothing. Then, I look again, and I see a large deer staring at me from the other side of the clearing. Its dark eyes fixate on me. I stop, not wanting to scare it. It's still staring. I look at Bee out of the corner my eye and he seems to do the same, like he's wondering the same thing: *why is that deer staring at us?* They usually run away before we can see them, leaving us to hear only the gentle patter of their hooves in retreat. I take a step forward and the deer mirrors my movement, making the distance between us smaller. Curiosity has started to burn in me now; I'm amazed that a deer seems so brave to be edging closer to a human. I search in my saddlebag for some carrot sticks (I keep some with me for Bee), never letting my eyes leave the deer's. I gingerly take a few more steps closer, as does the deer. I quickly look back to see that Bee has not moved. I stop, trying not to frighten the poor creature. I hold out my hand with the carrots in my palm. The deer stretches its neck toward my hand and sniffs at the carrots. The lip of its mouth picks at the carrot before it starts to chew. As its nose touches my hand, I feel that comforting warmth again, and as I look at my hand where the deer nibbles at the carrots, there's a glow, brightest where we touch, like a piece of sunshine with rays of light spinning off in all directions.

"Thank you," I hear a soft male voice say.

"You're welcome," I whisper in reply, so as not to startle him or myself. When the deer finishes the carrots it just stares at me, again, but this time it's comfortable being so close to a human.

"Can I?" I whisper, raising my hand as to touch him. The deer pushes its head into my hand and the glow shines brighter than before as we touch. I close my eyes, embracing the immense feeling of the deer. In my head I can sense the strength and grace of the animal and feel the speed of its run through the woods.

When I open my eyes the deer is gone, and I'm laid out on the ground. *Did I black out again?* I look at my watch. It's quarter to eleven. We've been out for over two hours. We don't seem to have got very far. I see Bee grazing on the other side of the clearing, and I start to walk over to him. Suddenly I'm right next to him. I look back to where I had been. It had to have been five hundred feet, at least. *Oh dear.* I think I might have banged my head pretty hard. I can't remember walking from A to Bee, and I'm having a weird hallucination. Maybe I'd better ride home. I check over Bee, thinking how loyal a horse he is for not wondering off while I blacked out. I mount up and we head home.

Sadness fills me as we plod along the main track. This will be our last time out together. Aunt D has suggested that Bee go for retirement and live out his final days in some sort of rest. He'd grown quite grey in the last few months and painfully slow, except for his occasional outbursts. The vet had said to have him put down, but I couldn't bare it. The vet asked me to consider that the winter months may not be so kind to him, and having him put to sleep would be kinder, but I couldn't. I didn't agree with it. It's not mine or even the vet's decision to end Mister Bee's life.

"Maybe you'll be reincarnated into a dappled Mustang. Then you could run faster than the wind." He snorts as if in agreement. I'd miss him so much. Our rides out together always have been nice: the surprising days of bolting across the downs, and the more peaceful times when we'd walked side by side along the canal. His temperament was a complement to my own: peaceful but strong willed with the occasional surprise that always brought a smile. In a way, Mister Bee was the way I imagined my perfect man. Strong and tough with an excellent sense of humour, but a sensitive creature that has the time to be at peace, taking in the views and appreciating the quiet, but also embracing the moment by sprinting down the beach to catch the perfect wave. Unfortunately, such a man doesn't exist.

As we stroll back into the yard I feel my eyes begin to sting with tears as our final ride out comes to an end. I lean down onto his neck and wrap my arms around him. Kissing his mane, I whisper in his ear "One last finale before we go." I stand up on my saddle and spring down to the ground, and for the first time I land with a gentle, almost graceful thud.

"Typical." I say out loud. "The first time I get that right and it's our last ride." Bee nudges me with his head and I ruffle his mane. Knowing what he wants, I dig my hand into my saddlebag to give him some carrots, but there are only a few there. I definitely only dreamed the deer. Didn't I? Maybe Jen didn't put many in there. I didn't check before we went out.

I lead Bee into his box, un-tack him, and give him some food while I brush him down. Then I put on his head collar and we head out to the paddocks.

Thick tears overflow from my eyelids as I prepare to say goodbye to my beloved pet. He pushes his nose under my arm, sensing my sadness. We stop at the gate as I turn to him and put my arms around his neck, resting my head on his shoulder. "I'm going to miss you so much, old friend. Thank you for being so good to me." I open the gate and let him through. "Now make sure you behave for Jen, won't you?" I take off his head collar and let him go. As I fasten the gate, I watch as Bee and the others graze happily in the sunshine. At least here he gets a peaceful retirement.

3: THE MAGIC OF A GREAT HAIRDRESSER

I park in front of the salon and send Ali a text before I go in: **Just going to have hair done, where do you want to go for lunch?**

As I walk in, Nicky's sweeping the floor.

I've been going to Nicky for my haircut for years; ever since she announced that she was going to train to be a hairdresser and needed models. She's only a couple of years older than me, and so good at managing my long, thick, wavy hair that I couldn't go to anyone else. Probably too scared, really. Another hairdresser would try to make my hair curly—poodle like—and I really didn't like that. People are always complimenting me on it. I really couldn't take the credit for its silky appearance; I just washed it, brushed it, and pulled it back into a ponytail when I was busy. Nicky was the real magic for my hair.

She looks up. "So, one last trim before you go?"

"Hopefully it won't grow too much before I come back," I say.

"I'm sure you'll do fine while you're away," she continues sweeping, "let me just sort this and we can get started."

"Actually, Nicky, can I quickly get changed?" I ask.

"Sure," she says, as she points down the stairs, "Use the laundry room. The others are out at lunch, so you'll be safe." I run down the stairs and barricade the door with some baskets, just in case. I step out of my jeans and pull my t-shirt over my head. I roll on some deodorant and slip on a denim miniskirt, a strappy vest, and flip-flops. As I look at my legs, they seem different. Maybe a little slimmer, or maybe the muscles seem more defined. Not like a body builder, but better than before—stronger. When did that happen? Maybe the exercises Aunt D and I have been doing have finally paid off.

We'd been doing some toning exercises in the evenings after I complained that my tummy muscles were slack. D had found a DVD for us to follow. It was quite easy, although I did feel self-conscious doing the routine with D. She has no need for such routines. She's already beautifully toned, even for a woman reaching her forties, and she doesn't look her age either. It's like she got to 30 and then stopped aging. The only sign of wrinkles she has is around her eyes when she smiles. People always ask her how she does it, especially when they discover her age. She always laughs with her reply and says, "Maybe because I'm trying to keep up with a teenager—maybe that's the key to a longer youth." I was sure it wasn't that. She was careful about what she ate, and she drinks mainly her special concoction of blended fruit and some other ingredients—I wasn't entirely sure what was in it. I'd never seen her make the drink from start to finish. It seemed such a long process. But maybe her key was that she was young at heart. Her fussing over riding accidents and my general safety was nonexistent when we're on holiday. We'd done cliff diving, rock climbing, rafting—loads. It was excellent.

***

I put my jeans and t-shirt into my bag and grab my wellies, dropping them off at the coat rack as I go to sit in Nicky's chair. Nicky washes my hair and then begins working her magic.

"So are you excited about tonight?" Nicky asks.

"Actually," I hesitate, "I really am." Nicky frowns at my answer. *What's that supposed to mean?* Hearing a gentle whisper in my head I answer, not wanting to be rude. "D's organized all of it. No expense spared." I can't imagine how much it has cost for us to have a party at home. "There's going to be a hog roast with all the trimmings. So don't worry about having dinner before you come over. There'll be a live band—D assures me that they're really good, so wear your dancing shoes. Emma and Sophie are there now doing all the decorations. So, fingers crossed, it will be a good night."

"You don't seem so sure." Nicky says.

"I feel like it's a bit more of a 'Good Bye' party rather than a 'Good Luck on your trip' party." Ever since my birthday I had been getting this worrisome feeling that my time of normality was coming to an end. Some of it I wasn't concerned about, but other things, like being with my friends and shopping and going out for drinks, I'd miss very much. I know I'm taking a gap year but I'll be back, right? It will all still be normal when I return, won't it? I'm worrying about nothing. I'm sure, sort of . . . but then there's . . .

"Plus, for the first time since I was about nine, I'm dateless. So I'll be a loner for my own party."

Nicky laughs. "Hope," she grins, "you're never a loner. Men pretty much throw themselves at you—you just never seem interested." She sighs. "When you were with Steve, it was like you were going through the motions—like you were just trying to keep everyone else happy, and when you two split up I wasn't surprised that it was you who had called it off." I look up at her, knowing full well what she was saying was true. "Sorry," she says apologetically, "but maybe you're too fussy?"

"I don't know, Nicky," I sigh. "Maybe I'm fed up with kissing the frogs to find my prince. Or maybe I expect more from a man than just good looks and a fast car. I'd like someone to connect with. Someone I want to spend time with. You know . . ." I smile at my reflection, watching her cut my hair, "someone to grow old with."

"Blimey, Hope. Aren't you a bit young for that?" She looks shocked.

Maybe I should have kept my thoughts to myself. "God, I'm not talking right now," I say, trying to reassure her that I haven't gone mad. I look down and start fiddling with my gown. "It's just that maybe I shouldn't be stringing blokes along if I don't feel the same way. It's not fair on either side if I do, so I don't."

"So no more fun?" she asks, raising her eyebrows at me, "or just no second dates?" Nicky continues to pull my hair into an elegant knot as I hear a whisper of *tart*, and I can see in my reflection a wide grin spread across my face.

"Well, I'm sure I'll have some fun, but as for second dates, I don't know. I think I'll just wait and see what comes along," I say, and we both laugh.

"What do you think?" Nicky asks as she holds a mirror behind me.

I turn my head from side to side. "It's beautiful, Nicky. Thank you so much," I say, smiling at my reflection; she always does a good job. Just then, my phone rings. The text message reads: **Can you come and get me? My car won't start. A.**

I send a reply: **Okay, nearly finished with Nicky. Be there in about 10 minutes. H**

I collect up my things and reach into my bag.

"Hell no," Nicky screams at me. "You're not paying today. If this is goodbye I want to at least give you something before you go."

I give her a tight hug and say, "Nicky, thank you, I'll see you later—and make sure you bring your lovely boyfriend with you."

"Of course I will. Although I think Elliot's only going because I said I'd wear a dress."

"Oh, right." I give her a wink.

"Go on," she says. "I'll see you later." And I'm out the door and in my car.

4: THE CRAVEN ARMS

I head out of town toward the village of Ham where Ali lives. Turning into the drive marked "Beaches," I find Ali on the front door step. Her old Fiesta is left abandoned on the front lawn. I park the car and get out. "What's wrong with it?" I ask as I walk over.

"Dunno. Don't Care. Damn thing's useless," she says in an angry tone. Oh dear. Ali's not in a good mood. When I look at her, she seems a sunburnt red. Don't mention it. She'll only get more wound up and then she'll be in a grump for the rest of the day and night. Just then, Ali's mum comes bursting out of the door. Ali's mum Claudia is simply an older version of Ali, with a slender figure, long blonde hair, and big blue eyes.

"Hello, Hope," she says as she waves at me. "Are you set for tonight?"

"I guess so," I say in reply, as I shrug and sit next to Ali. "D's done all of it, so I'm not sure."

"Got her clipboard?" Ali asks with a grin, knowing my reservations for the Sergeant Major D and her trusty clipboard.

"Yes," I respond, grinning back at her.

"Let's hope she's scheduled in some fun," she says with a sigh, "I need some."

"I'm sure there'll be some fun."

Ali gathers up her things and starts loading them into my car. "Mum, I'll see you in the morning, alright?" Ali shouts.

"Okay. I'm picking you up at eleven." Ali winces at her mother's reply. Claudia definitely noticed, and as I look at her I notice she's red too. Maybe they've got sunburn.

"Don't do that, Ali." Claudia bellows, "We're meeting your grandmother for lunch tomorrow. Like it or not." Oh dear. She seems as happy about the idea as Ali is.

"Fine," Ali shoots back in reply.

If she doesn't behave, she won't be going to London. I hear in a whisper.

"Don't worry, Claudia," I say in reply to the whisper. "I'll take care of her," and I get up and get in the car. Ali's strapped in already. She looks at me with one eyebrow raised.

More like I'll be taking care of her, says another whisper.

"Did you say something?" I ask, confused by the voice I heard and the lack of lip movement on Ali's face.

"What me? No," she answers, her eyebrows now furrowed.

"Do you know what? I fell off Bee today and I haven't been quite right since."

Ali laughs. "Maybe you knocked your brain out of gear?"

I laugh at her comment and say, "More like it's been knocked 'into gear.' No wonder I feel weird." I start the car and we're off down the drive and onto the main street of the village. I can hear the engine of a throaty sports car coming up quickly behind us. Don't get wound up. I try to persuade myself to just do the speed limit, but as the road widens, the car weaves around us. I honk my horn out of anger. "Bloody road hog, have some patience!" I shout out with annoyance.

"Typical," Ali says. "Nice car and there's an asshole driving it."

"Yep." We both laugh and watch the car speed off in the distance. It's one of those Audi convertibles in a beautiful royal blue color. "So where do you want to go for lunch?" I ask, slowing down at the village green.

"Well," Ali hesitates. I look at her out of the corner of my eye and notice that she's fidgeting; it's obvious that I won't like what she's going to say. I stop the car on the side of the road.

"Well what?" I ask.

"Well . . . do you mind if we meet up with Rob and his friend Phil?" She asks, still fidgeting.

"Oh god, Ali," I say, understanding her fidgeting. Rob, her boyfriend, I can handle—in fact he's a bit of a laugh—but his friend Phil is a leech, even though I've made it quite clear that I'm not interested. I take a deep breath and she pouts at me, which somehow gets me to give in to her. "Okay, we'll go and meet up with them."

She looks at me and says, "But. . ." She asks looking at me expectantly; she's my best friend, and she knows me well.

"Don't leave me alone with, Phil." Ali laughs. "Don't laugh!" But she continues to giggle. "He's a leech. He'd pretty much sit on my lap given half a chance. And he just really irritates me. You'd think he'd learn more about life, other than computers and beer."

"Christ, Hope," she says as she scowls at me. "It's like all men seem to irritate you these days. Anyway, I'm sure he'll be on his best behavior. He's got a new girlfriend, Chloe. She's working today, so him and Rob are having lunch, or just beer."

"Am I really that bad?" I ask, hating that my vow to myself to be better behaved is affecting Ali and her life.

"Honestly?" She asks, and I nod. "Men throw themselves at you and you just step over them like a bump in the road." I let out a long sigh as I look out the window. If only I could explain exactly what's been happening. How, before going out with Steve, I had been going out and drinking until I could barely focus, and then shagging any willing male that was available.

"Alright, I'll be good." I say with another sigh. "So long as he is."

"Okay, so now that's sorted, we'll go to The Craven Arms."

***

We park at the front of the Craven Arms. We get out and head over to the gardens.

"By the way," Ali says, "I love your hair. You're gonna look amazing tonight."

"Thanks," I say, touching the knot of hair on my head. "Pity there won't be anyone there to appreciate it," I say, sounding whiny as I start to feel sorry for myself for not having a date.

"Hope, you had plenty of offers. You chose to be single for your own party," Ali says.

"I know." She's right; the offers had been plenty, but somehow I felt that I shouldn't accept, that in doing so I'd miss out on something else.

"At least for your own party you get to dance with everyone rather than just one guy," she says, taking my arm. Ali can always find the positive in my decisions, even if she doesn't agree with them.

"What do you want to drink?" I ask, digging into my bag and trying to find my wallet.

"Can I have a pint of cider?" she asks, looking at her watch. I smile to myself; I bet she's working out how many pints she can have before the party and still look human—or at least like a relatively sober creature.

"Of course. I'll order some food as well. D said the hog roast won't be served until about half eight," I say, remembering that food for tonight won't be until late.

"Okay. We can share one of those platters." She gets her purse out of her bag.

"Don't worry, I'll get it," I say, putting my hand on hers and stopping her from getting her purse.

"Are you sure?"

"Definitely." I squeeze my hand on hers to reassure her. "Go and find the boys and I'll bring the drinks out."

I wait at the bar to be served. Out of the corner of my eye, I can see someone staring at me. I glance around, trying to act casual. When my eyes meet with the pair that is staring at me, an intense ringing starts in my ears, and I press my fingertips to my temples trying to ease the ringing. It doesn't help. I close my eyes, but then my head begins to hurt. Oh God, I feel sick. Someone bumps into me and a static shock runs up my spine. *Ow!* I open my eyes and look around. I can't remember the face that went with the staring eyes, but those eyes I've seen somewhere before.

"What can I get you, Hope?" Greg the bartender asks as he leans over the bar toward me.

"A large Coke for me." He raises an eyebrow at me and I smile back. I'm not drinking yet, and I don't feel too great at the moment. "A pint of cider for Ali, and can we have a lunch platter for 4?" I ask, knowing the platters are usually only done for two.

"Sure." He hands me a wooden spoon with a number 7 on it. "That's eighteen fifty, please."

I hand over some money. "Cheers," and I pick up the drinks and head out to the garden.

"Over here, Hope!" Ali shouts from the middle of the garden. I walk over to the table where they're sat and put down the drinks.

Both Rob and Phil are smiling at me. My ears start ringing again and I squeeze my eyes shut. Again, my head starts pounding. "You alright?" Ali asks as she takes a sip of her pint and notices me wince with pain.

"I don't know. My head really hurts." I rub the side of my head, but it really doesn't help.

"Sit down. Maybe you'll feel better when you've had something to drink. You're probably dehydrated," she says. That's why she's my best friend. There's no "suck it up you cry-baby"—she's actually concerned. I put my sunglasses on; the bright sunshine probably doesn't help. I start drinking my coke and the headache seems to ease; maybe I am dehydrated.

"So, tonight's gonna be fun," Rob says, breaking the silence.

"Let's hope so. D's organized the whole thing, so it will be a surprise, even for me." I take another large gulp of Coke. It's definitely helping. "She's promised a good live band. So, fingers crossed!"

"Do you know which one?" Phil asks.

"No I don't," I say, shaking my head. "The things I know are: live band, hog roast, large marquee, and a large dance floor."

"Blimey," Phil says, whistling through his teeth. "Bet it's costing a few pennies."

"Another thing I don't know." I say, feeling annoyed.

"Wow," Phil says, his eyes bulging. I put down my glass looking out toward the car park. I can see a guy leaning against the garden gate; he turns and looks at me. The ringing in my ears is getting louder.

"Oooh, I feel sick." I get up and run to the ladies.

"Hope!" I hear, as Ali runs after me. I make it to the loo just in time to throw up. Ali comes bursting in behind me. "Hope."

"In here."

"Oh dear," she says, as she moves the hair from my face.

"Ali, I'm sorry. I'm going to go home for a bit."

"Don't apologize. I'll get our things."

"Don't be silly. You stay here. I'll pick you up later."

"Hope, are you sure?"

"Yes. If you could get my bag for me that would be great."

"Of course," she replies. She darts off quickly returning with my bag. "Are you sure you'll be alright driving?"

"I'll take it steady." I straighten myself up. "I think I just need to go and lie down."

"Okay. Text when you're home, alright?" We walk out to the car and I get in and start the engine. "Just take it steady," she orders, and I nod.

"Ring me when you want picking up," I say as I reverse the car.

"Okay," she says as she waves me off. I drive slowly home.

5: EAVESDROPPING

I stop the car at the front of the house. Starting to feel sick again, I heave myself out of the car and head up the steps to the house. I can hear arguing from the kitchen. I creep through to the hall, listening.

"Why is he here?" That was D, she sounds angry.

"He said she needed him." Is that Terry?

"But it's not time yet." Time for what?

"He knows that. He's not come to interfere."

"Then why now?" That's definitely an angry Aunt D.

"He just said that she needed him, and maybe he needed her."

"I don't know, Terry. It might not be a good idea. She might reject him and then where will we be?" Is the 'she' me? And reject who?

"I'm sure it will be fine, and if not we'll just have to separate them until it's the right time." That's definitely Terry; I don't know anyone else who is so laid back and can actually calm D down easily.

"Okay. It's your head." D says, sounding a bit calmer. "Tell him not to come over until at least after nine. Is that clear?"

Oh no. My stomach does a complete summersault. I think I'm gonna . . . I clap my hand over my mouth and run through into the kitchen and throw up in the sink. I turn around and they both look at me, shocked.

"Sorry. I didn't think I was going to make it to the loo," I say, with my stomach still churning. I run the tap, trying to clean up.

"How long have you been feeling sick?" D asks as she rubs my back.

"Since we got to the pub."

Bet she's been drinking cider again. It always makes her sick. I hear her whisper.

31

"No I haven't. I've had such a headache and fuzzy vision that I didn't dare drink any alcohol." Annoyed by her assumption, my stomach squeezes in on its self and I lurch over the sink again, more sick.

"Where's Ali?" D asks.

"I left her at The Craven with Rob and Phil." D pulls the hair back from my face, wipes my mouth with a towel, and pours out some cold water from the fridge.

"Thanks," I say, and take a few sips from the glass. The cold settles my stomach. "I'm gonna go lie down for a bit." I say as I head for the stairs.

"Of course, get some rest," Terry says, guiding me to the stairs.

"Sorry. I don't know what's wrong with me." I drink some more water. "What time did you get here? I didn't think you'd be here until later." He's not usually early—in fact, quite the opposite.

"Well . . ." He hesitates, taking a glance at D, whose eyes are wide with anger. "My assistant wanted to get here early. There were some things he wanted to get sorted before the party."

"You have an assistant?" I ask, shocked; he doesn't usually like help.

"Well, he was too good to refuse," Terry says, shrugging. "I'm sure you'll like him. Jem's a little bit older than you." I suddenly feel jealous. Terry's a top DJ; he goes all over the place doing his thing, and gets paid pretty well too, and now he's got someone else to take with him. Why didn't he ask me? I would have loved to be his assistant. Terry's more like a big brother rather than an uncle. *He treats me like an adult.* D and I go and stay with him a couple times a year. He has a beautiful house that overlooks Newquay beach down in Cornwall. We've always had fun together, the three of us. Or sometimes D would go off shopping or walking while Terry and I go surfing or take out the motorbikes. It was great. I feel like I can tell him almost anything—probably more things than I could tell D. What's nice about Terry is that he's the one I'm most like. We both have a bronzed skin tone, brown eyes, and brown hair with sun bleached streaks. His hair is down to his shoulders, although he generally wears it up in a ponytail.

"Jem seems an odd name for a boy," I say, thinking out loud.

"Jem is short for Jeremy," Terry says.

"Hope, go and get some rest. Hopefully you'll be alright for tonight." D says as she shoos me up the stairs.

"I'm sure I'll be alright once I've had some rest."

"Sure." D answers sharply as she turns back to Terry.

I get halfway up the stairs and remember about Ali. "I told Ali to ring here when she wants picking up. Her car's broken . . . again. I said I'd go back and get her later on so we can get ready together."

"Alright," Terry says. "We'll give you a nudge when she rings."

"Cheers," and I continue up to my room.

I set the glass down on the bedside table and nip into the bathroom to brush my teeth. My stomach is beginning to feel much better. I head back into my bedroom, kicking off my flip-flops. I pull myself up onto my bed, and pull a blanket over me as I close my eyes and sink into a deep sleep.

***

I'm running as fast as I can through the woods of the Brail. It's dark and misty. The trees make scary shapes as I run—run as fast as I can. In the distance I can see the twinkling of lights. As I reach the edge of the wood there's a flash of light and I'm in the clearing, and its daylight, the sun shining in the clear, blue sky. I look out across the clearing and I can see a deer walking toward me. It begins to trot, coming faster and faster. I close my eyes, waiting to be bumped into, but I hear the feet stop. I open my eyes and I'm faced with the large deer, its head the same height as mine with large antlers. Is that the same one from this morning? I reach out to touch it. A crack of lightening snaps from my fingertips and connects to the deer. In a blink of an eye, the deer is gone and in its place is a man. He wears a deep purple velvet cloak, and as he lifts his head, the hood drops, revealing his roughly cropped hair, black and windswept. His smile shows brilliant white teeth. I look into his eyes; they're black too, sparkling like they're excited. He smells of earth and sweet grass. I reach my hand up to touch him and he presses his hand against mine, and a glow begins to shine from our touch.

The glow grows larger and larger. My hand starts to sting from the touch. The brightness from the glow becoming too much, I shut

33

my eyes tight. "It hurts!" I shout.

***

"Hope. It's all right. It's just a dream." Terry's voice sounds panicked, and as I open my eyes and look at him, tears flow over my eyelids. Terry cuddles me into his chest, comforting me.

"I'm sorry," I babble through the tears.

"Don't be sorry." He pulls away to look at me. "Did you have a nightmare?"

"No."

He raises an eyebrow at me. "Then why the tears?"

"Maybe because I woke up, I don't know." It wasn't a nightmare, but it did hurt. Terry passes me a glass of juice.

"I thought you should have this. It might make you feel better."

"Thanks," I say, taking the glass and having a sip. "This is D's juice," I say, looking at him with my eyebrows raised; she doesn't usually let me drink it.

"It's alright. It'll help."

"Where's D?"

"She's gone to pick up Ali."

"Oh God," I say, panic struck. I'd forgotten Ali. "What time is it?" I ask, looking around the room.

"Half five. I thought you might want to be awake before you start getting ready."

I take a few more sips of the juice. Actually this stuff is really nice. I can understand why D drinks so much of it. I run fingers into my hair and cringe. "Oh no. My hair's wrecked!"

"I'm sure it will be fine. I expect we could untangle it in time for the party." He grins at me. I get up and go over to the dressing table, investigating the extent of the damage in the mirror. Oh God, it looks like a haystack. I sit down on the stool, taking some more sips of the juice; I'm starting to feel much better.

"So where are you staying tonight, you and Jem?"

"Err, well." He runs his hands through his hair, which is no longer in his usual ponytail. "D said to stay here. There's the other guest room and the sofa." He shrugs.

"You don't seem sure." He seems nervous about something.

"D's not sure about Jem, or that he's here with us."

"I don't understand. Does she know him?"

"Not physically, but she knows *of* him."

"And she doesn't approve?"

"Not exactly."

"I'm sure it will be alright. She's been stressing about the party. I expect you just caught her off guard, that's all."

"We'll see how things go. If we do stay, don't go prancing about in the middle of the night. You might scare him." Terry says with a wicked grin, I frown back at him.

"I haven't done that for ages." I say in protest. Well, not since Thursday night, and that wasn't prancing about. I merely went downstairs to get a drink and found D in the garden, weeding. Not that that's odd, but it was 3 o'clock in the morning. She said that she couldn't sleep, and neither could I, so we sat out in the garden and read our books until sunrise.

"I know what you're like when you've had a few to drink." And he winks at me as he leaves the room.

I begin to pull the pins out of my hair, but it's too tangled. It's no good—I'm going to have to wash it out. Hopefully I'll be able to do something with it then.

I get the shower going and peel off my clothes. I step into the spray of the shower, letting the hot water pulsate onto my back. Washing through my hair, I pull out the remaining pins. I shave my legs and underarms; even though they're not bad, I just want to make sure. Something in the back of my mind is nagging at me, like I'm preparing for something or someone.

I wrap my hair up into a towel and dry my body off with another. Putting on my dressing gown, I walk back into my bedroom just in time to hear Ali running up the stairs.

"Hope!" I hear her shout.

"In here!" I shout back.

She bursts in. "How are you feeling?"

"Much better, actually. Sorry I left you with Rob and Phil."

"Don't apologize," she says, waving away my apology. "We were all right, just chatting, you know."

"What time are they coming over?"

"About eight; they left just as D picked me up." She looks at me a bit confused.

"What?" I ask, unable to understand her expression.

"Well, your hair. What happened?" she asks, looking at the towel on my head.

"I fell asleep and when I woke up it was a haystack," I say. After pulling off the towel, I begin to comb my hair. "Would you mind helping me to try and put it back into a knot?"

"Of course not, but do you mind if I have a shower first?" She asks, pointing her thumb toward my bathroom. "We were playing mini football with some kids at The Craven and I fell over a couple of times and ended up going barefoot."

"Go for it," I say, nodding towards the bathroom "Did you bring up your dress?"

"Oh no, I didn't." She turns on her heel to head back out.

"Don't worry. I'll get it while you get in the shower."

"Cheers, Sweet." And she skips off to the bathroom. I pull on shorts and a vest and dart downstairs. I take a quick glance through to the living room and see Emma and Sophie walking toward me carrying large bags of ribbons and confetti.

"No peeking." Sophie shouts as she walks along.

"It won't be a surprise if you peek." Emma says.

"It's not a surprise party." I say, annoyed. Why can't I?

"That maybe so but there's still no peeking." Sophie orders.

"Are you sure?" as I flash a cheeky grin.

"Yes," they both echo.

My ears pop and then start to ring. "Ow," I gasp, putting my fingers to my ears and trying to push the pain out.

"Hope, are you alright?" Sophie asks, looking shocked.

"Damn ringing in my ears." I scream, squeezing my eyes shut.

"Dion!" I hear Emma shout.

"What is it?" Her gentle footsteps come closer. She puts her hands on my shoulders, and my ears pop again, and the ringing stops.

"Oooh, it stopped." I say, relieved.

She looks at me with her eyes wide. Still holding onto my shoulders she says, "Ali said you fell off Bee today."

"Yeah. He had a bit of burst of energy and I clouted a tree." I wince slightly, realizing what I have said.

"Did you hit your head?" D asks as she looks over my forehead.

"Yeah, pretty hard, but I can't feel any bumps."

"Thank goodness you had your helmet on."

"Unfortunately the helmet doesn't stop you blacking out." *Oh Crap. You should have kept your mouth shut.* D runs her fingers along my wet hair.

"What happened when you came to?"

"I'm not sure." She holds my face between her hands and looks deep into my eyes. My mind starts going through my ride this morning. Her eyes widen as I think of the cloaked woman and the glowing ball of light and then the deer in the clearing. I wonder what she'd do if she knew what I'm thinking? She lets go and takes in a deep breath.

"Have some more juice. I'm sure the heat hasn't helped," she says with a sad sigh.

"I just need to get Ali's stuff from the car," I say. Feeling much better, I almost bounce my way out to the car. I open the car door and grab Ali's things. I can see Terry down the far end of the garden. He looks like he's talking to someone, but I can't see who. "Don't draw attention to yourself," I mutter, "you don't look fabulous yet." I go back through to the kitchen.

"Ali said she just wanted water," D says as she pours out some more juice for me. A glass of water already sat waiting on the table.

"Cheers," I say as D follows me up the stairs and I carry Ali's things in. We walk in the room just as Ali comes out of the bathroom, wrapped up in a large bath towel.

"Thanks. That's just what I need," she says as she takes the glass from D. I pop the telly on and flick through the channels. There's a re-run of *Friends*. Ali drops down on the sofa.

Seen this one—this is when you find out Rachel's pregnant.

Hearing Ali's whisper, I say, "Well, it's alright for background while we get ready." I turn back and sit on the sofa. Ali looks at me confused. "What?" I feel paranoid by her expression.

"I didn't say anything"

"Really?" I ask; I'm sure I heard something. It sounded like her.

"Honestly. Not a word."

I shrug. "Maybe I'm going doolally?"

"Too late for that," she smirks.

"Cheers!" And we just laugh. We gather up our things and begin to get ready.

6: PARTY

By the time eight o'clock comes around, Ali and I are buffed, polished, and sparkling. Ali's wearing a pale blue silk dress cut just below the knees with deep Vs cut into the front and back; it exposes her back and chest, and, combined with silver strappy shoes and her hair pulled back off her face with silver combs, she looks beautiful—proper jaw-dropping gorgeous. Rob is going to have a problem keeping other men off her. Mind you, he might just have a problem controlling himself.

My dress has a halter neck and is deep pink. Like Ali's, it's cut just below the knee with a deep V neckline, and provides "good boob exposure" according to Ali. We've managed to get my hair back into a knot pulled to the side with a large pink flower pinned into it. As I pull on my sandals, I start to feel excited. Ali pulls me up from my seat.

"Ready to knock 'em dead?" she asks with a large Cheshire cat grin across her face.

I feel my expression mirror hers. "Hell yeah."

We step out of my bedroom to find D dressed in a simple, elegant mauve dress. "Wait right there," she says, pointing her camera at us. Ali puts her arm around my waist and I do the same to her, posing. "Smile!" as the flash goes on the camera. My eyes start to sting, blurring from the flash of light. We head downstairs with D following behind. I can hear the buzz of chatter as we continue through the living room.

The three of us stand on the patio steps with a sea of people before us. They all turn and shout in chorus "Hooray!" I can feel my cheeks burn with embarrassment and as I look at Ali her cheeks are blushed too; although, when I look at her, her skin seems yellow—not sickly, but sunny and friendly. Maybe the lights are making her look like that.

Ali gives my hand a gentle squeeze and we walk down the steps and greet all of our friends. The Marquee has been decorated wonderfully with balloons and confetti in blue, pink, and white. Fairy lights are wrapped around every place imaginable. There's a large dance floor and a stage for the band, with tables and chairs scattered between the masses of people.

Everyone is here, all with hugs and kisses, wishing me well for my trip.

Sophie and Emma come barging through the crowd, arms spread as they walk over to me and squeeze me with their tight hug. "What do you think?" Sophie asks.

"It's lovely. Thank you so much."

"You're always welcome." And they both kiss me on the cheeks. Emma raises an eyebrow, glancing past my shoulder.

"What is it?" I ask as she steps back.

"Hope." Hearing the familiar voice, I gasp. It's Steve. I didn't know he'd been invited. I turn around to face him. "Wow." He says as he pecks me on the cheek. I twinge as I look at him. He's still handsome with his short, dirty blonde hair, his blue-green eyes, and his glorious muscular six-foot body. I swallow hard, trying not to think how long it's been since . . . since . . . I had felt those arms wrapped around me. I swallow hard again. *You broke it off with him for a reason. You don't love him. You don't have that feeling when you're with him.*

"Thanks," I say, trying to sound civil.

You shouldn't have let her go. You fool. I hear his voice whisper and I try to smile, but I know I've hurt his feelings, if not his pride.

"So when are you leaving?" he asks, his expression smooth in attempt to hide a frown.

"Monday," I reply. If I keep the answers short he won't stay too long, I say to myself. I cross my arms over my chest, trying to act casual. Gripping my arms, I try desperately not to let the animal inside of me out. I concentrate on his face and not his body; if I don't look at those arms and chest and . . . no. You promised yourself no meaningless sex. It's going to mean something next time.

So soon, I hear. That's not right. It definitely sounds like Steve, but his lips aren't moving. Where's that coming from? I look around, seeing if it could have been someone else, but we're surrounded by women. Looking back at him with confusion, I answer the whisper I had heard.

"It's been planned for months." I say, watching only his mouth. "I told you I was taking a gap year." *Doesn't he remember?* I continue to watch, waiting for his reply.

"I know. I just didn't think you'd go ahead with it," he says; his lips definitely moved then. I frown at his response. He fidgets as he avoids making eye contact with me.

"Why not?" I ask. Surely there's more to life than just here, but some people just don't seem to want to venture around this planet. I'm not one of those people. Don't get me wrong, I like it here, but I keep getting this overwhelming urge to go searching; for what, I'm not entirely sure, but it's an urge I'm finally going to be able to give in to.

"I guess I hoped you'd stick around a bit longer before you went off having an adventure," he says, finally looking at me. He looks hurt that I'm going. This surprises me after the things I'd heard he'd said about me when we'd split up—"Thank Christ the ice maiden is gone."

"Steve, now is as good a time as any. There's nothing to hold me back." I say, trying to sound cheerful.

She's still single. I hear. Okay, he definitely didn't speak then. What's going on?

"I guess not." He shrugs, but then he smiles and reaches over to me, brushing a lose strand of hair away from my forehead. His smile grows. I squeeze tighter on my arms, feeling no longer needy, but annoyed.

"You know I couldn't stick around here. You know me better than that," I say, stepping away from him.

"Do I?" he asks with a questioning eyebrow raised.

Because I wouldn't have said I did. Okay, this is getting a bit freaky.

"Steve . . ." I say, taking in a deep breath, "I have to go." I brush past him and step through the crowd to the edge of the dance floor.

My ears are ringing loudly. I rub my temples, trying to ease the buzzing, but it's no good. I look up and people are staring at me. I look over my shoulder, hoping that they're not looking at me. No wonder your ears hurt, you're stood right next to a loud speaker, I think to myself. I duck out of the marquee and head around to the bar. Maybe a drink will help.

Terry spots me standing in the queue for the bar and rushes over, pulling me to him in a big bear hug. "You look gorgeous," he says, looking at me admiringly.

My cheeks burn with embarrassment. "Thanks," I mutter.

"What do you want to drink?" Terry asks, stepping up to the bar.

"Can I just have a Coke?" I ask, still rubbing my temples; he looks at me with a quizzical eyebrow raised.

"Not in the party mood?" he asks, knowing how much I enjoy parties and alcohol.

"I was until my ears started ringing again," I say, holding my hands over my ears.

"Did you tell D?" he asks as he runs his hand along my forehead like he's checking my temperature.

"Yeah earlier on, but it stopped then."

He takes my hand. "Come with me," and he pulls me out of the marquee and back up to the house. As we walk through into the kitchen, D is already there waiting, holding a small box. I look at the two of them.

"What's this?" I say with a wince, pointing to the box.

"It's a belated birthday present . . . or maybe a going away present," D says as she passes me the box.

"But you can't. You've already done the party," I say in protest. "You can't do anymore gifts." But I smile back at them feeling spoilt, and I take the box from her.

"This was your mother's," D says, as she opens the box in my hands. Inside is a round, clear disc about the size of a two-pound coin, with a small hole where a chain loops through. D takes it out of the box and puts it around my neck. I look down at the pendent on my skin. It's so simple and elegant, and my mum's.

"I love it," I say as I give her a big hug. "Thank you so much for this. And the party."

"You're very welcome," she says, and we reach over and pull

42

Terry to us. All three of us hug together. "Look," she says and points at the pendent. It's pink; like a droplet of ink in water, the color bleeds through the disc.

"Wow. How does that happen?" I say, lifting the pendent to have a closer look.

"Magic," Terry states, and gives me a wink.

"How are the ears?" D asks, stepping away from me.

"Comfortable." I gently rub over my temples again; they're still ringing, but it's dull—like a background noise. "Maybe it's because we're out here and not in there." I point my thumb over my shoulder to the marquee.

"Maybe," and they both grin at me.

"What's that supposed to mean?" I ask suspiciously.

D gives me another hug and whispers in my ear: "Just go and enjoy the party." Headlights shine in through the kitchen window and I pull back from D, my frown mirroring hers.

"I thought everybody was here." Her eyes are wide in a sort of anger; I know she doesn't like people being late . . . maybe it's that. I look over at Terry and he smiles, taking D's hand. I'll steer the late-comers around the other way. Then they won't have to face Sergeant Major D. "I guess I'd better welcome them in." I turn on my heel and head back out the door.

7: JEREMY WINTERS

I stop at the bottom step, faced with an Audi Convertible in a beautiful royal blue color.

"Nice car," I mutter under my breath.

"Thanks." *Crap.* Where did he come from? I nearly jump out of my skin. He steps up next to me, standing a few inches taller than my 5'5", with his golden blond hair windswept (obviously from driving with the top down). He's wearing a pale blue short-sleeve shirt and black trousers. Smart but not overdone. Beautiful bronzed skin, and gorgeous. Nice car and not an asshole. That's a first. He smiles at me with gleaming white teeth as I look him up and down. *Oh crap. Am I gawking at him? Hope, you plum!*

"Hope?" he holds out his hand for me to shake.

"Yes," I say looking at his hand. *Work brain; he's just gorgeous, probably not nice really, or too self-absorbed.* "Yes. Sorry, I'm Hope. And you are?" I say, trying to collect myself. I don't recognize him, but there's something familiar about him . . . his voice—I'm sure I've heard it somewhere before.

"Jem, Jeremy Winters," he says, taking my hand. As our hands touch I feel a crack of a static shock; I quickly snap my hand back.

"Oh god, I'm sorry," I say apologetically. *Shouldn't wear silky knickers!* He smiles at me again and takes my hand, kissing the back of it. Pins and needles run down my fingers and into my arm. As he lifts his head from my hand his deep blue eyes sparkle, as if excitement is rising up from his insides. "You're Terry's assistant?" I ask with uncertainty; I thought he was much older. He doesn't look any more than twenty.

"Yes. That's me," he replies.

"Nice to meet you," I say as I shake his hand. "Are you coming in to join the party?" I ask, not wanting him to leave. I don't want him to go.

"If that's alright?" he asks, looking at me with a smile.

"Of course," I say with relief. He's still holding my hand, or am I holding onto his? It's comfortable—like how a pair of hands should fit together. Two halves making a whole. "Terry said you're staying with us. Did you want to bring your things in?" I ask, peering into the interior of the car.

"No, that's alright. I'll do it later." He pulls me close to him. We step off the stairs and walk around his car. Still holding hands, we walk quietly down the garden toward the far entrance of the marquee, avoiding a grand entrance from the living room. I can feel him watching me as we walk.

"What?" I ask, feeling paranoid. *Is there something stuck to my face?*

"It's just that . . ." He hesitates as we step through the entrance. "You're more beautiful than I expected." Expected? Why? What was he expecting? I frown, not expecting such a comment.

"Thanks." He kisses my hand again, and embarrassment turns my cheeks a glowing red.

"Hope!" I hear Ali shout as she barges through the crowds of people. "There you are." She stops short, gawking at Jem and then me.

"Ali. This is Jem. Terry's assistant," I say, lifting our hands together. Jem nods while Ali's eyes bulge as she looks him up and down and then fixates on our hands together.

Shaking herself, she collects herself together and says, "Wow. You're Terry's assistant?" Her eyes run over him again, suspicious. "He doesn't usually like help." Jem just smiles at her comment. With her hands on her hips she chews her bottom lip, either nervous or unsure. "Come on, you need to mingle," she says decisively. "We haven't seen you for nearly an hour. People are asking after you." I look down at our hands, still together, and then back to his face. I don't think I want to let go.

He smiles at me and gives my hand a gentle squeeze before letting go. "Go on. I'll catch up with you later," he says, and walks off towards the bar.

Ali looks at me, her eyes still bulging. "What?" I ask, waiting for the "Oooh" and "Hell-oo."

"Like what you see?" she asks with a large grin running across her face.

"I don't know," I say, watching him walk away. *Do I?* Ali raises an eyebrow at me. "Ali, I'm leaving Monday. I doubt I'll see him again." Although I think I'd quite like to.

"So a drop dead gorgeous guy really isn't enough?" That's more of a statement than a question.

I take a deep breath and grab her arm. "Come on. Let's mingle," and I pull her into the crowd. Ali stays nearby as the questions start from all directions. "Where are you going first?" "What are going to do there?" "Why are you visiting that?" The questions are repetitive and my answers get less enthusiastic the more times they're asked. The crowd loses me in their discussion of where I should go; I try to pay attention but fail miserably and stand up on tiptoe trying to see where Jem has gone. I catch sight of Nicky, and she kindly interrupts while I'm being harassed by some of D's friends.

"Hope, what happened to your hair?" She asks as she wraps her arms around my neck. I touch my knot of hair, checking that it's still together.

"I fell asleep this afternoon and when I woke up it was a state. Ali had to help me fix it."

She smiles. "It's not bad," *for an amateur,* she says, the sentence finishing in a whisper. Huh? Her lips didn't move for that bit. Did they? I wonder who said that. It sounded like her. Ali grabs both our arms and pulls us to the dance floor, rescuing me from internal questioning.

"Come on, let's dance!" She squeaks. Ali, the biggest kid I know, just can't resist a good song to dance to. We start bopping about in time with the music. "That's a nice necklace. Who gave you that?" she asks as she lifts the pendent up to look at it.

"D gave it to me as a belated birthday present," I say with a shrug.

"It's an amazing color."

I look down at the pendent and suddenly stop dancing; it's white with pink swirls in it. "It was pink just a minute ago," I say with confusion. Ali lets go, leaving the pendent to fall to my chest.

"Maybe it's one of those mood things. You know, they change color to suit your mood."

"Maybe . . ." We both shrug. Out of the corner of my eye, I see Rob step up onto the dance floor and sneak behind Ali. He winks at me and picks her up, spinning her round and around. She slaps her hands around the back of her head, screaming.

"Put me down! You're gonna make me sick." He puts her down, spinning her round to face him, and wrapping his arms around her again, he kisses her hard on the lips before lifting her off the ground. They're so happily in love. It's a bit sickening, really. But he is perfect for her. Just as crazy and childlike as she is. I love to see her happy. It makes going away that much easier, knowing she's got Rob. I feel my heart sink, longing for the same happiness that Ali has—jealous of it, in a way.

The music begins to calm and flows into a slow dance, Elliot joins Nicky and the two couples twirl together happily. *Time to make an exit,* I think. I turn on my heels and head toward the bar, passing the band as I go. I step over some loose leads and get another static shock. "Ow. Christ Sake. What's causing that?" I say with irritation. I look down at my clothes. "I'm sure it's got nothing to do with what I've got on." I look up and Jem is stood right in front of me, smiling. I can feel my cheeks warming with embarrassment again. *Caught right in the act of talking to yourself—well done!*

"Would you like to dance?" Jem asks as he holds out his hand to me. I look back over at the dance floor, watching the happy couples still swaying. I let out a sigh.

"No, thank you. I was heading to the bar to get a drink." And I step around him.

"Maybe the next one?" he asks, following me. I shake my head. What's wrong with you? There's a seriously gorgeous guy asking you to dance and you *do* want to dance. But you still won't, will you? I'm even questioning my own thoughts. Not good. "Hope?" Jem reaches for my arm, but I pull myself away before he can touch me. I look him in the eye; he looks hurt. What would dancing achieve? It's for the best if we don't tempt fate.

"Sorry. I don't mean to be rude, but I'd like to just get a drink and then some air," I say, stepping out of his reach. I turn on my heel once again and head for the bar. I stand in the queue waiting to get served, and let the guilt rise up in me. Jem seems nice, but I don't know him. I'm leaving on Monday. I don't . . .

"What do you want, Hope?" Tommy asks with his usual long, friendly smile. I just hold out my arms. He comes rushing around from his side of the bar and gives me a big hug. His lanky body towers over me as he tucks me under his unshaven chin; he's nice smelling—like sandalwood, or something. I hug him back, enjoying the friendly embrace. "Anything else?" *'Cause I'm so up for it.* The end of his sentence finishes in a whisper, and his smile grows further.

Ignore it—you're just imagining it, I say to myself. *He's a friend—just a friend.*

"Could you do me one of your monster cocktails, please?" I ask, grinning at him.

"There's a jug ready for you." He drapes his arm around my shoulder and leads me up to the bar. "Help yourself." He passes me a fresh glass and moves the jug toward me.

"Really, are you sure?" I ask, unsure of this large jug of cocktail.

"Hell yeah," he says with a grin. *We like it when this one's had a few.* His lips didn't move then. Filling up the glass, Tommy drops a straw into the cocktail.

"Cheers, Tommy!" I give him a peck on the cheek, which makes him blush. He turns away from me quickly, making his dreadlocks rattle around his head as he serves someone else.

8: COCKTAILS

Outside there's a few people sat out on the lawn—couples chatting and enjoying the sunset. I walk down to the far end and lean on the fence. The view across the meadow is beautiful in all shades of orange as the sun drops down behind the downs.

I can't help it; the tears begin to flow, the sadness inside me squeezing at my heartstrings. "This is what you wanted," I whisper to myself. Travelling around to see your family and do amazing things on the way—a year out to have an adventure. You need to get out and about while you're still young. That's why you've stayed single—nothing to hold you back. Obviously it's just my nerves kicking in. I pat round my face trying to mop up the tears and not smudge my make-up. I take a few more gulps of my drink and then take a deep breath.

"Time to go back in," I say to myself. I hear someone clear their throat behind me. I turn, faced with Jem, who is holding my nearly full cocktail jug. "What's this?" I ask as I point to the jug. "Trying to get me drunk?"

"I thought you might need a refill," he says as he takes my glass. He glances at me while he pours out the cocktail. "Are you alright?" He asks frowning at me; *didn't I mop the tears away enough?*

"Aren't you having some?" I ask in reply, ignoring his question. I sit down on the grass. Maybe I need a little longer before I go back in. Let my face calm down.

"Are you sure it's safe?" he grins at me, pulling a glass out from his back pocket.

"It's not that alcoholic," I say as I take a sip. *Oooh, that burns.* "Take that back, no it's not safe". But I'll drink it anyway—anything to cheer me up. Jem chuckles and sits down next to me, resting the jug in the grass.

49

"Terry said you liked your cocktails."

"He did, did he?" I ask with a smirk. Trust Terry. His smile puts me at ease. "What else did Terry tell you?" I ask, knowing Terry wouldn't have said just about me drinking cocktails, although he is right—I certainly do like my cocktails. I sip some more while I watch the sunset.

"Lots of things." He shrugs.

"That's comforting," I say sarcastically. "He's never mentioned you before," I say, turning to look at him. It's odd; Terry and I tell each other so much—why didn't he tell me about Jem until he turned up here this afternoon?

"I only joined Terry a few months ago." Maybe that's why he hadn't said anything. Maybe he wasn't sure about him.

"Do you like it?" I ask, trying to figure out why Terry had chosen him.

"Very much so. Terry's a good teacher."

"How come you're here?" I say, speaking my mind out loud. *That's a bit blunt—he's going to think you're rude now.*

"Terry said I should meet his family, seeing as he talks about you and D nearly all the time."

"I'm surprised you wanted to meet us if Terry's told you all about D and me. Most people would run a mile." He chuckles and lies back on the grass. He looks amazing out here with the last pieces of sunlight bouncing off him, showing his toned muscular body against his clothes. Perfect. I lie on my side, resting my head in my hand. Watching him, wanting to wrap myself around him, wanting to kiss him, wanting to . . . I shake my head. No. Don't think about it. You don't do one-night stands; not anymore. You're not that kind of girl. I take another sip of my cocktail. Blimey this is strong. What did Tommy do, double the shoots? I keep sipping. Maybe it will loosen me up. For some reason I feel really tense tonight. Jem turns onto his side and faces me, his blue eyes serious.

"I came here to meet you, Hope," he says and leans over to me. Without thinking I close my eyes and let our lips touch. A tear escapes the corner of my eye; I'm disappointed with myself for not having better control.

You pushover.

Maybe the extra shots in the cocktail helped?

The question enters my head, but I didn't think that. It definitely wasn't me. I pull back from Jem and look down at his hand, which is now resting on my hip. I shake my head. "You spiked my drink?" I shout, the anger in my voice getting louder. "To persuade me to . . ." I get up and start walking back towards the party. You let your guard down for a second and then you figure out he's only getting you drunk so he can get into your knickers. I shake my head, wiping away my tears. You idiot, you shouldn't have drunk the cocktail. You know what you're like when you've been drinking. I can hear Jem running up behind me.

"Hope, that's not it!" He shouts as he reaches out to grab my arm and another shock cracks between us.

"What the hell?" I shout back as I snap my hand away.

"Please. That's not what I want," he says pleading with me.

"Really?" *Because I doubt it,* I say, half speaking and half thinking. He reaches for my hand and the static happens again. "For God's sake!" I shout out with annoyance, but he takes my hand and I feel a tingling in my fingers like having pin and needles. "Then what do you want?" I say, the anger still loud in my voice.

"I just wanted to meet you." I look up into his eyes; his expression is sad—heartbroken.

"Why me?" *Is it because I'm leaving? So you don't have to see me again?*

"Because I needed to . . ." he says, his voice pleading. *Because I'm not whole without you.* I hear his voice in my head but I'm watching his face and his lips don't move. Is that him?

Yes, it's me you can hear. They definitely didn't move.

"I beg your pardon," I say, trying to pull my hand away, but he leans in to kiss me. I turn my head so he can't kiss me on the lips. "No!" I shout. "What's going on?"

Jem looks around us. "Maybe this isn't the best time to explain," he says as he continues to look around.

"Explain what?" I ask, annoyed.

"After the party," he mutters looking around again.

K. M. Buckland

"Fine." I pull my hand away. *After the party, then you can explain what the hell is going on. Make sure you keep away from my friends; I don't want them having to deal with this freaky shit as well.* His eyes are wide with shock as I spit my thoughts to him. I turn and head back into the marquee, leaving him gobsmacked.

"There you are!" Terry shouts, holding up a fresh cocktail for me. "I was just coming to look for you." His smile fades as he watches a frown rise on my face.

"Really?" I ask as I take the drink from him. "Or were you checking on your assistant—checking on his progress?" My angry words bite at Terry.

"You were with Jem?"

I roll my eyes at Terry's question. "Like you didn't know," I say, my sarcasm dulling the venom in my tone. I down my drink quickly, grateful that it's not as strong as the previous one.

"Take it steady." Terry nags.

"Nope." As I start to turn he grabs my shoulder.

"What happened with Jem?"

"He spiked my cocktail. So that I would . . ." Terry starts to smile and then lets out a light chuckle. "It's not funny, Terry"

His expression is smooth, but only just. "Hope," he puts both hands on my shoulders, looking me straight in the eye. "The guy likes you."

"That doesn't mean he should spike my drink"

"No. But . . ."

"But what?" I ask, folding my arms in front of me. Terry shrugs, releasing his grip from my shoulders.

"Just give Jem a chance." I shake my head. Now I see why D wasn't sure about them staying. Terry's trying to set me up. But why, why now?

I march off to the dance floor, seeing D with Ali. I take a deep breath and squeeze my way through to them. D catches a glimpse of my anger, and then, looking over to where Jem has entered the Marquee, she reaches out, pulling me closer to her.

"Is everything alright?" she asks with real concern in her voice. I look at her, but I can't say anything. I try to smile but it doesn't work; in the end I sigh and look over at Jem.

"After the party," I say, squeezing her to me and feeling her calm saturate me.

"Of course, after the party. Later on we'll have a talk." Comforted that she would listen and maybe even help, I let her go and watch as she walks over to Terry. I can see Terry cringe as she seems to give him an ear full.

Trying to blend in and possibly cheer up, I start dancing with Ali. Nicky, Emma, and Sophie join in and we all mess about bouncing into one another, generally being silly rather than dancing. It works, and within minutes I'm laughing so hard I can barely breathe, but the music then changes tempo and flows into some soppy song.

Ali claps her hands over her face. "I've got to find Rob, he's so got to dance with me for this!" She runs off to find Rob. Nicky, Emma, and Sophie try to find their other halves too, leaving me all on my own and taking my cheer with them. I turn to walk off the dance floor, knowing that this song is for couples and knowing full well that I wasn't part of one.

9: DANCING

I hear the crack of another static shock before I feel it pinch at my skin. Whipping round, I slam right into Jem.

"Stop doing that," *because I know it's got something to do with you,* I shout, finishing the sentence in my head. His smile only makes me more annoyed. Obviously he finds it funny that we get static shocks.

"Dance with me," he says, his voice almost firm. It sounds more of a demand than a request. He takes my hand and then wraps his arm around my waist. Terry's words echo in my head. "Just give Jem a chance!" I shake my head. My heart is pounding so hard; I want so badly to kiss him again. But I'm so cross that he spiked my drink. I try to push away, but he just holds on.

"I'm sorry about the drink," he softly whispers in my ear. My anger melts with his words as his warm breath rolls down my neck. How does he do that? And how come I can be this close to him? I'm attracted to him and I'd willingly sleep with him but it's not uncontrollable. I just have that feeling again.

Just let go. I hear in my head.

Why can I hear what he's thinking?

Because you let me, I hear in reply.

It's a pretty weird thing to hear voices, you know.

You'll get better at it.

"What?" I shout as I pull away from him, not noticing exactly how close we'd become.

"Dance with me." He says again, but this time he's asking. I take a deep breath, debating if this is a good idea or not. I place my hand on his shoulder and brace myself for another shock, but there's nothing—just some pins and needles like before. Jem looks at my hand and then back to me, a soft smile rising on his face. "Dance with me," he implores. The music changes tempo again; it's still romantic, but a little faster. *Just let go*, I think to myself. We begin swaying and twirling; not once does his hand let go of mine and every time he pulls me in close to his chest my eyes gently close as I feel his soft lips against my neck and cheek.

As the song draws to an end he drops me back, cradling me from the small of my back with one hand and pulling my knee up to his hip with the other. We're both breathless as he pulls me upright and a loud applause begins. My whole body turns scarlet with embarrassment; I hadn't realized that we'd cleared the dance floor.

Ali comes bouncing over from the edge of the dance floor. "I didn't know you could dance like *that*." Her eyes bulge as she stares at Jem's arm wrapped around my waist.

"Neither did I," I say, as I glance over my shoulder at Jem.

That was you, not me, I hear him think.

I look over Ali's shoulder, seeing Rob creep up behind her. He grabs her around the waist and pulls her to him. Ali lets out a loud scream before shouting "Rob!" and smacking him round the head. He kisses her on the cheek, which somehow always soothes her. Rob glances over at us watching them.

Who's this guy, then? I hear in my head.

"Sorry, Rob. This is Jeremy, my uncle's assistant." They politely shake hands.

"Wow. That must be interesting," he says with enthusiasm.

"Yes. It's definitely an eye opener," Jem says, and I look at him with confusion.

What's that supposed to mean? I ask. How is DJ-ing an eye opener?

Later, I hear in reply.

"Well. It's nice to finally meet someone who can melt Hope." And he flashes me a cheeky grin and winks.

"Thanks," and I childishly poke my tongue out at him. He must think I'm a real ice maiden. Ali wraps her arms around Rob's neck and they dance off slowly around the dance floor. Jem pulls me back into his arms and this time I don't hesitate. "You're not an ice maiden . . ." He hesitates to finish as he looks past my shoulder. I look up at him, feeling concerned as his expression changes to hard and tense.

"Can I cut in?" I freeze, recognizing the voice. It's Steve, my ex-boyfriend, wanting to cut in. Jem steps away from me, and I look at him confused. Doesn't he want to dance with me?

He just wants to dance with you one last time.

I don't know that I should. Remembering how hard it was to control myself earlier.

"Yes of course," Jem says politely to Steve, passing him my hand. "Terry's been signalling me anyway." And with that, he's gone.

"So he's Terry's assistant." Steve says as he nods his head in the direction that Jem had left.

"Yes. Jeremy." I say with a hint of pride and a tiny bit of annoyance. I'd let go and he'd left. Why?

"You two seem quite cozy," Steve states, pulling me possessively closer to him.

"Do we?" I ask, feeling a frown crease my forehead.

Yeah ya do. I've never seen you like that. Not even when . . .

"Steve, you're not jealous, are you?" I ask, a small grin now pinching at my cheeks.

"No," he says as he shakes his head, "not jealous of him, per-se. But that he could make you happy. Dance the way you like to. You looked comfortable with him." That's a rather honest thing to say. How much has he had to drink? But he is right, I did feel comfortable.

"I'm sorry that I hurt you." I say, apologizing for the first time about how I had treated him. He is a nice guy and I had done nothing but treat him like a piece of meat. He looks at me with his eyes wide with shock.

"I don't think you meant to, Hope," he says, finally letting his shock subside.

"But I did nonetheless," I say, looking back at him. From this angle I remember why I had chosen him. He was strong; his beautifully toned muscles were proof of that, but he was more than just a flawless body. He was sensitive and creative, but more than anything, he fascinated me. He could be as filthy minded as me, but he was also open minded . . .well, at most things he was.

"I don't think you were ready for a boyfriend, or commitment." I shrug at his comment. It was true that at the time I hadn't been ready for . . . well, anything remotely permanent.

"Or maybe some things are just not meant to be. We want different things." His arm wraps tighter around my waist, reminding me of a time long ago when it was just us. "You want to settle down. Have children. Have a wife sat at home all day." With a sigh I stop moving and look at him straight, knowing I'm going to have to repeat what I had said before—what had ended our relationship. "I'm not that kind of person. I'm sorry," I say with a sigh, and I was—truly and completely sorry. I was ashamed of what I had done to him and wished for maybe the millionth time that we could go back to the time when we were just friends. He was a brilliant friend—better than most men. He could make me laugh at the stupidest things but he could also argue with me and that was what I loved about him; that somewhere amongst that nice guy was a lump of courage.

"You're too much of an adventurer," he whispers in my ear, pulling me that last bit closer to him. I smile up at him, hearing the smile in his voice.

"For you, I am." I say as the song ends. He pecks me on the cheek, moving that loose strand of hair from my forehead again. He looks at me with a sad smile, but somewhere in that sadness, I see forgiveness. I smile at him even though my eyes are beginning to sting as tears pool at my lids. I reach up on tiptoes and kiss his forehead.

Steve catches a tear before it runs down my cheek and then looks at me with a happy smile.

"I hope you find the adventure you're looking for," he says before giving me one last squeeze and walking away.

10: PICNICS & RACES

"We're having a bit of a picnic in the garden," Phil says as he stands behind me. *Upsetting Steve again, are we?* As his thoughts sneak into my head, I sigh, knowing how good of friends Phil and Rob are with Steve and how good they have been since I split up with him.

"Excellent. I haven't eaten anything yet," I say, ignoring his thinking comment. Steve will be all right, I hope. I follow Phil out into the garden. Nicky and Elliot, Ali and Rob, Sophie and Ben, Chloe, Emma and Jason, and Jem sat on the edge of the circle, laughing and joking. They're drinking cocktails and nibbling at the mass of food they've collected from the buffet.

I sit down next to Ali and avoid eye contact with Jem. I'm feeling guilty, in a way, for dancing with Steve. It's odd really, I've only just met the guy and yet I have this feeling . . . *that* feeling, again.

"So you two are going to London on Monday?" Emma says before filling her mouth with a sausage roll.

"Yes. A bit of retail therapy before my Aunt and Uncle take me to France."

"No partying then?" she asks, dropping another roll in her mouth. I turn to Ali and grin.

"Oh, I expect there'll be some partying," I say, seeing Ali grin back.

"I wonder if we could get into that new club where Terry's been working," Ali says. I didn't know he'd been working in London. Why didn't he say? I shrug, more concerned that he hadn't said anything. "Maybe we could ask about some V.I.P. Passes," she adds, looking at me hopefully.

"I guess if you'd like to." I say with a shrug.

Hell yeah. At a new club like that we might meet some celebrities. Her thoughts amuse me. She'd do almost anything to get in with the 'red carpet' crowd.

"So are you all packed"? Sophie asks, her tone expecting a "no."

"D's sent a lot out already, so I don't have so much to take with me. I've just got my suitcase for London to pack and some bits for when I get to France."

"Are you going to Paris?" she asks with enthusiasm.

"I believe so. Kirk's doing some exhibition there, so I guess I'll be tagging along."

"You'll love it there. We went last year, it was lovely. And the shops . . ." she takes a quick look at Ben, "are excellent."

"Yeah, *excellent*," Ben says with sarcasm. "Her credit card got a serious bashing."

"Where else?" Nicky asks, changing the subject of shopping before Ben and Sophie begin arguing.

"Prague. I think."

She doesn't know much about where she's going, does she? Nicky's frown reflects her thoughts.

"My aunts and uncles have organized my travelling arrangements until Christmas. So I'm sort of in their control until then."

"And after Christmas?" Nicky asks, still frowning.

"I thought I might go to America. D has some friends there that I could stay with. So I might go there, and then maybe Italy."

Not Italy. Jem's words enter my head with a stern tone. Shocked, I turn and look at him.

Why not Italy? I like the idea of Italy. I've never been.

Just don't go to Italy, please, his thoughts reply, pleading with me.

"Where in America?" Rob asks through a mouth full of food.

"North America somewhere, I think."

"So not Hollywood," Phil says. *Would have thought that would have been the first place she'd go.* Phil's thoughts make me chuckle.

"No, not Hollywood," I say, still amused by his thoughts.

"Would have thought you'd hit the beaches of California or somewhere hot—flash your skills at surfing in a bikini," Rob says, a large grin pulling across his face. I throw a sausage roll at him.

"Just because you can't keep up doesn't mean I'm flashing."

"I can keep up." Rob's voice rises into a squeak, and I laugh. "I'll prove it." *I'll race her 'round the garden now.*

"Don't you think you've had too much to drink to be running about?"

"Nope." He gets to his feet.

"Fine." I undo my shoes, never able to resist the chance to embarrass Rob. I can see Ali's smile grow; Rob is unfit and she always finds it entertaining when I show him up. Poor guy. I stand up next to him. "So where do you want to race?"

"How about a lap around the house?" he asks with a shrug.

"Sure."

Phil gets up and stands in front of us. Counting on his watch, he holds up his hand.

"Ready . . . set . . . go!" I stride off, Rob staying level with me until we pass the front of the house. I jump over the small wall in the front lawn and turn around the end of the house and then back down towards the garden. As I appear around the corner I hear everyone roar with laughter, and I hear Rob's heavy breathing behind me. I continue down to the end of the garden and turn along the fence to head back to where Phil is standing. I make an abrupt stop right in front of Phil.

"Hooray!" Emma, Sophie, Nicky, and Ali all cheer as they rise to their feet in a victory dance. Rob drags himself to where Phil and I stand.

"Show off," he says between gasps of air.

I help him to his feet. "Maybe you should get some practice while I'm away," I suggest, but he only grins.

"Alright, we'll have a re-match at Christmas." I hold out my hand for agreement and Rob shakes it. *I'll be ready to beat her at Christmas.* I chuckle at Rob's thought. "What's so funny?"

"You are," I say, chuckling again. He grabs my arm and flings me over his shoulder, running down the garden with me in tow.

"Rob!" I shout out in protest. "Put me down!"

"What are you gonna do about it?" he challenges, spinning around. Instinctively I slap him round the head and he drops me on the floor. "Blimey. You've got a slap on you," as he rubs his head. I didn't hit him hard; I was only playing.

"Maybe you're just a wimp," I say, feeling a sly grin extend my comment.

"I'm not a wimp." He offers his hand out to me to help me up. He drops his arm around my neck, squeezing me close to his side. "We're gonna miss you. You know that, don't you?" Rob theatrically whispers in my ear.

"What? Miss me embarrassing you?" I say, trying to sound cheerful but actually feeling the need to cry.

"Ha ha," and he jabs me in the ribs. I sigh; thankfully the need to cry evaporates and I smile up at him. "I know what you mean. I'll miss you guys, too." I look over at Ali. "You will look after her won't you?" I know that despite whatever happens between them that he would, but I still needed the reassurance.

"Definitely," he says with the shy smile of a guy who's totally smitten.

"Thank you," I say as I wrap my arms around his waist.

"Why are you two being cuddly?" Emma asks.

"Rob just needed a little comforting for losing so badly," I say sarcastically, giving Rob another squeeze. Jem gets up and walks over to us, making everyone around us fall silent as they listen to what the 'new guy' has to say.

"So, are you a bad loser?" Jem asks with a challenging smile brightening his face. I shrug and quickly glance up at Rob, who is grinning at Jem.

"It's been a while since I've been beaten," I say cheekily, feeling a grin pinch at my own cheeks. Rob lets me go and walks over to Ali, quietly chuckling and muttering "good luck."

"Up for the challenge?" he asks, grinning back at me.

"Sure. Do you want to do the same lap?" I ask, looking him up and down and trying to figure if he's actually fit or not.

"Okay. What do I get if I win?" Jem asks as he folds his arms over his chest and watches me watching him.

You need a prize? I ask with shock, "What do you want?" I say, becoming suspicious of his motives. He puts his hand to his chin, pondering.

"You have to kiss me," he says as his grin grows. The girls muffle their giggles and I look over at Ali, whose eyes are wide.

She wants to, I hear her think.

"And if I win?" I ask, trying to sound more confident than I actually feel. *Make it good*, I think to him.

"You can take my car out for a drive," he says confidently. Now there's a good prize, I do rather fancy a drive in a convertible.

"Done," I say, holding out my hand for him to shake in agreement. Jem looks at my open hand with curiosity. "You don't get a chance to kiss me if we don't shake on it," I say, still holding my hand out to him.

What about the shocks? Jem asks my mind.

Oh, shocks . . . I hadn't thought about them. I close my open palm into a fist and step that last bit closer to him. Looking into his eyes I feel that feeling again and realize how much I want to touch him, but another part of me shouts out—the part that likes to rise to the challenge. I playfully punch his arm as I walk up to where Phil is standing.

"It's not like you're going to win, anyway," I say over my shoulder to him. Jem spins around and walks purposely toward Phil with a cheeky grin smacked straight on his face.

Much better; I don't like it when men don't try.

"This should be interesting." I hear Rob whisper in Ali's ear.

"I don't know . . . she's very fast," Ali says in reply.

Phil steps up to us. "Ready?" We both nod, standing ready to run. "Ready . . . set . . . go!" And we're off, neck and neck. We reach the corner of the house where it's now completely dark. I look round to see where he is, but he's gone. I can't even hear his footsteps. Jumping over the small wall I reach the next corner in zero time. As I turn I clout straight into Jem.

"Ow. Crap." *How did he get there?* I fall to the floor. Looking up at him I can make out the shape of a grin across his face. He offers his hand for me to get up but I ignore it and struggle to my feet. "You're not going to win," I shout with venom in my voice.

"Are you sure about that?" he asks through a chuckle.

"Yes." I run off around him, round the other side of the house, and sprint out toward the garden.

I'm gonna win. His thoughts sing in my head as he sprints past me. I push myself harder, coming up neck and neck again as we run along the side of the fence. Turning again back up to the others, he's gone, and I don't want to keep up. I hear a loud "Hooray!" from the boys as I stroll up to the picnic gathering. I stop a couple of feet away and Jem walks over to me.

"Can I collect my prize?" he asks, his voice soft and comforting. Suddenly I feel not like a loser but a winner, because I do want to kiss him, but maybe not with such an audience.

What about the shocks? They can't see that. If my friends had witnessed the shocks and pins and needles, they'd probably freak out.

We can do it. Just let go. Watching him walk closer to me, I try desperately not to be forward and run full speed into his open arms.

If you want it, you'll have to come and get it. He carefully places his hand on my arm and pins and needles tingle through my skin. I can feel my heart start to pound; it's beating so hard that my ribs are beginning to ache. He leans in and gives me a peck on the lips.

He caresses my cheek with his nose, and whispers in my ear, "Amazing," with a contented sigh.

"What's amazing?"

He looks me in the eye, his deep blue eyes mesmerizing me as he responds: "You are." Well, that does it. I wrap my arms around his neck and cease my struggling.

"You'll only get one chance," I whisper before letting our lips meet again, but this time there's no fear—no restraint. His mouth claims mine and we pull ourselves closer to each other until I can feel the beating of his heart against mine; the pins and needles are almost comforting, just because I know that he is the one holding me. The tears begin to escape from my closed eyelids as I realize that I don't want to let go, but that I have to. Jem pulls back and wipes away my tears.

"Why are you crying?" he asks, quiet fear sounding in his tone.

"Because I'm leaving," I say as I rest my head on his shoulder.

"Hope, it's not forever." He pulls his arms up around me and kisses my hair.

"No, not forever," I agree with an exasperated sigh. We let go of each other and turn to face the picnic crowd. All of them are standing up in amazement, howling and whooping at the two of us. I look over at Ali and see her smile is huge as she claps her hands.

She likes him—she really *likes him.*

Then, Jem and I become dazzled by the two sets of headlights heading down the drive. "That's our taxi," Emma says, recognizing the cars that have arrived. I walk back over to them and, taking in a deep breath, I brace myself to say goodbye to my friends. Emma, Sophie, and Nicky pull me into a big squeeze between them.

"Keep in touch," they all say. I feel my eyes start to well up with tears as I try to say goodbye. Ben and Jason each give me a peck on the cheek as they leave.

Phil pulls me into a tight hug and kisses me hard on the lips. "Have fun," he says, suddenly looking sad.

I kiss him back and smile, stepping out of his arms to wipe away my tears. "Definitely. I'm sure Ali will keep you informed of my whereabouts." Then, all of a sudden, Rob pushes Phil out of the way and lifts me up off the ground, squeezing me so tightly that I can barely breathe.

"Take care of yourself," he says, and he kisses me on the lips.

"I'll be back for Christmas, Rob," I say through gasps of air.

"Yeah, you will. We've got to race again."

"Make sure you get some practice. I don't want to have to beat you again." He lets out a loud burst of laughter as he puts me down.

"See you at Christmas," he says, and Ali and I follow them out to the taxis parked in the drive. Ali and Rob cuddle together as they say their goodbyes.

"See you tomorrow night," she says as we wave him off.

11: TRUTHS

I turn around to see where Jem has gone and sigh as I watch him walk back into the marquee. Ali and I make our way back to the picnic and fill up our glasses again.

"Great party, huh?" Ali says as we sit down on the grass.

"Yeah, really great. I really enjoyed myself," I say, thinking happily of how well the evening had actually gone.

"Well, I think a certain assistant had something to do with that," she says, grinning over at me.

"Maybe." My grin mirrors hers. "So, are you and Rob going to do anything special over the summer?" I ask, trying to change the subject.

"We've talked about going away for a weekend." She cringes. "I guess it depends on work."

"Ooh . . . weekend away—that's serious," I say mockingly, seeing her blush out of the corner of my eye. Why did she cringe? "Ali, Rob's a nice guy. I can see he makes you happy."

"Yeah I'm happy. But weekends away are . . ." she sighs, "serious."

I let out a little chuckle. "What's wrong with that?"

"I'm going to uni in September. It's going to be difficult to have a relationship."

"Jeez, Ali, you'll find a way 'round it. I'm sure." She has a natural ability to balance her life. I drink more of the cocktail, which is luckily not extra strength this time.

"I should say the same to you," she says as a giggle escapes through her grin. "I mean seriously, Hope. I've never seen you like that with anyone before."

"Like what?" I ask, trying to sound like I don't know but failing.

"Like sat on cloud 9, head over heels, can't be without you." This was the subject I was trying to avoid: Ali's evaluation of Jem . . . and me.

"Really obvious," I cringe, "bet everyone's whispering about it now."

"Yeah, but not in a bad way." *He's perfect for her.* Looking out across the garden, I sip more of the cocktail. "So, do you like him?" she asks, watching me.

"Ali," I groan, and her grin grows even wider. "I don't really know him."

"But you'd like to," she says confidently. *The way she kissed him earlier proved that.*

"Ali, you were the one who just said long distance relationships are difficult. At least you and Rob are going to be in the same country."

"True," she says in agreement, but grabs my arm and makes me look into her serious eyes. "But honestly, Hope, if he makes you feel like the way he looks like he does, you should find a way to make it work."

"I don't think he'd be patient enough for me to go travelling and still be sat here waiting for me to come back," I say, trying to think how I am going to be able to travel now that I've just met him. Again, odd; I hardly know him, and yet the thought of being away from him is almost unbearable.

"Yeah right," she says through a mouthful of food. "You've obviously not seen how he looks at you." But she's been watching him, hasn't she? Checking him out, even. "You should have seen him when you were dancing with Steve. He kept checking over to see where you were." He was, was he?

"I've only just met him," I say in protest, not just to Ali but to myself. This isn't possible—it's too fast.

"So . . ." Ali says as she eats some more.

"So . . ." I lie back on the grass. "You don't just meet a guy and—bam—that's it." Do you? I wonder. "Surely relationships grow. You know like you and Rob. It was nearly two weeks before you two really kissed and now . . . well, look at you! You're well on your way to a happily ever after."

"God, Hope, it sounds like you've married me off already," she says with a cringe. Her cringe sends a sudden shiver down my spine.

"Maybe," I say, sitting back up and looking at her. Am I missing something? Is she not thinking of staying with Rob? I know we're young, but I thought she was happy.

"The thing is, Hope, you're a bit of an all-or-nothing kind of gal," she says, her serious face back again; I recoil at the truth in her words.

"Okay maybe that's true. But . . ." I take a deep breath. "I don't think it's a good idea." I say, trying to convince myself.

"Hope, I'm not saying marry the guy. Just let him in, and if you don't like him it won't matter because you'll be travelling, and if you do . . . well, maybe you'll be home quicker." I can see her peeking out of the corner of her eye at me, waiting for my reaction.

"Is that what this is really about?" I ask, feeling upset that maybe she thought a man would stop me from what I want to do. She shrugs, wrapping her arms around her knees.

"You've said you'll be back for Christmas, but I know full well that you'll pop home for a couple of days and then be off again." What she says is probably right. But . . .

"Ali, I need to do this."

"I understand that," she says as her eyes begin to water. "It's just that . . . you'll be off having an adventure and meeting new people." She takes in a jagged breath. "And what if you forget me?" I pull myself up close to her and wrap my arm around her shoulders, feeling my own tears start to flow.

"I could never forget you. You're a part of me," I say through my tears.

"And you me," she says, wiping away my tears. I hold up my glass and Ali does the same.

"To friendship," I say, and we crash our glasses together and both finish our drinks. "The next six months are going to be good. And I'll ring and e-mail, so you know where I am and what I'm doing."

She rests her head on my shoulder. "I'll still miss you, though"

"Me too." We sit in the darkness for a long while, letting the silence say our goodbyes for us.

Ali wipes away her tears and looks at her watch. "I'd better go to bed. I've got lunch with my Gran tomorrow."

"Okay. Has D put you in the room next to mine?"

"Yes. Jem is staying in the bedroom at the end of the hall," she says, a smirk rising across her face. My mouth drops with shock; Ali wouldn't usually condone one-night stands.

"I'll see you in the morning, Ali." I say, trying desperately to put her last comment out of my mind.

She gives me one last squeeze and whispers in my ear: "Let him in. Just once, let go," she says, her tone almost pleading.

"Good night, Ali." And she gets up and walks back into the house.

I undo the pins in the tight knot and let my hair fall down my back. Lying back on the grass, I shut my eyes, listening to the noises of the night, and begin to feel almost relaxed. A warm hand brushes against my cheek. Knowing that it's Jem, I squeeze my eyes shut, refusing to open them; I'm still deciding if letting him in is such a good idea. I feel his warm fingers run along my forehead, removing the hair from my face and leaving a tingling sensation from his touch. Then, it becomes clear in my head. Ali's words ring through my mind. *If he makes you feel like the way he looks like he does, you should find a way to make it work.* I open my eyes and pull him to me, kissing him gently.

"We'll make it work," he says softly. Looking into his eyes I can see that he means it, but a part of me is still concerned that this feeling happened too fast. Jem lies down next to me, taking hold of my hand, and the pins and needles run up my arm. I turn on my side, resting my head in my hand, watching him.

He is certainly handsome. And I do like him, but . . .

"How did this happen?" I say out loud. Jem lets out a huge sigh and then rolls onto his side to face me. "You and me, for instance. We only met tonight, and, well . . ." Don't blush, I think to myself. "You seem to have swept me off my feet." *Is that really what I wanted to say? Or should I have said the complete truth: can I keep kissing you until my lungs run out of air? Because I've never felt like this before.* I catch Jem watching me. *No, stick with the 'swept me off your feet' and have some self-control,* I say to myself, trying to convince myself that I can.

"I guess that's as much my fault as it is yours," he confesses.

"How is it my fault?" I ask. *What the hell did I do? I didn't even invite him.* He rolls onto his back and tightly closes his eyes.

"It's my fault because I wanted to meet you before you left to go on your trip." Opening his eyes, he turns his head to me. "And it's your fault for being so . . ." Hesitating, he closes his eyes again. "For being so beautiful," he says with a sigh.

He thinks I'm beautiful. My face warms. "How is that my fault?" I ask. To be fair, there were some beautiful girls here tonight—far more beautiful than me—and I'm sure they would have taken him.

"God, Hope," he says, covering his face with his hands. His voice is angry.

Is he angry with me because he thinks I'm beautiful?

"No, I'm not angry at you," he says through his fingers.

Crap. He can hear my thoughts. Note to self: have good, clean thoughts when around him. God, that's going to be hard. "Then why are you angry?" I ask, feeling that he's still tense.

"I'm angry at myself for not having better self-control—for kissing you, and for knowing how badly I want you right now."

Okay. That's a little intense. I feel a little shocked by what he's said, but also sympathize with him. I had felt the same, but now . . .

Do you not feel the same way? I hear in my head. I roll over onto my front and dangle my cocktail glass in front of me.

"Did Terry not tell you everything about me and drinking?" He rolls over so our bodies touch.

Smiling, he says, "Something to do with going like mush and giving in." *Hence the extra shots in the cocktail.*

"So you were trying to get me drunk?" *And get into my knickers.*

"I was trying to soften you up. You play quite an ice maiden, you know."

"Yes, thanks, nice of you to highlight that," I say sarcastically. "Softening me up is not a good idea." I scare most people when I'm drunk, which is why I usually drink cocktails that aren't too strong. *God, he must think I'm a lightweight.* I shake my head. I've stopped drinking so much or so bad because of what happens—I'm a crazy person when I've drunk too much.

69

"Something happened before?" he asks as he sips at his cocktail.

"Yes," I respond, although I'm not too sure that I should tell him. But my mind is already flashing through my past instances of drinking (heavily) and men—of waking up a couple of times next to some guy that I'd met in a club or bar—and then, of course, there was Steve. My mind's eyes runs through the last few times we had had sex; I had been drinking and pretty much tore him to pieces. No—me and drinking and men were definitely not a good combination. My hormones would take over. "I don't trust myself." *Because the next time I have sex, I want it to mean something—something that I feel rather than just need.*

"And you don't trust me?" Jem asks sadly.

"I don't know you or this thing between us. It's rather intense."

"I think that's just how it is," he says with a shy smile.

"How what is?" I ask, feeling a bit dumb.

"When you fall in love," he says confidently. Swallowing my mouthful with a loud gulp, I shake my head in disbelief. *It can't be love. Can it? Maybe it's just lust?*

"It can't be lust, Hope." He looks like he's trying to convince himself as well as me.

"Why not?"

He looks away from me and sighs. "Because if it was just lust we'd be upstairs now, alcohol or not."

"Probably," I say, sipping my drink. *Hope, you whore.* Even my thoughts tell me off. Jem turns back, looking at me with a sly grin; I can't help but grin back, wondering if he's thinking the same as I am. What would it be like? Especially with shocks and pins and needles, that could be quite interesting. My little bit of self-control begins to slip as I lean toward Jem. I want him more than I've ever wanted anyone. But something deep in the pit of my stomach is screaming: *No! Don't sleep with him. You'll ruin everything.* But can't I just......... Before I can finish my train of thought Jem kisses me hard and urgent running his hand up into my hair pulling me closer to him. It's not enough. I roll onto my side, taking his arm and wrapping it around my waist. The pins and needles intensify from his passionate hold on me. Pulling his body closer to me, I roll onto my back.

Our lips mold together until he breaks away and whispers, "Hope, my love," breathlessly. I look deep into his eyes. I love how that sounds and that he is the one that said it. Could I really love him? Or have I really had too much to drink? "I'm not going to take advantage of you. You've been drinking." Pulling himself away from me, he sits up and looks out at the meadows beyond the lawn, now only just lit by the moonlight.

"Thank you," I say, sitting up next to him. I probably would have regretted it in the morning. We sit in silence for a long moment. A list of questions grows in my mind, but there's only one I can ask out loud. "Why you?" Jem's head snaps round to look at me, his faced screwed up.

"Don't you like that it's me?" His voice sounds hurt.

"I didn't say that, I—"

Jem interrupts before I can finish. "—I know I'm not Vin Diesel, or whoever you'd fancy, but . . ." His voice is now sounding hateful.

"I didn't say that I didn't like that you..." I run my hand along his arm, the tingling of pins and needles running into my fingertips. *You make me feel amazing.* "I just asked why it's you. Or maybe why it's me?" He turns himself round and crosses his legs; watching him, I do the same. He takes my hand and places it on his chest and then places his hand on mine. He takes in a deep breath and with his other hand he holds my hand over his heart. Fascinated by his motions, I do the same to him.

"Listen," Jem says softly. I close my eyes, trying to identify the drumming noise that I can now hear. Da da dum, da da dum, da da dum.

It's a heartbeat, I realize, hearing the familiar steady beat.

"It's our heartbeat," Jem says, correcting my thoughts.

"How does that work?" I ask, feeling confused. How is that even possible?

"Well, I guess in simple terms, the pieces that we carry sing for each other. So when we get close to the other piece we don't want to let go." I open my eyes and look down at my hand on Jem's chest. It's glowing as if sunshine is caught in my hand, radiating from his chest.

"Wow," is the most I can manage to say, but somehow, although the glowing is strange, it feels right. It's as if it proves something—like it's meant to be. *Is that why I feel like this?*

"Yes, definitely wow." Jem agrees with a huge smile on his face. I frown at his response. Why isn't he freaked out by the glowing? Does he feel the same? Like it's meant to be?

"But how did you get a part of my heart or vice versa?"

"I'm not entirely sure how it works, but I'm pleased that it does." I watch my hand glowing.

"Why does it glow?" I ask. Is it magic? It doesn't hurt; in fact, it feels nice—cozy. Jem shrugs and takes his hand away from my chest. *Oooh, not so cozy now.* I drop my hand from Jem's chest and lie back down on the grass. Twiddling with my hair, I start running through the things that have happened today. So much has happened since I woke up this morning. The more I think about it, the more I start to realize.

This morning when D and I were talking about the party, she could hear my thoughts. Only Ali knows about the Sergeant Major and the clipboard, and she wouldn't have blabbed. Can D read Ali's thoughts too? That would be scary. Took Bee out, crashed into a tree, blacked out, cloaked woman with glowing ball of light. What did she say? I wrack my brains but I can't remember. What happened after? The deer in the clearing, then I blacked out again. Didn't know how I got to Bee so quickly, and then jumping off the saddle in the yard. My legs—I sit up and look down at my legs—they definitely seem fitter. I look at my arms and feel my stomach; in fact, I feel fitter all over. How? Hearing voices. Weird? But it's not continuous. I can't hear everybody. Some fuzzy vision, but again, it's not all the time. It's really only been when I look at Ali, and then there's Jem, who can read my mind; can he read everybody else's? He gives me static shocks and makes my heart glow. Or apparently makes my half glow. I can answer back telepathically as well, which is peculiar too.

Jem moves round and sits next to me. "I can only read your thoughts because you let me. You can shut me out as well."

"That's good to know." *That could save me from some serious embarrassment.*

"It takes practice though," he says with a knowing tone.

"I'm going away. I'll have plenty of time for practice," I say, feeling confident that I could master it with some practice.

"Don't you like that I can hear your thoughts?" Jem asks, interested.

"Some things aren't too bad, but girls do need their privacy—even in their heads."

"So do boys," he says with a shy smile.

"I can imagine," I say sarcastically. *Hair gel, pants, fantasy dreams with Angelina Jolie.*

"You're taking this very well," Jem says, smiling at me proudly.

"Am I?" It's a part of me—this mind reading, fuzzy vision, and whatever—I can't deny what I am; I can only accept it, right?

"Hope, you've been hearing voices. Not only did you not freak out about it, you also replied telepathically, like you had been doing it for years," Jem states enthusiastically.

"It seemed a natural thing to do. It could be quite an advantage, being able to communicate telepathically. Does it work on animals?" I ask curiously.

"I can't, but you might be able to."

"Cool," I say, thinking of the possibilities. Just imagine—it could be amazing! I could talk to Bee. Now that would be absolutely incredible.

"You truly are amazing," Jem says, looking at me with admiration.

"If you keep saying that my heads gonna swell," I say sternly at him.

Wrapping my arms around my legs, I rest my head on my knees. Why me, though? I'm just some hormonal teenager. There's nothing special about me.

"D and Terry will explain," Jem says as he gets up and offers his hand to me. "Well, at least they'll explain what they know."

"So they don't know what's happening to me?" I ask, feeling a bit disheartened.

"Not everything. That's why I'm here," he says.

"Do you know why I'm like this?" I ask hopefully.

"Not really." He shrugs, still holding out his hand. "I'm here because I didn't want you to go through this on your own."

"Thank you," I say, as I take his hand and get up.

"I have to confess that you scare me a bit though." His admission seems flippant, but I notice that his expression is firmly set, as if he's hiding something.

"I scare you?" I ask, shocked.

"Yes, you scare me," he says, smiling down at me. "Your self-control is brilliant—it scares me that you won't need me."

Ah; he likes to have a woman who depends on him. "That's not a bad thing though, surely?" I ask, knowing that I'll be leaving Monday and that I'll need my self-control; if only I didn't have to keep pinching at my subconscious every couple of minutes, I probably would have jumped him by now.

Me too. Jem's thought replies to mine.

Really going to have to work on the blocking out thing—this stuff could be embarrassing. Jem bursts into laughter. "What's so funny?" I ask.

He wraps his arm around my shoulders and pulls me to his side. "Only you," he responds, and kisses the top of my head.

12: EXPLAINATIONS

When we reach the patio, D and Terry are coming out with a tray of tea and biscuits.

"Are you tired?" D asks as she pours out the tea.

"Not really," I say, smiling up at Jem as he squeezes me tighter to his side. "I think my nap earlier helped." Jem smiles back at me, making me melt just that little bit more.

"Jem, can you give me a hand for a minute? We'd better let these girls have a chat alone." Terry says as he takes his tea from D.

"Sure," he says, and gives my shoulder a gentle squeeze and then follows Terry into the house.

D and I sit next to each other on the bench, holding onto our warm cups of tea.

"So, can you explain what's going on?" I ask, before sipping my tea.

"I'll explain what I can."

"That would help," I say, sitting back into the seat. *Anything would help at the moment.*

"The thing is, Hope, you're sort of unique." D seems to squirm as she speaks.

"Sort of unique." I frown as I repeat, not liking the sound.

"Well," D lets out a long sigh, "your mother was one of The Sabbath Court."

"One of what?" I ask, already not understanding her. D frowns at me, showing that she doesn't appreciate the interruptions. "Sorry," I say, pinching my lips shut tight.

"The Sabbath Court," she repeats, her single raised eyebrow awaiting another interruption.

"You mean like witches and spells and stuff?" I ask, remembering something about a book I once read—The Sabbath something, about witches and their histories.

"Yes."

Okey dokey, she's gone crazy.

"No, Hope, I haven't." She puts her hand on mine.

"Oh great," I sigh. "*You* can hear my thoughts, too." I sigh again; I knew something was up this morning.

"Yes, but only for the past couple of months." D smiles back at me as I rapidly run through the things I could have thought that might have shocked her.

"Why only the past couple of months?" I ask. What's happened in the last couple of months?

"Our powers don't 'show' until we're eighteen, or when we mature. Boys seem to gain their powers later than girls," she explains.

Ah, I get it, I turned eighteen in March. "So there are a lot of people like this?" I ask, feeling concerned but also a little relieved that what I've been experiencing isn't too unusual.

"Magical beings?" D asks, and I nod. "A few, but no more than a couple thousand, and we're spread all over the globe, so you don't encounter many that often." She shrugs at her answer like it means nothing, but somehow that still seems a lot.

"This Sabbath Court . . . can they all read minds?" I ask, feeling concerned that what's in my head is not private.

"No, and I can only read your thoughts, no one else's," she says reassuringly.

Well, that's a relief but . . . "Why?" Why only my thoughts?

"We guess it's because I've been your guardian for so long. It is rare but it is possible that your powers *rubbed off* on me." D frowns at her own words.

"But Jem can read my thoughts," I say, wondering if he can read my thoughts because they rubbed off on him, too.

"Yes, I noticed that," she says, her voice sounding annoyed.

"He said it was because I let him in," I say, ignoring her tone.

"Not exactly." She hesitates and takes another sip of her tea. "Terry invited him so that he could try." D suddenly sounds tired and old.

"Try what?" I ask. If this is going back to the seducing thing I'll be well pissed off.

"Have you not noticed the changes in the past three months?" she asks, looking back at me. I shrug; *I don't think I have. D and I have been getting on a bit better.* "Yes we have. But I think it's because I'm not so stressed out anymore." D smiles at me weakly.

"Am I really stressful to live with?" I ask nervously. Poor D— I've been an absolute bitch at times.

"I've been shielding you since you were born, trying to keep you safe. The day you turned eighteen you woke up with a shield around your body, and as time has gone on you've also put one around the house, around your friends, and me. The amazing thing is you do it subconsciously." D looks out over the garden, letting her moment of pride hang in the night air.

"So, I *am* stressful to live with?" I ask, watching her, but she doesn't respond. "I am sorry," I apologize sheepishly. D looks at me in shock. "What?" I ask defensively, "I didn't know you were trying to keep me safe. You could have told me—given me some sort of warning."

"Well, it was necessary at the time," D says with her loving, parental smile.

We sit for a while in silence, my mind still going into overdrive. "This shield *thing*—is that what Jem was trying to break?" I ask, feeling troubled that someone would need to break a shield to get to me.

"Yes. It was dangerous for him to try," D says, looking away from me again.

"Because of me—am I dangerous?" I ask, feeling concerned; I was only worried about myself and not what could happen to someone else. D shrugs in response.

"I'm not entirely sure." D turns and looks at me, her face looking sad. "My theory is that you automatically defend yourself. I think that's why I can hear your thoughts when I'm with you; and like tonight, with the ringing in your ears." D points to her ears, trying to explain. "You see, a shield is like a bubble and when someone is within that bubble you can hear him or her. That was everyone's thoughts you could hear." She sighs as she glances over to the patio doors. "But when Jem arrived, you formed a second shield close to your body."

"Is that why we've been getting shocks and pins and needles?" I ask, wondering, if i didn't have a shield, would everyone get shocks from me?

"I don't think so," D says, pondering. "A shield can only be broken if permission is granted or its creator is killed."

"Nice," I say with sarcasm. Great bit of info that—not!

"You being unique makes a difference." D smiles at me proudly. "The problem is, you could have many skills, but they need to be unlocked, hence your trip. Our family is going to help you—train you," further pride makes her voice rise.

"Train me for what?" I ask, feeling unsure of what she's saying.

"To follow in you mother's footsteps." *Huh?* "She was the peace keeper. Your mother was a very talented witch, and a soul seeker. When she looked into a person's eyes, she said she could see the very essence of them: the good and the bad, the regrets they had, and the dreams they hoped for. That's how I met her. I was working in some woods in the midlands. There had been a problem with tree fever and I had gone to encourage new growth in the land. Your mother was organizing a treaty between the fairies and tree elves there. They had been fighting for years, and your mother had helped them resolve their differences and live in peace."

"Hold up." I put my hand up to make her stop. "Did you say she was working with fairies and elves? And you make the trees grow? Like mother nature?" I ask.

"Yes," D says with personal pride. "I am a nature whisperer and a shield. I inherited the skill from my mother. Your mother asked me to protect you when you were born, from that first day in the woods we became friends."

"And the fairies?" I ask, unsure of her sanity. Because fairies . . . and elves . . . they don't exist. Right?

"Yes, they do exist, but they generally keep to the woods," she says matter-of-factly.

"Really? Why haven't I seen them? I spend loads of time in the woods," I ask, suddenly feeling offended that I haven't seen them.

"I expect you're not ready to yet. Or maybe you have and didn't realize."

"I don't think so." I've never seen anything out of the ordinary in the woods—never. Okay . . . until today, that is.

"They might be a bit scared of you. You are your father's daughter," she says, shrugging again.

"What does that have to do with it?" Like the guy actually stuck around to find out what I'm like.

"Your father is an absorber." D's matter-of-fact tone returns.

"An absorber? That doesn't sound nice." Is that why I shield myself?

"He wasn't always." D sighs like she's finally giving in. "An absorber can digest or absorb another being, taking all their powers. Although he didn't kill them, the people were left with nothing. They would become hollow and would start to age. You see, Hope, we're born with our powers, inheriting them from our parents. We can also gain one as a gift, usually from a relative. They *must* be given and not taken, but your father had taken so many that he had immense power and only one weakness—your mother."

"But they weren't always together. How did Mum meet him? Why would she be with someone who was so dangerous?" I ask, concerned about how my parents had met and how things were for me to be conceived.

"Magical beings, or witches at least, come as a pair. Usually, a heart is shared with our kind, and the half that we carry yearns for the other; when we find that other half, we tend not to let go, like being married. Your mother's heart didn't sing for any of us. She consulted with the Grand High Witch of The Sabbath and requested that she leave the court to find her other half. She travelled for many years, and while she was looking for her other half she discovered other beings that lived independently from the Sabbath. She found witches coexisting with other species, like vampires, fairies, and shape-shifters. She began documenting her findings and reporting to The Grand High witch. The Grand High was pleased with her work, but also amazed. Witches haven't coexisted with vampires for thousands of years. Neither have shape-shifters, for that matter. The Grand High pronounced your mother the peacekeeper and gave her

K. M. Buckland

the authority to set treaties and keep the peace.

"That's how our family was made. Your Mother brought us together. We're all different, as you know. Not technically related. But we share and love just like a normal human family. She only ever asked us to love and respect one another, and we have now for many years. The sad thing is that we have been in hiding since you were born in order to keep you safe.

"When your mother met your father, it was a dangerous time for witches. The vampire Masters had declared war on the Sabbath and its kind. Your mother went to make peace, but the Masters rejected her request and imprisoned her. That's how she met your father. He rescued her and brought her back here to England. The Masters tracked them for years, but thankfully never found them. They were very careful not to use their powers. Your father even stopped absorbing, but that was probably because your parents had performed a union.

"That's how we found out you were on your way. Your parents went to the Grand High Witch to announce their union to the court and that they were expecting a child—you. The Court didn't approve of the union and demanded that the Grand High break the union and destroy you. Your mother begged The Grand High to not break the union, knowing that she could not exist without your father. Thankfully, the Grand High was fond of your mother and asked her teller to foresee your mother's future. The teller confirmed that you would be born and that you would be no harm to our kind, but she did warn your mother that she would be the sacrifice for such a creature being born. She knew it to be true, but she also knew it couldn't be stopped. She loved your father very much, even if he is a monster. The Grand High took your mother's authority for treaties and advised that your mother never return to The Sabbath Court. Your mother agreed and asked The Grand High to grant her one other request: that when you were born, you could continue her work. The Grand High agreed but would not consent to the authority for treaties. It's hard to explain, but you're not a member of The Sabbath, so for you to create a treaty on their behalf would be forbidden," she says with a shrug. "She also advised that a child of such parents will be sought out by both sides and must be shielded until their powers are under control. That's where I come in," she says, pointing to her chest.

"Although I didn't live with your mother until her final months of pregnancy, when I arrived here, she had already prepared everything ready for your birth and her . . ." I turn to D, sensing her sadness, and watch as a single tear wells in her eyelid and falls down her cheek. With a sigh she wipes it away. "That's when your father left. They travelled for nearly fifty years before they settled here."

"Fifty years? But Mum was in her twenties when she had me." She's wrong—I've seen pictures of her and she looks like she's in her mid-twenties, certainly not reaching her sixties or seventies.

"She *looked* like she was in her twenties," D says with a grin.

"What are you saying? I don't age?"

"You will age, Hope, but after so many years it slows down. We're not immortal, but we do live a very long time." She sighs again, drinking more of her tea.

"How long?" For how long would I have to live like this?

"For you, I'm not sure, because you have your father's powers. But for me . . ." she hesitates, looking away from me. "Well, The Grand High Witch has recently celebrated her 1,372nd birthday."

"What? One, three, seven, two?" I ask, completely shocked at the number.

"Yes."

"That's really old."

"Yes, but she's very powerful, so her life expectancy is much more."

"So the more powerful you are the longer you live?"

"Something like that."

"So this heart yearning thing is that what Jem is?" Because although he said it and I accepted it, there's something else—something more—and the feeling I have when I'm near him is . . . indescribably amazing.

"He believes so, but we're not sure. Tellers haven't been able to see you."

"And the fact that his chest glowed when I touched it . . . is that normal for two pieces?" I ask. The glowing felt good for me, although it was weird, but then, the whole day seems to have been weird.

"They glowed?" D says with shock. *Obviously not normal, then.*

"Yep . . . freaky," I say, trying to sound unbothered, but D's still tense.

"What color was your I-stone when you touched him?" she asks through clenched teeth.

"I-stone?"

"Your mother's pendant. What color was it?" D asks impatiently.

"Umm, white with pink and blue spots in it, I think. Why? I thought it was a mood indicator or something. What's an I-stone?"

"An I-stone indicates your heart motions. It also helps with concentrating on a singular person's thoughts rather than an overwhelming continuous buzz."

"Heart motions—is that like mood changing?" I ask, still confused.

"No. A mood is triggered by the brain, but the heart changes color when it feels a transformation, and your heart seems to change more frequently than any other."

"So when I put it on and it changed to pink . . . that meant?"

"Pink is family."

"And when I met Jem and it turned white. That means what?"

"White *usually* means a balance."

"Usually?" I ask; the way she says usually is a little unsettling.

"Your motions are very quick. That's why you must be careful with Jeremy, if he is your other half."

"Would I hurt him?" Even though I don't really know the guy, I still don't want to hurt him.

"Not intentionally, but until you have control of your powers you must not unite." D's tone is stern.

"Right. No union until I have control." I don't know how I'm going to do that; my self-control isn't that good. And what exactly is a union?

"You'll find a way, I'm sure." D says, trying to sound reassuring. "The thing is, Jeremy's heart is very strong and bright, and yours . . ." She takes a deep breath.

"Is not," I say, finishing her sentence. *Ice maiden—that's me.* But somehow I know that *that* coldness in me is for a reason.

"The heart motions that you have are too fast, but they're also not complete."

"Why's it not complete?" Shock makes my voice squeak.

"I'm not sure, but Hope, be careful. Make sure that you are absolutely positive before you accept his union," she says, pleading with me.

"Alright," I say, agreeing to what she asks; anything to get her to calm down. D gets up from the bench and tidies up the cups.

"I'll make some more tea."

"Okay." I curl up on the bench, letting my mind process the information. Being a peacekeeper could be pretty cool. But what skills do I have exactly? If my Dad absorbed so many talented creatures, what will I become? Am I dangerous? Will I be an absorber too? Sucking the life out of people . . . I can't do that. I'm not a murderer. My eyes begin to water and the tears slowly soak my cheeks. I wipe them away with irritation. I can't believe how much I've cried tonight. I'm not usually so soft. I close my eyes tightly, trying to make the tears stop.

I feel someone sit next to me. Not caring who it is, I ask out loud, "Am I dangerous?"

"Only when you're angry," Terry says through a chuckle. Opening my eyes, I look at him, feeling a wave of relief that it's him; I rest my head on his shoulder.

"Am I like my dad?" I ask, concerned.

"In many ways, you are. But not in a bad way."

"What was he like?" Terry's the one who tells me about my dad; D has never really spoken about him and I've never questioned it, more because I didn't want to upset her. She seems disappointed in him for leaving me.

"When I first met your father he wasn't with your mum. He was still very hard-nosed then. He'd been trying to stop with the absorbing, but he said it was very hard when the powers were so tempting. However, when he met your mum, she gave him a reason to stop—a reason to live in peace. Your mum always thought it was because of their union that he had found that peace, but I think it also had to do with becoming a parent.

83

"When your parents were together their abilities were great, and they worked hard toward getting different species to coexist. You see, your father had absorbed an ancient vampire and a shape-shifter, so he could *shift* his powers from one to the other. It was quite helpful sometimes, but dangerous too. If your father remained a vampire for too long, he'd become thirsty, just like a normal vampire. That's where your mum comes in. She gave him a reason to shift back to his normal self."

"So they balanced out?" I ask curiously.

"Sort of," Terry says thoughtfully.

"Why did you bring Jem here if you knew he thought I was his other half?" I ask, trying to understand Terry's motives.

"Incentive, I guess," he says with a shrug.

"What do I need incentive for?"

"An incentive for the magic within you to be good," he says positively.

"So I'm not good, then?" I ask, waiting for confirmation.

"Well," he grins at me and wraps his arm around my shoulder, "you're a bit better now, but before you were going out with Steve, D was ringing every week saying you'd been out drinking and up to no good."

"I'm sorry. I didn't mean for you to worry," I say, feeling ashamed of what I had put them through.

"It's alright," he says, giving my shoulders a gentle squeeze. "You've been better since your birthday. Well . . . until tonight."

"That wasn't me, Terry," I shout out of protest as I lift my head from his shoulder. "Jem spiked my drink. You suggested that he should soften me up." My voice gets louder.

"Yes. Sorry. That is true. But I didn't expect you to react the way you did." He looks at me as if he's seeing something new for the first time.

"So when two halves meet they don't . . ." *automatically want to jump into bed together.*

"No," Terry says with another chuckle. "But the thing is Hope, you fight it as well, like it annoys you." A singular eyebrow lifts on his forehead, questioning me.

84

"It does, a bit," I say in agreement, resting my head back on his shoulder. "It seems too much like an arranged marriage."

"Yeah, I guess it is, a bit."

"Would it hurt him if we don't unite?"

"I don't know. I've never known a union to be denied." Terry turns my shoulders so I face him. "Hope, your powers will grow, but only you can decide how you use them. Your coming visits with our family are to help you, because although you are rightfully a member of the Sabbath Court, your mum had also made other acquaintances which will lead you to your fulfilment.

"D told you that the Sabbath is a group of witches and that their rules are followed by all of the craft and those who don't are removed?" he asks.

"Removed?" I ask with fear; she didn't tell me that bit.

"Removed, disposed, or imprisoned," he says with a shrug.

"But mum followed the rules. She helped keep the peace," my voice squeaks with fear.

"Yes. You see, in our world, there are many species and different courts. For thousands of years there have been wars. When your mum left The Sabbath on her travels, she found that most of the wars were caused by their rules, and had tried to make the different courts change their rules so the species could coexist, keeping one rule for all. Keep the humans out of it. Keep our existence secret. She had reported it to The Grand High Witch, but she didn't approve. Her and your mum argued continuously about changing the laws; your mum insisted that the Court that had created the laws was misinformed, and that most beings could coexist when they had a common goal."

"That must have been hard to do," I say, admiring my mum's bravery.

"Yes, and sometimes dangerous. Her presence wasn't always welcome."

"People tried to kill her?" I ask, feeling sorry for the life she must have led, but proud that she had survived long enough to give birth to me.

"Tried but failed. She was very clever." He smiles fondly.

"Did she really want me to continue her work?" Something about the idea doesn't seem right to me. Keeping the peace sounds like quite a job, but something in my gut argues the title for me.

"Yes, but only when you're ready."

"Does the Grand High Witch know that Jem thinks he's my other half?"

"Yes she does." Terry sighs unusually. "That's why she sent him to work with me."

"Why would she do that?" I ask, trying desperately to understand.

"Well, Jem's her son, and . . ."

"What? Why did she send him here?" I interrupt, shrieking.

"Because he asked her to. The future of you two cannot be seen; her teller has tried for years."

"That doesn't sound good." My voice sounds calmer than my body feels.

"I guess not. That's why you must be positive before you unite,"

"Then why let him come here?" I ask, still not understanding why.

"Because she trusts her son, and although your mum and The Grand High didn't always agree, she did think highly of her."

"I guess that's a relief." I get up and start pacing on the patio slabs. "It's a lot to take in," I confess. "I was normal this morning. Well, at least I thought so." I stop briefly, "What about Ali?"

"Hope. You can't tell her about this. It would be too dangerous for her to know," Terry says sternly.

"Dangerous for Ali? Would I hurt her?" I ask, feeling terrified of what I could be capable of.

"No, you and Ali have a connection. I'm sure you wouldn't hurt her." He looks toward the door.

"But?" I ask, concerned by the way he's checking.

"But others might."

"Because of me?"

Terry nods. "Your future, your powers—everything about you is uncertain. We've done research for years and found nothing.

There are beings out there that'd destroy you the second you step out of line, and others who just want you. The theories people have are endless," he says with another unusual sigh.

"They'd use Ali to get to me?" He nods. "And Jem if we unite?"

"Probably, but Jem is very talented, and we keep an eye on Ali," he says, sounding positive.

Feeling a bit more comfortable that they are watching over Ali, I continue to pace. "What's Jem's talent?" I ask, suddenly curious about his unique capabilites.

"Well, he can do a lot, really. The mind reading you already know about and . . ." Terry gets up from the bench and holds out his hand. "Come with me. I'll show you."

13: MAGIC

We walk up the patio steps and into the house. I can hear soft, gentle music coming from the marquee. D meets us in the living room, carrying a tray with four mugs of tea. They both nod in the direction of the marquee. I let go of Terry's hand and walk 'round to the entrance of the marquee. The music is so sweet that it's enchanting—beautiful and familiar like a lullaby. As I walk down the steps I notice that all the tables have been moved and stacked up neatly in a corner. Walking into the centre of the marquee I can see Jem sat crosslegged on the floor with his eyes closed like he's mediating. I tiptoe closer to him, trying not to disturb him, and I realize the music is coming from him; he's humming. He lifts his arms up to shoulder height and as he does so, so do the chairs that are scattered about. He brings his hands together and the chairs come together into a line, and then one by one they stack into piles next to the tables. With his eyes still closed, he pushes his hands up above his head and the decorations and fairy lights unravel from the marquee supports and float down to the ground. The balloons and ribbons shrink until there is nothing. The fairy lights then begin to wind themselves up into a small, tidy, and organized hoop—a task that would take a couple of people to do. When all the decorations have gone and the fairy lights tidied away, the ceiling of the marquee begins to twinkle with little white lights. I reach up to touch it, fascinated by what the lights could be. The small lights fly into my hand, making my whole hand twinkle. Looking closer at my hand I see that it's not random specks of light but tiny insects, like lightning bugs, only smaller. Real magic.

Oh dear. My head starts to feel light and my eyelids heavy. *Oooh. I feel . . . faint.*

A warm pair of arms cradles around my shoulders and gentle tingling runs over me where the skin touches mine.

"I think she just fainted." I can hear D's voice next to me, her tone concerned. "She's had a lot to take in."

"How did she take it?" Jem's magical voice asks.

"She's worried that she's dangerous." Terry's voice comes from past my feet.

"But she's not." Jem's tone is enthusiastic and proud. "She has excellent self-control. It's amazing."

"Jem, you're going to have to give her some time before you two unite. Her heart motions are too fast. If you unite too early, I fear that her mind will take over and you'd be left with nothing." D's voice is stern, but also worried.

"That's a risk I'm going to have to take." The arms holding me shrug.

"Jem, please think about it first." D's voice comes closer to me, worried still.

"Okay. I hear what you're saying. Give her some time. But it is her." The arms cradling me lift me up and a warm set of soft lips kiss my forehead. "She made my heart glow."

"It's not normal. What if she had drawn from you?" D's tone is so panicked it's scary.

"I don't think she can," Jem says, pride perfectly clear in his voice.

"Look." That's Terry's voice again, but it's coming closer to me now.

"She's finding a balance." D whispers.

I open my eyes, but my vision is a bit blurry.

"Are you alright?" Jem asks, his voice soft with concern. I reach up to touch his face but my hand feels like a lead weight. Jem takes my hand and holds it into his chest. Tiny shocks run through our hands and his warmth fills my whole body.

"That was amazing," I say, smiling at him. He smiles down at me and then looks at our hands twinkling with the little lighting bugs.

"They're pleased that you're finally here, but they didn't mean to scare you," Jem says in a translating monotone. I shake my head; it wasn't fear that had made me faint, just the inability to breathe while

I watched in awe of the amazing creatures. I struggle to get my mouth to speak and eventually my words come, even if they are very quiet and hoarse.

"They didn't scare me," I say, shaking my head in protest. "I just think I forgot to breathe."

Jem tucks his other arm under my knees and lifts me up. "Maybe it's time you went to bed." I nod, feeling totally relaxed in his arms; the pins and needles from his touch are comforting as he carries me up to my room, and as my eyes become heavy, I drift off to sleep right there in his arms.

***

"Hope!" That's a new sound for an alarm clock. Then there's a nudge in my ribs. Oww! "Hope, wake up." Another nudge. I stretch up and open my eyes. The sun is shining brightly through the windows.

"Ali?" I say through a yawn and blurred vision.

"Yes, sleepy head," she says and laughs.

"What's so funny?" I ask, frowning at her perkiness this morning.

"You look a state. Did you stay up drinking?" She asks. I can just about see one blonde eyebrow rise with her question.

"A couple. What time is it?" I ask, still feeling disorientated.

"Nearly eleven," Ali says confidently.

"Oh god." I sit up quickly with the shock and feel the blood rapidly leave my head. "Is your Mum on her way?" I ask, holding onto my head, trying to steady it.

"Yeah, D said I should wake you before you sleep the day away."

"How are you feeling?"

"A little hung over, but it was worth it," Ali answers with a happy smile.

I stagger out of bed and over to the window, opening it wide to allow the breeze to rush over me. "Ah . . . fresh air," I say, letting my lungs fill with the breeze. The sound of a car pulling up the side of the house and then honk its horn makes Ali jump to her feet.

"That'll be Mum," she says, skipping over to me and giving me a hug.

"I'll see you tomorrow morning," I croak.

"See you in the morning," she shouts over her shoulder, and she's gone.

I lie back on the bed and shut my eyes. I can hear the mumbling of chatter downstairs—D and Terry, no doubt, and there's the sound of the marquee people clanking about. I squeeze my eyes tightly, trying to shut out the noise. "It's no good," I say to myself after a few minutes. With a long sigh I heave myself out of bed and unzip my dress, which I had actually slept in last night, and walk over to my bathroom in my underwear. "Oh my god!" I say in a hushed shriek. "What are you doing?"

"I just had a bath," Jem says with his back to me, wrapping a towel around his waist.

Entranced, I walk toward him. *I want him. I want him.* I shake my head, trying to snap myself out of it. *What if I hurt him?* Jem turns to look at me. His body is still wet, with water running down his bare, toned, bronzed torso. My breathing is getting faster and it's taking all my strength to stop from wrapping myself around him. I put my hands over my eyes, hoping that not seeing him will help.

"Hope." I can hear him walking toward me.

"Please don't," I beg. *Please. Please—you're half naked.* I can even smell his mesmerizing warm skin. I hold my breath and try to back out of the bathroom, but I bump into the door.

"Don't go." His footsteps come toward me.

"Don't touch me, please." I say, knowing that as soon as he touches me I'll have no hope of controlling myself.

"You won't hurt me," he says confidently.

"You can't be sure of that," I say, my hands still covering my face.

"Maybe not, but what does your heart tell you?" he asks, the hint of a smile in his voice.

"It's pounding so loud. I don't think it's saying anything," I say, my voice now shrill.

"Open your eyes," he begs, and I hear him walk closer to me.

"No. If I open them, I might do something I'll regret," I confess. My thoughts flicker between *'kiss him'* and *'don't touch him.'*

"Don't think about it; just follow what you feel," Jem says, taking my hands from my face; I squeeze my eyes shut tight. There's no shock—just the pins and needles, and they're only slight.

"What if something happens?" I ask, relaxing my eyelids.

"Then we'll deal with it," he says confidently.

I take a deep breath and open my eyes. "You've still only got a towel on," I say, looking down at his body.

"You're only in your underwear," he says, counter-commenting. I look down at my body. *Well, at least it's a matching set.* I look up into Jem's eyes; the deep blue in his irises is sparkling. I put my hand on his chest, checking that what happened last night wasn't actually a dream, and as Jem places his hand on mine, my hand begins to glow on his chest.

"It's all true. You weren't dreaming," Jem says softly, sounding almost in awe of what he sees. My hand feels warm and cozy, like when you warm them in front of a fire. He takes his hand from my chest and the feeling stops. "It is you," he says, and he kisses me gently on the lips. A small snap of static cracks between our noses. The power of the shock breaks my self-control and then I just can't help myself. Flinging my arms around his neck, I kiss him hard and urgently. Jem kisses me back. Kissing down my neck, he swiftly picks me up and carries me to the bed. As he lays me down on the mattress, I pull him to me. Our arms and legs are entwined as we kiss each other everywhere; his lips are like butterfly wings caressing my skin. He moves down my neck and along my collar bone, nestling his nose and lips into the satin and lace covering my breasts. As his lips move down my stomach, his hands move up my back, and a quiver of ecstasy runs down my spine. His lips hesitate at the band of my knickers and then his hands follow, tucking between the lace and my skin.

You promised yourself no random sex, least of all in the middle of the day with a house full of people. My subconscious is speaking out. *I know this, but I can't stop it. I want this. I want him,* I argue back. Jem's hands pull down at my knickers. *But not yet.* Suddenly, the sharp pinch of a shock runs into my fingers.

"Move!" I shout, clenching my hand into a fist and trying to hold onto the shock, feeling the sheer strength of the power that's growing in my hand.

Jem looks up at me. "Hope?"

"Move!" I shout. *Nope, too late.* A large static shock runs off my hand and into Jem's chest, and a stream of lightning connects us. *It's not hurting me, is it hurting Jem?* I look up at him; there's a slight smile on his face and his complexion is pale. Then his smile drops and his eyes roll into the back of his head, and he drops to the floor with a loud thud. *How do I make it stop? The stream of lighting is still connected between us. Is it a union? Why has Jem blacked out?* I scramble over next to him. His body is limp on the floor. *I'm hurting him. I'm like Dad. I'm absorbing him. Aren't I?* "Not him, please . . . please, no." I curl up into a ball next to him. What do I do? I shut my eyes tightly, trying to stop the stream of lighting. But it's not working. It won't stop. My tears are thick and heavy as I look over at him.

D bursts into the room. "What happened?" she shouts. I look at her and lift my hand, showing her the stream of lightning. She follows the stream to where Jem is lying limp on the floor.

"It won't stop," I mumble through the tears.

"Terry!" D shouts out down the stairs. Terry comes bounding up the stairs. His jaw drops when he looks at Jem and then at me.

"Help him, please. I can't stop it. I don't know how," I plead with Terry. He runs over to Jem, trying his best not to touch the stream of lightning.

"I think he's just blacked out," Terry says, examining him. He gently taps Jem on the face, trying to wake him. D crouches down next to me.

"Hope, you need to shield your powers in," she says.

"I don't know how," I say, sobbing harder.

"Close your eyes and listen to me and only me," she commands. Doing as she says, I close my eyes. "Now imagine you're holding out your hands and the lightning is cracking between your fingers." I concentrate on her voice, envisaging the lightning caught between my fingers. "Good. Now imagine a glass ball, and the lightning in that ball." I can feel the tingling of the lightning start to fade. "That's it, Hope. Now, imagine moving your hands and the ball floating in front of you."

"Okay," I whisper, confident of what I see in my head.

"Now, just let go." In my head I can see the ball floating away from me. I open my eyes and look at D; she's smiling.

"Did it work? Is Jem alright?" I ask, trying to find reassurance in her expression.

"I'm sure he'll be fine. Probably shock more than anything," Terry says, looking over at D.

"What happened here?" D asks, looking at me in my underwear and Jem in just a bath towel. I look at her feeling a bit sheepish, thinking of what happened in the bathroom. "Oh . . ." she says, her cheeks reddening with a blush. One advantage to mind reading—I don't have to explain my embarrassing moment of sexual urges. "You didn't want this?" D asks, and I shake my head.

No I didn't want sex. It was like being enchanted. I couldn't stop.

"You tried to hold onto the shock." D says with amazement.

"Yes. But I wasn't strong enough, and . . ." I look over at Jem still unconscious on the floor and cringe at what I've done. I'm the one who's put him there—me and my powers.

"Hope, it was an accident; you didn't mean to hurt him," Terry says, trying to reassure me.

"It still happened, though," I say, my eyes starting to water again. *I've turned into a monster.*

"Did the shocks start when it wasn't what you wanted?" D asks, her eyes flicking between me and Jem. I squeeze my eyes shut, trying to replay what happened.

"Yes. But it was worse. Look at him." I inch myself away from him, ashamed of myself; I could feel the power grow through the shock and I couldn't stop it. It came from me and I couldn't stop it.

"He was warned," D says, standing in front of me with her hands on her hips.

"It's not her fault," Jem croaks as he lifts his head.

"No. It's yours," D shouts at him angrily. "What were you thinking?" D pulls me up to my feet and stands in front of me. "We told you to give her some time. Now do you see why?"

"I wasn't thinking. I didn't expect her to come into the bathroom. I . . . I—" He rubs in head with confusion and looks up at me.

"Well, you should have had better control."

"Yes, I know," he says as Terry helps him up and faces D.

"Don't be hard on them, D," Terry pleads.

"Don't be hard on them? You of all people know the possibilities," D shouts back at Terry.

"Look, no harm done. Jem merely blacked out." Terry says, facing D.

"Fine." Her voice is still angry. She looks between Jem and me. "The pair of you get dressed before something else happens." She leaves the room.

"Hope, I'm sorry." Jem tries to apologize, holding onto Terry for strength.

"Why are you sorry? I'm the one who hurt you," I say in protest, but before he can say anymore, Terry's pulled him out of the room.

I quickly get showered and pull on a pair of shorts, a vest, and slip on a pair of flip-flops before I run down the stairs. *I need to get out of here.* I run through the kitchen, trying not to touch anyone. I grab my keys and jump off the steps and run over to my car. I can see Jem standing at the doorstep. I look at him and shake my head.

I need to be alone. Please, I beg with my thoughts. A heavy tear escapes from the corner of my eye; I can't hurt him again.

14: CONNECTIONS

I drive up the long track from the house and escape from the shadows of the woods into the blazing sun. *I just need to get away—away from everyone.* I turn toward the Gibbet and put my foot down, my tears now coming thick and fast as I drive. I yank the steering wheel, pulling the car off the road and onto the old dirt track leading to the Gibbet; the car skids on the gravel as I slam on the breaks.

"Why did this happen to me?" I ask out loud. "Why am I the one who hurts Jem?" Even the thought of him lying limp and unconscious on the floor makes my insides twinge with guilt. "Why can't I be normal? Why can't this be normal?" My tears are so heavy I can barely see. Squeezing my eyes shut, I curl up in the driver's seat, hating myself for being the monster that I am. For the first time in…well, forever, I've met someone I really like and I can't touch him. I can't be with him, but how can I not be with him? I shake my head; I knew that even from the seriously short time we had spent together, I couldn't, even though I knew we'd have to. I'd have to go away to master these *powers;* I'd have to find a way to not hurt Jem again, but what about Terry and D? Do I hurt them? Obviously not the same as with Jem earlier, but my shield thing—does it really protect them, or does it imprison them?

Am I like my Dad? Do I absorb powers? Could I continue my mother's work?

"I don't know . . . I don't know!" I shout into my hands. I need answers; I need someone who knows me. D and Terry had told me some things, but what about the rest? What about what I am inside? The only real people who'd know about that are my parents, and mum's gone and no one's seen Dad since before I was born. How do I get through this? Can my family really help me? I take a couple of deep breaths and try to calm myself down.

Collecting my thoughts together and stopping with the tears, I

dig the through the pockets of the car trying find a tissue. Nothing—
D has obviously been cleaning in here. I open up the glove box,
certain that I'd left a handy pack in there, and as the door drops on
the glove box, a large, white envelope falls onto the floor.

"I'd forgotten about that," I say, looking at the envelope
curiously. Giving up on the tissues, I wipe away my tears with the
back of my hand. Picking up the envelope, I look at the address; it's
hand written in beautiful penmanship. The paper feels thick and
expensive, sort of like what I'd expect official papers to be on.
Maybe it is official; I did have to sign for it. I turn it over and run my
fingers over the wax seal. A sun and moon are imprinted in the red
wax.

"What is this?" I break the seal and open the envelope. I tip the
envelope on its side and a large coin falls out into my palm. I've
never seen a coin like this before; it's the same size as a two-pound
coin, but it's completely silver. On one side there's a series of circles,
each with a different image engraved within them: a tree, like a
simple version of an oak, a bird in flight, not a dove but maybe an
eagle, a shining sun with rays pointing off it, two simple figures that
look like people, a fish tail poking up out of water, and a crescent
moon. On the other side is a pair of hands holding a heart, and
above it reads:

To find peace, you must follow your heart.

I pull out the note that accompanies the coin. Again in the beautiful
handwriting as the address, the note reads:

My Darling Daughter Hope,

I give you a piece of our world.

Embrace it.

With all my love.

William.

Dad? How is that possible? No one has seen him for years. Well,
at least I never have. Why has he waited till now? I put the note and
the envelope on the passenger seat and look at the coin again. A
piece of our world—a world that could be dangerous, a world that

might not welcome me—how can I embrace that?

I get out of the car and put the coin in my pocket. I stroll along the dirt track to a five bar gate and climb up, perching myself on the top rail. I close my eyes and try to clear my mind, trying to figure out what to do next.

The sun is shining brightly and warms my skin. I let out a deep sigh. It's beautiful up here—peaceful. In the distance I can hear the sounds of cars driving about in the village at the bottom of the hill, and I listen to the buzz of people pottering about in their gardens. Peaceful. No wars, no fighting. Just people being people, getting on with their lives—normal, human lives. Could I not go back to that? My eyes begin to water again. No, I don't think I can, but how do I go on? I need help.

"It's beautiful up here, isn't it?" The husky male voice startles me so much that I slip off the gate and land on my knees in the dry mud. Struggling to my feet I brush down my knees, looking around to see who had made me jump. There's no one there. I lean over the gate and look up and down the track, but there's no one. I turn back to the field that I've fallen into. I really can't see anyone, anywhere.

"Who said that?" I say out loud, and as if it was answering my question, a large deer steps up the steep side of the field and looks at me. Is that the same deer from the woods yesterday? He looks the same. The deer then snorts in the air and runs off. "No, wait!" I shout after it. *Great move, you loud mouth, now you've really scared it.* I start to run after it. If it is the same deer from yesterday, maybe it can answer some questions, like what happened yesterday in the woods. I sprint after the deer, following it to the edge of the woods that leads down the side of the hill. Once in the shadows of the trees I stop; I can't see him. I look around frantically, but he's gone. I slump down to the floor, leaning on a thick tree trunk, and my eyes begin watering again as I curl my arms around my legs and push my head on my knees.

"I need help," I sob. "Help me, please." I don't know who I was asking; maybe it was the deer, or maybe some magical god, but in that moment I felt scared and unknowing as the wind brushes over me, pushing my hair away from face. Looking up, I can see the deer coming toward me, the sun glowing so brightly behind him that I have to squint to see the figure. Squinting doesn't help; the brightness seems to grow and make my eyes sting. I squeeze them shut, hoping that when I look again, the deer will be in the way of the sun. I wait for the lights to stop burning through my eyelids, but it's gone. I carefully open my eyes and look up. Stood before me isn't a deer, but a man. He's tall—maybe six foot—with short, black hair that is ruffled and wind swept, and his features are softly wrinkled. He walks closer to me and I can see that his eyes are dark just like the deer's, and when he smiles, a flash of perfectly white teeth show beneath his long, friendly smile. This is a smile I've seen before—a smile that's just like mine. The man crouches down next to me, and although I've been taught to keep away from strangers, I don't feel unsafe anymore. In fact, I feel more than safe; I feel home.

"Hope, you don't need help," he says as he shakes his head. "You didn't hurt him. Your mother made sure you couldn't hurt him."

"My mother is dead," I shout, suddenly feeling angry that she's not here to explain, to help, to be my mum. And then, my brain clicked into gear. "How do you know my mother?" I ask, squinting at the man I don't know.

"Hope," he turns my shoulders so I'm facing him. "I'm William, your father." I shake my head, letting the tears flow even more.

"You can't be. He left me . . . he left because he knew what sort of monster I'd become." I say, my hands covering my face and my whole body shaking as I sob.

"You're not a bad person," he says, moving the hair away from my face.

"I am. I hurt him. What if I'd killed him?" Even the thought squeezes at my insides. If Jem had died, what would I have done?

"He was warned. He was informed that you'd be different than any other." His voice is soft and tender. I look up into his dark eyes.

"I don't want to be different," I say, the anger still apparent in my voice.

"How about unique?" he asks with a smile. That does sound better, I think, wiping the tears away with the back of my hand.

"But why me?"

"Because the ancients chose you; they chose you to bring peace to our world and to bring order back to the people." People that want to kill me—people that don't want me to be like my mum, and people who are more powerful than I could ever imagine.

"But I'm not powerful. I zapped a guy for trying to get into my knickers," I say, sounding completely flippant that a guy was trying to get into my knickers and even worse saying something like that in front of my dad. *My Dad.*

"Maybe you should have done that to the previous guys. Then you wouldn't have such a long list of them," he says, his voice sounding mockingly stern.

"Have you been spying on me?" I ask, ashamed to admit that I did have a bout of one-night stands. Well . . . a large bout. But it wasn't love, it was just sex, and I haven't had sex since I broke up with Steve, which was soon after my birthday. So, three months, and it's been difficult—like an animal within me is only at peace when it's had a good orgasm. Nonetheless, I've been holding onto my sexual urges for a while now, promising myself that next time I have sex it will be for real—for love.

"Not completely spying. I was concerned when you started staying out and drinking before you turned eighteen." I bow my head in shame, realizing for the first time what hell I've really put D through. "But what amazed me is that you don't drink to get drunk. You drink to soften yourself up, so, you're not so hard and cold." Even my own father thinks I'm an ice maiden. "But you've been holding back for a while now. I know it's eating you up. I see it every time you go running."

"You followed me when I was running?" I gasp. I run to wear myself out. In recent months I struggle to sleep for very long, but last night I slept really well. No dreams, no nothing, just sleep. Is it because of Jem? It's like he does something to me that puts me at peace.

"I only follow you to make sure you're safe. To make sure you're careful." He looks at me with a soft smile. "But it seems that you're mother's lessons have paid off."

"What? My mother is dead," I shout. "You would have known that if you'd stuck around." Anger shoots through me when he mentions my mum.

"I'm sorry I couldn't stay with you while you grew up, but I have always been nearby. I've always been close enough to keep you safe." He takes my hand and looks at me, "And yes, physically your mother is gone, but she lives on in you, in your subconscious—guiding you, teaching you. Have you not ever wondered why school seems so easy?" I shrug. It's not that easy. I do have to study, but I generally pass with good grades. "Have you not ever thought about how fast you could truly run? Because I know you don't push yourself. Or how about how strong you are?" I shrug again. I know when I run I only jog, but I don't push myself to get completely out of breath and sweaty; it's just to wear me out. And as for the strength, no, I've never really thought about it. I can pick up a couple of hay bales easily, but Jen always says that I've been doing it for so long I was bound to build up some muscles.

"What are you saying, Dad? That I can run fast and pick up cars and stuff?"

"I don't know about picking up cars, but running fast I would say is definitely possible."

I feel my face screw up with confusion. "But why?" I ask. Dad leans back on the tree trunk next to me. Looking out into the distance, his mind seems to be far away.

"Because you're my daughter . . . because I took so many powers." His voice is low as he lets out a long sigh.

"D and Terry said that you're an absorber," He cringes when I speak his label, and then the question that I really need answered falls from my mouth. "Am I an absorber?" He shakes his head. "Then what am I?" *Because if I'm different, I want to know who I'm different from. Is there someone out there like me? Am I really not a bad person? I'm not so sure sometimes.*

"I'm not sure what you are exactly," he says, still looking out across the fields. "But you definitely don't absorb. But then, I guess I had taken so many that you couldn't possibly fit any more power into your body." That actually sounds a bit scary—like my whole body might suddenly explode. "You started showing signs of a vampire soon after your seventeenth birthday, which is very early for a gifted being." I take in a deep breath of air as shock fills my body.

"Vampire?" I ask. *Oh god, have I been sucking blood in my sleep or something? Oh my god, I really am a monster.*

"Luckily you don't have any thirst." I let out a huge sigh of relief. "But I think you could run as fast as them and possibly be as strong, too. You've definitely already discovered their ability to enchant." *Huh? Enchant?* My brows pin together as Dad turns and grins at me. "Yes, Hope. Enchant."

Nope, still don't get it. How do vampires enchant? "I don't understand. Vampires don't need to enchant, do they?" From what I've read in books and seen on telly, they're handsome or beautiful with no tacky chat-up lines, and people just are drawn to them. Oh, people are drawn to them.

"Yes they do. That's how they beckon their prey." A shiver runs down my spine at the scary thought of seeing a vampire suck a person's blood—gross and scary.

"But if I don't have their thirst then why would I enchant?"

"Hope, vampires don't just crave human blood. They crave human contact, human pleasure. Like you have been," he says, grinning some more. My cheeks burn with embarrassment; although it's embarrassing that my dad knows that I've been sleeping around, it's actually a relief to know that my bout of 'hump 'n' go' was because of some vampire power and not because I'm a revolting tart. Another click in my brain triggers more questions.

"If vampires crave sex and blood, surely there would be things on the news about it. Vampires are too strong to handle a person to just have sex. Wouldn't they drink from the person too?" Dad's eyes grow wide with shock. Did I think too much or did I say something dumb?

"Vampires of today are less civilized—less humane—and thankfully because they feed from humans, they don't feed too often. A month is probably the maximum they could last, but those that feed off humans don't crave human contact; it almost disgusts them. So the most you see on the news is suspicious murders or accidents." He lets out a quiet laugh.

"So there are vampires that don't feed from humans?" I'd seen some sci-fi programs where vampires drink donated blood, but surely that's just as bad.

"Yes, a few. They hunt animals, like humans do, but obviously they drink the animal's blood and don't eat the meat." I nod, understanding that would be necessary.

"But that doesn't make them strong." A human's blood, from what I understand, would be the best way to maintain strength and speed.

"They need to feed more often—about every two weeks—but they crave the human contact. They can also live as a unit—a civilized family."

"So vampires who drink human blood can't do that?" I ask, finding the subject intriguing. The idea that there are vampires out there who aren't blood-sucking monsters is beyond me. Well, not sucking the blood from humans, anyway.

"Four is probably the most you would find in a coven, although a lot of vampires are nomads. The Masters control the largest coven."

"The Masters?" I repeat, feeling a little intimidated by the name.

"The Vampire Masters are four brothers. Or were . . . I haven't seen them for a very long time. They also have a full guard of forty vampires and a following of gifted vampires of about ten." Oh my god—fifty-four vampires, all together. I really don't want to go where they are.

"Terry said you absorbed an ancient vampire, that it was dangerous for you to be one for too long." He looks away from me again; ashamed maybe of what he had done.

"Yes, being able to shift to and from a vampire is easy enough, so long as you want to." Another sigh escapes him "If I'm a vampire for too long I start to get thirsty . . . agonisingly so. It's like the worst heartburn, burning through your throat and chest." I see a tear escape from the corner of his eye. I gasp, realizing what he's saying.

"You drank human blood." He nods shamefully. "But how did you stop?" I ask, hoping that he *has* stopped.

"Your mother," he says, wiping the tear from his cheek and turning to me again. "And you." He cups my cheek with his hand and kisses my forehead. "My dear, sweet, amazing daughter." Looking up at him and feeling my own tears wetting my cheeks, I fling my arms around him and hug my dad for first time. For a long moment we hold onto each other, until Dad breaks away. "So, what exactly happened with you and Jeremy this morning?"

Leaning back against the tree trunk, I fiddle with the hem of my shorts. "I wish you could mind read. It would make things less embarrassing." Dad chuckles and kneels in front of me.

"So, the telepathy kicked in?" I look up at him, shock obviously showing on my face as he cringes at my expression. "Your mother could. It stands to reason that you can as well." I lift the I-stone from underneath my vest. The round pendent is showing a candy pink color; I guess it proves he's family, but it wasn't that shade when D and Terry were near me.

"Could you take it off for a minute?" Dad asks.

"But won't my ears start ringing again?" He leans forward and undoes the chain from around my neck.

"I shouldn't think so. There's only you and me here for about a mile or so."

"Oh." So there is a distance thing on it, then. That's a relief.

"You're also holding a shield close to your body, so I doubt you'll hear me until you extend that shield."

I look over my body, but I can't see anything. "How do you know I'm holding a shield to me? I can't see anything," I ask, rubbing my hands over my arms and legs to see if I can feel anything, but there's nothing.

"Because I can't hear your thoughts and because I can't feel any of your powers," he says, his smile gone again. I'm still not sure that I really have any.

"So, how do I extend my shield so you're within it? D said I do it automatically. Apparently there's one over her and the house." I place the I-stone on the ground next to us. Dad takes my hands and sits crosslegged in front of me.

"I think you'll be alright, just think about keeping me safe." I squeeze my eyes shut, trying to imagine the bubble D had explained the shield to be and Dad and I sat within it, safe from the outside world. "That's it," Dad says with pride in his voice. "As long as we are within it, no one can hear us. So only you and I can communicate." Makes sense, I guess. "Now think about this morning and what happened with Jeremy." I let my mind go back to this morning when I woke up . . . talking to Ali, listening to the chatter of people downstairs, and then walking into the bathroom. Jem wrapping a towel around his body, me clapping my hands over my face, trying desperately not to think of Jem in just a towel, bumping into the doorframe, and then Jem kissing me, and me kissing Jem, and then the burst of energy from within me, Jem falling to the floor, and the stream of lighting flowing between us. I pull my hands away from Dad.

"Sorry. I can't show you anymore." My tears start flowing again. It hurts too much to keep replaying the part where I hurt him.

"That's alright," Dad says as he gets up and walks to the edge of the woods. "You definitely didn't hurt him. He enchants too, you know." My heart starts pounding harder, realizing that what I feel is not real—it's just magic. Dad looks at me and shakes his head. "The connection wasn't an enchantment." Looking up at him, I feel my chest on the verge of bursting as my heart continues to pound.

"It wasn't an enchantment?" I ask, my breathing short and fast. "Did I do something worse to him?" My tears are so thick and heavy that I can barely see.

"No. An enchantment doesn't manifest once inside a shield. And you shield Jeremy." He starts pacing back and forth, rubbing his temples. "Could that be possible, so quickly," he mutters. His pacing starts to concern me after a couple of minutes, so I get up, wiping my face for the millionth time, and stand in front of him, making him stop.

"Dad, what's going on?" A singular eyebrow lifts to his forehead. I guess I should be able to hear him really, shouldn't I? "I can't hear your thoughts, are you shielding?" Dad closes his eyes and puts his fingers to his temples.

"I think I am." He smiles at me and then looks away. "I'm sorry." I take his hand and make him look at me.

"Dad?" My thoughts barely a whisper: *did he absorb from me?*

I can hear you. His smile returning, "I didn't absorb you. I don't think I could even if I wanted to." I snap my hand away from his.

He'd want to absorb me? Fear suddenly floods my body.

"Hope, no. I honestly couldn't. You're my daughter, even if you are very powerful. There's something holding onto you, almost like there's something you're waiting for." He starts pacing again. He stops every now and again and looks up at me. "What happened when you first met Jeremy?" I close my eyes, thinking back to when we first met on the doorstep, when I was admiring his car.

"We got a static shock," I say, answering his question. "Actually, we had several static shocks throughout the evening, and then it started to dull to pins and needles. Well, until this morning; that was more of a 'stick-your-finger-in-a-socket' kind of shock," I shrug. Static shocks are surely common enough, as are pins and needles.

"What happened when you touched his chest?" How did he know about that?

"My hand glowed. I think the way it glowed when I touched you yesterday in the woods, like a cup of sunshine." He nods at me.

"Our touch was recognition—real family. Not our honorary family. The glow happens when we first meet."

"So I could have more family?" Nobody told me about brothers or sisters, but mum's dead—how is that possible? "Dad, was that Mum I saw yesterday when I hit that branch in the woods?"

He sits back down on the ground. "Yes. Your mother gave you your heart motions. Making sure you were ready for . . ." He hesitates to finish.

"For what?" I ask.

"For meeting your other half, which I think you have: Jeremy." My heart lifts a little as I smile at the thought. So, Jem was right.

"But why did it glow? D was shocked when I told her."

"That doesn't surprise me. We generally only glow when we find our 'soul twin,' or like when you touched me. You touched my soul, and the idea is that it glows because your soul recognizes it. That's how I met my brother, and how your mother met her sister. Soul recognition also occurs between parents and their children." So I could have an aunt and an uncle—real ones. No offense to D and Terry and the others, but real relatives would be something. Someone I could be similar to.

"Do I have a soul twin?" I ask, my voice squeaking with

excitement; the possibility of a sister would really be amazing. Dad shakes his head and when he looks back at me, my excitement disappears.

"I'm not sure, sorry," he says with a sigh. "Unfortunately my brother never had any children before he passed away, and your mother's sister lost her son in the 'great war' between the witches and the vampires. She sadly fell terribly ill after receiving the news, and died."

"So, a 'soul twin' for me would have to be a child of your 'soul twin'?" I ask.

"That's generally how it works with gifted beings. I guess we'll wait and see for you. But you'll know when you find them," he says, trying to sound positive.

"But Jem's not my 'soul twin,' is he?" I ask, suddenly feeling quite disgusted with myself. That really shouldn't happen between a brother and sister; surely that means that he's not my 'soul twin,' right?

Dad shakes his head and chuckles. "No, the poor guy isn't your 'soul twin.'" My whole body relaxes as I let out a huge sigh of relief. "The pair of you are very gifted. It makes sense that you would belong to each other." We belong to each other, which is so much better than being related.

"I still don't get why our chests glow when we touch. If he's not a 'soul twin' and he's not family, why would it happen?" The pins and needles I can handle, but if the shocks happen again like this morning, it wouldn't be much of a relationship. Would it?

"I don't know why it glowed . . . maybe because the pair of you are as bad as each other. Maybe you needed reassurance," Dad says, trying to understand. "Our kind don't have the sex drive that you have, and Jeremy, for that matter." Well at least I won't seem so much of a tart next to him. "From what you showed me, you and Jeremy made a connection, but not one that I've seen before." I curl up into a ball, thinking of Jem. We belong together; we've somehow made a connection.

I lie back against the tree trunk, relaxing ever so slightly, because although it seems impossible, considering we only met last night, it feels right. It's that feeling again.

"Dad? D said something about my heart motions being too fast

. . . that it would be dangerous for Jem and me to form a union." Not that I'm entirely sure what a union entails, but nonetheless, what does it have to do with my heart motions?

"Yes. Your heart motions are fast—faster than mine, for that matter. That's why you must go on this trip and visit with our family. Learn about your powers and yourself. If your heart motions remain too fast, a union could break between the two of you."

"And that would hurt Jem?" I ask, and Dad nods. I can't do that—not again. Terry was right: I did need incentive, not just to be good, but to be me—all of me. I need to face this world for what it really is, and figure out if Jem and I can be together. If my heart motions will slow enough for a union, I need to find my 'soul twin,' (if I have one) and eventually continue my mother's work.

I get up and dust down my legs, rubbing off the dry mud. Picking up my mum's I-stone, I fasten the chain around my neck.

"Where are you going?" Dad asks.

"I'm going to finish packing. Then I think I might go for a run."

Dad stands up next to me and takes hold of my arm. "How about we wait until nightfall to test your speed?" Dad asks.

"Okay. Will you show me?" I ask, smiling at him.

"I'd like that," he says, smiling back at me. "Bring Jeremy with you," he says. I cringe at the idea. "I'd like to meet my future son-in-law," Dad says with a grin.

"Dad, it might not happen yet," I say, cringing again. The idea of marriage really does send a shiver down my spine. "It might not be possible," I say, hoping that a union has nothing to do with white dresses and saying "I do."

"I'm sure you'll find a way. You're clever. You'll figure it out." We hug like a father and daughter who had done so for many years and not for their second time.

"What time shall I meet you?" I ask, feeling excited about seeing him again and having the opportunity to test my speed.

"If we meet up at the Gibbet at about ten that would be alright," he says, looking up at the sky.

"Okay, I'll see you later," I say as I make my way back to the car, feeling much less like a monster and more like the real me.

15: WANTING & WAITING

I park my Land Rover next to Jem's Audi, grateful that it's still here and that he will be, too. Walking up into the house, through the hallway, and into the kitchen, I find D and Terry sitting at the kitchen table, looking up at me anxiously. I try to smile to reassure them but their faces are still solemn and unsure. I pull the coin Dad had sent me out of my pocket and drop it on the table, letting it spin and spin until it begins to wobble and eventually stops flat on the table top. Terry leans in and looks closely at the coin, then sits back. D picks up the coin, checking both sides, and then puts it back on the table top.

"He can't go with you while you're travelling," she says sternly. "Not while you're learning, and you'll have to make sure that your heart motions slow down." Giving the proper mum lecture, I walk over to her chair, wrap my arms around her shoulders, and kiss her on the cheek.

"I'm sorry to have scared you. I promise, while I study, Jem will stay away, and I'll work on the heart motions. I promise," I say feeling positive. "Don't worry. I'll find a way to regain a balance." She puts her hands on my arms and leans her head into my elbow.

"I know you will," she says lovingly. Looking around the kitchen, I let go of D and wonder where Jem is. How is he feeling?

Answering my thoughts, D says, "He's in the garden. I think he's still on the phone."

I turn to make my way through the living room when Terry shouts, "When should we expect William's arrival?" With shock, I turn back and look at him. Terry's face is lit up like a small kid with a new toy. I walk around and look at D, who has deep lines creasing her forehead.

"I don't know. Did you want to see him?" I ask both of them. I don't think D does, and Terry knew him before. I don't know . . . is

D scared of him? She shakes her head. Then why?

"What if he absorbs from you?" she says in a low mumble. "What if he absorbs from Jem?" I shake my head. From what I had seen of my Dad today, he was not the monster they had portrayed. But even so, somehow I had shielded him, so I don't know if he could absorb now. Not unless I released him of his shield, or I died.

"Or he absorbed you," D says out loud.

"He can't, D. Not just because I'm his daughter, but also because it won't let go of me. Like my powers are waiting for something." Maybe it's waiting for Jem. If he is as powerful as what I could become, then wouldn't the powers want to unite? Join forces? There's so much to figure out. I just hope I can do this. "How's Jem feeling?" I ask, looking at Terry, who's still smiling like a Cheshire cat.

"He's fine. A little bit tired maybe, but other than that, no harm done."

D looks up at me again, her face much calmer this time. "Terry and Jeremy are going to join us in London. Terry is going to take me in the Land Rover and Jeremy is going to take you and Ali in his car."

"Why?" I ask in annoyance. "I thought Ali and me were going to go alone. You know . . . retail therapy before the trip really begins," I say, sounding like a whiny teenager. Taking a deep breath, I suddenly realize their intentions. "You're coming to make sure I don't hurt anyone, aren't you?"

"We can't lock you in the house every time something like this morning happens, so we're going to stay nearby until you can control yourself." The 'we' as in the 'royal we,' meaning all the family. Terry takes D's hand, looking at her.

"Hope isn't bad; you can trust her. She just needs guidance." Placing my hands on both their shoulders, they look at me.

"Come to London. I'm not promising that the same thing won't happen again, but I will try my best to make sure it's not in public and if you're nearby, I'm sure we can handle it together." Leaving them to their mumbling, I make my way out to the garden.

As I walk closer to the open patio doors I can hear Jem talking.

"No. She's beautiful, alright . . . clever, tough. She'd run rings 'round you . . . not for a while. She's leaving in the morning . . . we're going to London. I don't think that works with her. Though I'm not entirely sure, if she does the same to me . . . ha ha ha, you wish . . . I'll see what I can do. Yeah. Bye."

I step out into view. Jem turns and looks at me as a large smile spreads across his face—a beautiful smile that lifts my heart and makes me feel like a million bucks. His eyes sparkle with excitement.

"You're back," he says, walking to the bottom of the steps and stretching his arms out wide. With no fear that I could hurt him or that it was wrong for us to be together, I skip down the steps and into his arms, flinging my arms around his neck. He lifts me up, swinging me 'round and 'round until we fall on the lawn with dizziness. Resting himself on top of me, he kisses the end of my nose, a smile still wide across his face.

"How are you feeling?" I ask, running my fingers through his hair.

"Embarrassed more than anything. I can't believe I blacked out," he says, his cheeks blushing into a subtle pink.

"I think we'll have to make sure that doesn't happen again."

"Which bit?" Jem asks with shock.

"Any of it," I say, pulling myself away from him and sitting up.

"Hope, what happened this morning . . ." I'm shaking my head before he can say any more, remembering him lying unconscious on my bedroom floor. It hurts me so bad. He turns my chin so I'm facing him. "You didn't hurt me, honest." Looking up at him and into his deep blue eyes, I realize that he's still touching me, and there's no shocks, no pin and needles. I place my hand over his heart, and it glows.

"Soul recognition," I whisper, smiling at my own understanding.

"What did you say?" Jem asks, suddenly pulling away from me, his eyes wide with shock or maybe fear.

"Soul recognition." I say again.

"But you're not my 'soul twin,'" Jem says, his voice squeaking with fear. I shake my head again.

"No. Not a 'soul twin.'" But soul recognition sounds familiar—like something I've heard before. Not just from Dad, but I've heard

111

it in a movie or something. How random is that? Maybe 'soul twins' aren't exclusive to witches; maybe what happened didn't have anything to do with witchcraft, or maybe it's something else. Or it could be like Dad had said, that we're "as bad as each other and needed reassurance." I let out a little chuckle and Jem looks at me, shock still stretching his face. "A pair of sex-crazed loonies," I say through a chuckle.

"I guess sex-crazed lunacy is one way of describing it," he says, his face no longer shocked, but sad. He starts pulling nervously at the grass. "Did you know that I've never spent this much time with a girl and not slept with her?"

"Ha ha, we've already done the sleeping," I say, trying to make a joke of his seriousness.

"You know what I mean," he says, smiling back at me.

"Yes. You mean that you've been a sex-crazed loony like me and you've been resisting temptation for a while." Hoping that he has been resisting temptation, I see Jem cringe as he continues to pull at the grass. Okay, maybe he hasn't been resisting temptation. "You can't be worse than me," I say, but even though I've said it, I'm not too sure.

"How did you stop?" Jem asks, beginning to make a bald patch on the lawn.

"I stopped because of Steve. I used him, literally. That's when I promised myself the next time I was with a guy it would mean something—that I'd stick around and maybe get to know the guy first. I was doing well until you came along."

"Is that why they call you 'The Ice Maiden'?"

"That's me," I say with a sigh. "No feelings. Just hump 'n' go."

"I confess that I've been the same."

"It's different for men, though. You don't get branded a tart or a whore. Mostly you get called a hero."

"I'm no hero."

"I guess if you're as bad as me, I can't be much of a tart, then."

"Have you ever 'made love' before?" Feeling my eyebrows pin, I think, didn't we just discuss this? "No. I mean 'made love.' No sexual urges. No enchantments."

"I don't think so . . . mind you, I've only just found out that I can enchant, so, I guess love was never necessary before, and I guess being the Ice Maiden I've never been affectionate enough to 'make love,'" I mutter, shrugging off quite a personal question.

"Neither have I," Jem says as he looks up at me.

"Virgins in the 'Love Department,'" I say through a laugh.

"A 'do over' or a clean slate." Jem says in reply. That would be quite nice—a clean slate. No magic, just us.

"Just us," Jem whispers. "Hope?" Jem asks, his voice now sounding shaky and nervous.

"Yeah?" I say, already envisaging Jem's next question.

"Do you want to go out for dinner tonight?"

I look over my shoulder toward the house and then back at Jem. "I don't know if we'll be allowed to go alone," I say, wondering if actually we should go anywhere alone together. Would it be safe if we did? Would Jem be safe if he was alone with me?

"I'm sure I can control myself, if you can." His grins touches his eyes, making them sparkle again. Feeling my own grin I look away from Jem, trying to conceal my thoughts; deep down I know that I probably can't. *For God's sake, it sucks to be me right now. He's gonna run away screaming if he sees my crazy thoughts.*

"I won't run away screaming," Jem says through a soft laugh.

"You probably will. My head is full of crazy, scary things."

"I guess it won't be long until you can hear all my thoughts, and then we'll see who's running away," he says, facing away from me. I wonder if he has the same dreams that I do—the one that seem so real that it frightens me—the one that scares me enough to make me not want to sleep ever again.

"We'll see," I say, and I kneel up next to him and kiss him on the cheek. Standing up, I head back to house.

"Where are you going?" Jem asks after me.

"I'm gonna pack now if we're going out for dinner tonight." I'm sure he can find a way to persuade D and Terry to let us go out for dinner on our own.

***

I begin emptying my drawers, figuring out what would be the best to take with me to London. D has already sent most of my clothes out; my ankle walking boots, shorts, and t-shirts have been sent to Olly. I can then take that with me to Julian and Helen's. My long boots, heavy coat, and jumpers have been sent to Peter and Sarah; when I get to them it will be late November and starting to get very cold. So really, all I want to take with me to London is bits for going shopping and something nice for going out in the evening. I open up my wardrobe—what to wear tonight? Nothing tempting—something that I can run in for when we meet Dad and something I can eat dinner in safely.

I begin pulling out different outfits and placing them on the bed, darting back and forth between my wardrobe and the mirror. Caught up in my own thoughts of pedal pushers and skirts, I don't notice Jem in the room until I hear him gasp for air. Stopping in my tracks, I turn to the direction of the gasp, seeing Jem holding two glasses of water with his jaw dropped wide open. His eyes are wide with shock, looking like they're on the verge of popping out.

"Jem?" I ask, taking a step toward him. His posture stiffens and his eyes are still wide with shock.

"How did you do that?" he asks, his voice barely a whisper. Jem closes his eyes and then in less than a second I can see myself in my mind's eye, moving so quickly between my bed and my wardrobe that I'm a blur—ghost like.

"Cool," I say out loud. I am fast; I wonder how far I can go like that?

"You're a vampire?" he shrieks. I cover my mouth to muffle the giggle that wants to escape me.

"No, silly."

"But you just moved like they do. How is that possible?" he asks, looking at me curiously.

"I do have some vampire *in* me, but I'm not *a* vampire. Well, not a thirsty one." I see him relax slightly, putting the glasses on the chest of drawers next to him.

"I don't understand. How can that be?" he asks, curiosity still clear in his voice.

"I don't really know myself. But I'm going to test it tonight if you'd like to come with me." Part of me hopes he will, while another part hopes he won't.

But she's not cold. Not dead. Does she enchant like them? Jem's thoughts become faster the more shocked he becomes. Without looking away from me, he backs toward the door.

"Jem, don't," I plead as I walk toward him, consciously making my stride human like. Jem backs himself against the wall. His eyes are closed tight as a tear escapes the corner of his eye.

It's not real. It's not real. His thoughts repeat in my head.

"Look at me, Jem, please," I continue to plead, but he shakes his head, squeezing his eyes tighter. "Jem, please. An enchantment doesn't work inside a shield." Doesn't he know that? Can't he feel that it's not an enchantment?

"Vampires are different to witches," he says in reply to my thoughts.

"But it is real. I promise you, Jem. This is real." I step up closer to him, taking his hands and wrapping his arms around my waist. I can feel pins and needles tingling through my fingertips as both pairs of hands come together. Opening his eyes, he looks at me; he's still scared and confused. I run my fingers along his bare arms, up onto his shoulders, and down onto his chest. The glowing of his heart begins to show. "It is real," I say softly, leaning closer into him, letting my nose caress his jaw. "You were worried that I could make you feel something that you wanted?"

"Yes," he whispers back, wrapping his arms tighter around my waist.

"And now?" I ask in a whisper, kissing the hollow of his neck. Jem shivers from my touch and a small shock runs up my nose. "Oooh, that tickles," I say, pulling away and rubbing my nose.

"That wasn't the same as before," Jem states as he watches me.

"That was you. Not me," I say through a chuckle. *He can shock me back. I wonder if he was thinking the same thing that I was when I shocked him this morning.* Jem runs his hands up my back, pulling me closer to him. "Please don't be scared of me. I don't know if I can do this without you," I say, resting my head on his chest.

"Do you really mean that?" he asks uncertainly. I lift my head and look deep into his eyes; I don't know if I was looking for an answer or maybe the right thing to say, but as he looks back at me I knew that deep inside of me, I did. Without him could I really be good?

We tenderly kiss again and again until our lips mold together. Pulling my hands up into his hair, our kiss becomes more urgent— needed. I pull away, gasping for air.

"We need to wait," I say with a struggle. *Too soon and I fear I won't want to stop; too soon and I might not go. Go away and find my powers . . . and then where will be?*

"Right here," Jem whispers, pulling me back to him and kissing down my neck.

"But that would be it, though, wouldn't it?" Jem looks at me, his expression hurt. "Don't get me wrong. Kissing you is definitely something that I could keep doing. But . . ." How do I say this without sounding hurtful? I'm not going to stay at home and produce children and do nothing but look after him. I'm not like that. Before I found out about these powers, I was going for a trip just to be with my family—to know them better. I guess I'll really be doing that now. To just stay here with Jem would make our relationship just about sex, and if this is forever, then I don't want to do that either.

"So we'll wait," Jem says. "If this is forever, then we can wait until you've mastered your powers."

"And get to know each other better?" I ask, as his smile stretches across his face.

"I'd like that," he says, and kisses me on the forehead before letting go of me.

Jem takes one of the glasses of water and sits down on the sofa, flipping through the channels on TV. I begin organizing the clothes I've pulled out of the wardrobe, making piles of outfits, wrapping up shoes, and laying out plenty of socks and underwear. Ali and I will be having retail therapy, and some clothes had better stay here. I begin emptying my make-up bag, again resorting to what's best to take and leaving what I can buy while I'm away.

"So what's the plan when we're in London?" Jem asks, still watching the telly. Oh dear; I hadn't thought about him joining us while we shop and do girly things. Maybe he won't be a typical man and moan and just tag along.

"Um . . . Ali said she wanted to get some fabric for a pattern she has." She's very creative and clever with fabric and doing womanly things like dress making, unlike me, who can barely cook. "So, I said I'd take her to a place I know in Soho. And there's an exhibition of 'fashion through history' or something like that at the V&A museum that we're going to see, and then of course, the essential retail therapy." Which he probably shouldn't witness. "Oh, and I wanted to get a couple of books as well. There's a bookshop near the fabric place in Soho, so I'll probably go in there while Ali's looking at fabric." When I'd said it, I suddenly questioned why Ali agreed to go shopping with me. It's a rarity for us to physically shop together. We generally enter a shop together and then go our separate ways, finding what we want. Meeting in the changing rooms, we'd show each other what we've found, and then pay for it separately. Maybe not how best friends should shop, but it works for us. We always have fun, and that's the point, isn't it?

"Well, if you don't mind, I'll join you when you go to the bookshop?" he asks, looking over at me.

"Sure," I say with a shrug. *I guess someone has to keep an eye on me.*

"It is for your safety," he says, sounding almost like an authority.

"But why? Okay, I understand that I'm new at this . . . and that I could hurt someone. But will I always need to be chaperoned?" Jem gets up from the sofa, pulling me to him and hugging me. His touch is so warm and welcoming that I can't resist hugging him back.

"It's just for now," he says, trying to reassure me. "You have to remember that you're different from anybody else—that you're the first child to be born from a Sabbath member without a Sabbath partner and that you're foretold to restore peace to our world. Our species has been waiting a long time for you."

It's a heavy burden to bear, and am I really capable of such a thing? Restoring peace . . . humans are always at war somewhere, how would magical beings be different?

"But you're part of The Sabbath Court; being the Grand High's son, doesn't that become automatic?" I ask.

"No. It's different for me because *I am* my mother's son. I'm not part of the court until my mother passes her leadership to me." *So until she decides to retire or she dies, until then he's a free man? But he will eventually be part of The Sabbath. But if we have children, won't they end up*

117

being the same as me? "When we can perform a union, you will join the court when I do."

"And if we can't?" I ask, unsure if that is really possible for us. Can we still be together? Can we have a normal life? Maybe like humans? Rather than a 'union,' we could get . . . nope, can't even think the word. That kind of commitment is still a bit iffy, even if he is the one for me. I think I'd rather live in sin than do that. Oooh. Gives me goosebumps just thinking about it.

"Considering we only met last night you've really accepted that it's you and me, haven't you?" I nod, feeling my cheeks burn with embarrassment. He kisses me on the forehead and looks deeply into my eyes. "Thank you," he says, kissing my forehead again.

"You're not freaked out?" I ask, knowing full well that I am. *How can I rationally belong to someone I've only just met? How can I be with someone I can't always touch? And how can I be with someone now, when I'm just about to leave? The other thing of course, is that I feel like one of those desperate women lusting after a guy they've just met, thinking it's "love at first sight." Surely something like this is going to scare him away. It scares away all of the other guys; what makes Jem any different?*

"Because I've been waiting a long time to find you—waiting to find someone that wants me and not my magic." He lets go of me and walks over to the window.

"How long have you been waiting?" I ask, never before actually thinking to ask how old he is.

"I'll be 140 years old next March."

I clap my hands over my mouth, trying to quieten the popping sound of my jaw dropping. *Holy fuck, that's old.* But then, I guess witches or wizards or warlocks or whatever do live a long time. Then another question springs into my mind.

"Do you want me? Or do you want my magic?" With his back still to me I see his shoulders lower as he lets out a deep sigh.

"That's why I'm here now," he confesses.

"Oh, I get it. Check if you'd like me before I have too much power." Seeing his head nod, I shrug; I would have done the same. "And?" I ask.

"The same as last night, and it was the same this morning. I thought it was an enchantment at first, but when our hearts glowed I knew it was you. I had been tricked before because people know who I am and they wanted that, but you didn't. You just saw me and from that first time we got a shock, I was amazed, and then with what happened this morning . . ." I clutch at my chest, the sharp pain of guilt stabbing me in the heart. Jem rushes over to me, pulling my hand from my chest, but the thought of him unconscious because of me still flashes in my head. "What happened this morning made me more certain that it is *you*."

"What, you were looking for someone to zap you until you were unconscious?" I ask, feeling a little sick.

"No," he says through a chuckle. "I've been waiting for someone to get into my heart without breaking it—someone who can melt me." I'm not sure that I've melted his heart . . . probably just woken it up with a large bout of electricity or something. Accepting that it's him and me is one thing. But love is something I'm not sure of yet. I do really like him, and maybe I could love him, but. . . the bit that keeps pinching me is something in my subconscious. To love him would be nice, and I have thought about the forever part, but my forever might not be as long as his. *What if it's another lifetime before I truly love him?* I've definitely thought of the having children and living together, but do I crave to be with someone rather than loving them? Is it what he does to me that I really love? I could really do with a magic ball or something that could come up with the simple "yes" and "no" answers, rather than "I'm not sure" or "I don't know." *Will he wait until I'm ready to be in love?*

"I'll wait as long as it takes," he says, gently squeezing my hand.

"What do we do in the meantime?" I ask, wondering if it would be possible to be without him until the New Year. No, that didn't seem possible, but D said he's not allowed to be near while I study or train. Or could I simply wake up one morning and bam—that's it—all fallen in love and head over heels. No, that didn't sound like me.

"Maybe we'll just wait and see what happens," Jem suggests with a smile.

"One step at a time?" I ask. Jem nods in agreement and sits back down on the sofa. *Okay, that I can do.*

16: CONTROL

"Suitcase," I say out loud, and turn back to the door; Jem follows closely behind me. "Aren't I safe enough to go up in the loft on my own?" I ask, feeling a bit irritated that I need a bodyguard. Even if it is Jem it's not like we can do anything . . . can we?

"I'm sure you are," Jem says with a chuckle, "I just think that you'll need more than one considering the amount of clothes you've laid out." I shrug; there's not that much there, and I'd rather be prepared. *A girl has to have her essentials.* "Well, you have a lot of essentials," he says, smiling at my thoughts, and very childishly I turn around and poke my tongue out at him.

We climb up into the loft and find boxes upon boxes scattered across the boards. I turn on the torch (D always leaves one by the hatch) and shine it around the loft. The beam of light passes over dust-covered cardboard boxes and old leather suitcases. As the beam runs over the corner of the loft, I start to hear a humming sound.

"Did you hear that?" I ask in a whisper. Jem shakes his head in silence. I walk over to the corner where the humming is coming from, moving boxes and cases as I go. The humming sound is getting louder the closer I get to the corner. I push away a large box and reveal a wooden trunk with the initials E.W. carved on the side. The humming is like a velvet trace of notes—a tune I know, but I can't remember the lyrics. I pull the trunk away from the wall and blow at the blanket of dust that has settled on the top. "Can you hear it now?" I ask as I turn to Jem; he's a couple of feet behind me and he looks pale, stood motionless by the hatch. I turn back to the trunk and carefully lift the lid. It can't be anything dangerous; it's my mother's trunk—E.W.—Eleanor Wood. She wouldn't keep some-thing dangerous for me to find, would she? Of course not. I pull the lid back and gently rest it against one of the roof's beams. The trunk is fairly empty considering its size, and I wonder if she used it for when she was travelling. Would it be a bad thing if I used it to do the same? I carefully lift up the large folded paper and as I do, a purple, velvet bag rolls toward me. As I pick up the bag the humming gets louder, and I undo the knot around the opening and look inside. Inside is a clear ball; as I slip it out of the bag and into the palm of my hand, the humming stops. I look closer at the ball; it's heavy—maybe crystal. But crystal balls are bigger, aren't they? This is about the size of a tennis ball, or maybe a fraction smaller. "What is it?" I ask, still whispering. Jem takes a cautious step toward me. The core of the sphere begins to glow, but for some reason it doesn't panic me. The glow is like a gentle flicker of a candle flame, soft and comforting and a little exciting, like watching the candles on a birthday cake before blowing them out.

I can hear Jem trying to tip toe toward me while I muse over the glowing ball. As he steps closer, the glow of the ball brightens. "Did you do that?" I ask, but Jem doesn't reply. I glance up at him standing just inches away from me; his complexion is still pale. I raise my hand to touch him—to reassure him—but as I move closer to him, the glowing ball brightens again. "It's us," I say, amazed. Two powerful beings surely belong together, but what does a glowing ball of light have to do with it? I wonder if it's like the same ball of light that Mum had for my heart motions—a piece of me.

Just then, a crack of static snaps from between my fingers and strikes Jem's hand. I curl my hand into a ball, trying to take back the shock, but it's too late. Jem drops to his knees and I drop the glowing ball into the trunk just in time to catch Jem before he falls face first into the floor. As I cradle him in my arms, I can feel a current running through me. It doesn't hurt like the shocks, but it's not comfortable. I run my fingers across his forehead and then down onto his neck. He's breathing and I can feel a pulse, but it's very weak. *He fainted, but why?* I look back at the trunk; I can still see the glow from the crystal ball. *Did it do this to him?* I carefully rest his head on the floor and release my arms from under him. The glow in the trunk dims as I pull away from him. Peeking over the edge of the open trunk, I can see the ball sat on the folded paper at the bottom. I pick up the velvet bag that it was in and wrap it inside out over my hand so as not to touch it. *If I put the ball back in the bag, will it turn off? Jem was fine until I took it out of the bag, maybe he'll be all right when I've put it away.* I grab the ball with the hand that's covered in the velvet bag and carefully turn the velvet edges so the ball falls to the bottom of the bag. Looking into the open bag, I watch as the crystal ball's glow dims and dims until it's clear once more.

I turn back to Jem; he's still unconscious. I don't know if I should touch him; what if there's another shock? It will hurt him. I kneel down next to him, keeping my hands behind my back. "Jem," I whisper by his ear, but he doesn't move. I wonder if the trunk and the ball being so near doesn't help. I get up eyeing up the trunk, trying to figure out how to get it out of the loft. Maybe if I can get it down to my room he'd feel better, but the trunk looks rather heavy, even if it is nearly empty. *Could I lift it on my own?*

I tug at the handle; it doesn't feel too bad, but I need to lift it over Jem and the mountain of cardboard boxes before I get to the ladder, and then, how do I get it down through the hatch? I stand for a while contemplating how to get to the trunk down to my room, my eyes flicking from the ladder to the trunk.

Dad said that vampires were strong. *Could I tap into that to get the trunk down to my room? And then maybe get Jem to his room?* I think about how I moved earlier in my room, but the thing was, I wasn't aware that I was doing it. Maybe I don't need to be. Could it just happen? When I need to go fast, I do, and when I need to be strong, I just am. Could it be that simple? I stand in front of the trunk and grab both handles. Taking a deep breath as I normally would when picking up something heavy, I bend my knees and then take on the weight of the trunk, straightening myself out as I hold the trunk at my waist. *Wow,* I can feel the weight of the trunk, but it's no burden, just like carrying a large, empty cardboard box—awkward, but light. I scan the floor, figuring out my path to the ladder. I lift the trunk up onto my right shoulder and hold out my left hand to balance myself. I swiftly tiptoe around Jem and over to the ladder. Pulling the trunk down off my shoulder, I maneuver it through the loft hatch using one end. I get down on my knees and hang myself down through the hatch until the other end of the trunk rests on the floor. I jump down with a light thud, feeling proud of myself for being able to use my powers so well. It's a shame it's not for the right reasons. Swiftly again, I carry the trunk to my room, setting it down on the floor near my bed. I turn and run back to the ladder to the loft. I move the ladder, feeling confident now that I can carry Jem to his room; I'd do better at not waking him if I don't have to move around the ladder. I lightly jump up, grab the frame, and pull myself up. *This is actually quite easy, but why does it scare Jem so much?* I move over to Jem.

Ah . . . how do I pick him up without giving him another shock? I kneel down next to him, leaning over him to check that he's still breathing. As I do so, my mother's I-stone falls out from under my top. Dangling from my neck, it swings between Jem and me. It's black; I don't know what that means. As the stone gets closer to Jem, the color starts to change; its movement is only slight now, and the end closest to Jem gets paler and paler, eventually turning white. The I-stone is now half black and half white. The white I understand, but why are the colors split in two? Before, there's been a main color and then specks or swirls of another color. Maybe D or Dad will know what it means. I tuck the pendent back under my top; questions will have to wait until later. I need to get Jem downstairs before D and Terry see him and get more panicked. I take in a deep breath; clearing my mind, I try to think only of keeping Jem safe. It had worked with putting Dad into a shield; hopefully it will work with the shocks. I lift his head and slip my arm under his neck. *Phew—no shocks.* I tuck my other arm under his knees and lift him up; again, the weight isn't a burden. I swiftly move over to the hatch, squeezing Jem closer to me and cradling him like a child.

"Hope," Jem croaks. I look at him in my arms; he still looks pale. Maybe he'll be all right when he's had some rest.

"Hold onto me," I say quietly, trying not to scare him with the fact that I'm carrying him. He wraps his arms around my neck and looks down at the hatch. Seeing him wince, I whisper "close your eyes," and when he has done what I ask, I jump through the hatch, landing with a gentle thud. *Oh dear; someone would have heard that—move before you're seen.* I dart along the hall and through the door to the guest bedroom. I smoothly place him on the bed; his arms are still around my neck and his eyes are still closed.

"You can open your eyes now," I whisper in his ear. He opens his eyes and stares at me and then at his hands gripped together. "How are you feeling?" I ask. *He still looks really pale. . . maybe the shocks are doing more than hurting him.* He shakes his head as he lets go of his hands around my neck.

"I feel embarrassed more than anything," he says, lying back on the bed. "Girls are supposed to faint and then the boys carry them to bed."

I smile. At least he's embarrassed rather than angry; most men would be infuriated to have a woman stronger than them. I sit on the edge of the bed and look at him. "Are you sure about this?" I ask, not wanting to ask, but knowing that I have to. "Twice in one day I've knocked you out . . . that can't be good, and what if it gets worse?"

Jem sits up, cupping my cheek with his hand. He kisses my softly on the lips. "Yes. I'm sure about this," he says as he kisses me again. I no longer feel strong, but rather so weak that I can barely breathe. I blink hard, concentrating; *giving into a moment's temptation will end up the same as this morning.* Taking in a deep breath I get up from the bed, but Jem takes hold of my hand, holding me back

"Where are you going?" he asks, his voice a sweet, seductive purr. I look down at our hands together, trying to think clearly.

"I'm going to pack," I say, desperately trying to not give in and hop into bed next to him. "Maybe you should get some rest while I do."

"Are we still going out for dinner tonight?" I wince at his question; I don't know if it would be safe for him. Even though I could pull the shock back into my hand, he still blacked out. He didn't get any more when I thought about carrying him and keeping him safe in my arms. "You've almost mastered the shocks already, haven't you?" Jem says, smiling proudly at me.

"I have to concentrate," I say not feeling as proud as he looks, but instead feeling more disappointed with each shock I give him. Why do I give Jem shocks? It's like Dad said: *There's something holding onto you. Almost like there's something you're waiting for.* I wonder if my powers have been waiting for Jem. Maybe that's what the shocks are? "What happens when I give you a shock?" I ask. Jem's eyes widen from my question. *Didn't he hear my thoughts about Dad?*

"No, I didn't hear your thoughts just then. It kept breaking up, like some sort of interference." Okay, that's a bit weird; I thought I'd already let him in. Dad said he couldn't hear my thoughts until he was within my shield, and now he has a shield over him because I apparently put it there.

Ignoring what he's said about my thoughts, I ask again, "So, with the shocks, what happens to you?" I sit down on the bed, watching him. He leans back on the pillows, avoiding making eye contact with me. "Jem, what is it?" I ask, concerned. He sighs and then finally turns and looks at me.

"I'm somewhere else. I'm . . ." he hesitates and looks away again.

I take his hand. "Jem, do you see a woman who looks like me? Maybe a little older, with a long purple cloak, and a purple tint to her eyes, like mine?" His head snaps around, facing me, and his eyes are so wide that they look like they might fall out of their sockets. He nods his head. "I think that my Mum watches over you when I shock you. Does she say anything to you?" He shakes his head. "Well, at least you're safe when you black out."

He blinks hard, refocusing himself. "How did you know about that?" he asks, shock making his voice squeak. I shrug, letting go of his hand, and get up from the bed.

"Because she was with me yesterday when I blacked out; but she also gave me my heart motions, apparently getting me ready to meet you." Then I have another thought—*are my heart motions too fast to share with Jem? Are his too slow?*

"Your mother knew I was coming?" he asks, shocked.

"Apparently so," I say, frowning at him. He didn't say anything about sharing heart motions, and he didn't say anything about Dad, either.

"I can't hear you very well, there's something blocking me," Jem says. This could be an advantage, I guess—save me from some embarrassment. And maybe sometimes it would be helpful—*could I block him out completely?* Walking back over to Jem, I cradle his face with my hands; *could I kiss him just enough to not give him a shock?* Jem pulls me closer to him, understanding what I'm trying to do. As our lips touch, I can hear every thought he's had through our conversation, and I wonder if he can hear mine, too. Our lips mould together, our kiss becoming deeper and deeper. Still with no shocks, but it's not about sex, it's about being close to him—as close as possible.

You've still got to pack. Hearing his thoughts in my head, I smile, hearing him as clear as a bell.

"That was still a bit fuzzy, but it was better." I lean in and kiss him again.

Then you get some rest and we'll meet in the garden at about seven o'clock. Jem pulls away from me, looking at my hands on his chest.

"So we *are* going to dinner?" he asks, sounding unsure.

"As long as D and Terry agree, I think we can handle it." *Mind you, either way I'd still have to go out so I'm at the Gibbet for ten o'clock.*

"What's at the Gibbet?" Jem asks. I smile at him, happy that some things are still private.

"I'll show you later," I say, kissing him on the end of his nose, and I make my way to the door.

Walking back down the hall to my bedroom, I tidy away the ladder and shut the hatch door to the loft. As I reach my bedroom door, the house phone rings; I hover near the stairs to see if it's for me.

I can hear D talking. "Oh, all right. Well come for the one night. We'll sort out getting you back here." *Who's she talking to?* "I'll just get her." D comes running up the stairs. "It's Ali for you," she says as she passes me the phone. I walk through into my room and D follows.

"Hi ya, are you alright?" I ask. Why is she calling? I only saw her this morning.

"Hope, I can only come to London for one night," Ali says, her voice sounding sad.

"Why? What's happened?" She was as excited as I was about going to London.

"My Gran has summoned us to her house up north somewhere," she says with resentment. "We have to be there Wednesday afternoon and it takes nearly all day to drive there, apparently."

"Oh, okay," I say, feeling disappointed that she won't be able to come along for long.

"D said that Terry and Jem are coming with us as well," she says in the exact opposite tone—happy and cheery. I know what she wants to know, but I'll ignore answering it for now.

"Yes, apparently so," I say in an annoyed tone, still irritated by the fact that I need to be watched. I know it makes sense, but I do like to have some privacy.

"So where are you and Jem going tonight?" she asks, her voice getting higher in pitch. I turn and look at D to give her a stern look but she's frozen, staring at my mum's trunk sat next to the bed. I turn back. *Keep things normal for Ali,* I think to myself.

"Um . . . I'm not sure, actually. We're just going out to for some dinner."

"Ooooooh!" Ali's overactive mind goes into overdrive.

"Ali," I say, scolding her. Does she really have to do that?

"You like him," she says triumphantly. *Don't answer that,* I think to myself.

"So you don't mind them coming with us? The retail therapy might be a bit limited."

"So, Jem will be with us most of the time, will he?" *She's a nightmare.*

"I guess so. But if it's not Jem then it will be either Terry or D."

"Oh. Being overprotective again, are they?" she asks, her cheery tone gone again.

"Yep," I say with disappointment; she knows what it's been like. She even noticed when D loosened her grip and started letting me go out. "So if your Gran has summoned you 'up north' for Wednesday afternoon, that means we'll only have Monday night together. There won't be any decent clubs open," I say, successfully changing the subject but sounding a bit whiny at the same time.

"I'm broke, anyway. Maybe we could just go to that karaoke bar near your uncle's apartment. It's always fun in there."

"Okay, let's do that," I say in agreement; that would be good for our last night out. Well, not forever, but for a while, at least.

"Sorry to have to change our plans," she says with sadness in her voice.

"Ali, it's all right. We'll have fun with the time that we've got." It's probably better that she's not staying for so long, now; at least if she's away from me and with her family, she's safe.

"I've got to go," she says suddenly. "Rob's picking me up in a bit."

"Okay. We'll see you in the morning," I say calmly.

She lets out a giggle and then squeaks into the phone, "Oooh, I'll see you in the morning, *Mrs. Winters.*" With that, she hangs up. I bet her and Rob have got money on Jem and me; I obviously looked melted last night, then.

Turning back, I look at D, who is still frozen and staring at Mum's trunk.

"Ali's only coming for one night in London now. Her Gran has summoned her up north. Will it be all right if one of us drives her back?" I ask, putting the phone down on the side. "I don't like the idea of her travelling alone on the train." Claudia, just the same as D, has always made sure we don't go anywhere like London on our own. So of course, when Ali and I were old enough, Uncle Kirk very kindly consented to lend us his apartment and his housekeeper. We've got somewhere safe to stay and D knows where we are. But now Ali will be going on her own, and, while I know D says I put a shield on her, it won't protect her from everything. To be honest, I'm not sure that having a shield over someone is always a good thing.

Interrupting my errant thoughts, D says, "Yes, one of us will bring Ali home. I'd already spoken to Claudia before you spoke to Ali." That's a relief; I hate worrying about how people are going to get home. "That is your mother's trunk," D states, pointing at the trunk.

"Yeah. I found it up in the loft when I was looking for a suitcase."

"Really? I've never seen it there before."

"It was buried behind a mountain of boxes." I shrug, accepting that D never really went through the loft. Mum would have put it there when they decided to settle here.

"How did you find it?" she asks, still frozen like a statue, her eyes wide with fear. I kneel down in front of the trunk.

"It was humming a song I know but I can't remember the words to." I open up the lid and the humming begins again. D's frozen posture breaks and she backs away a few steps. "D?" I ask, quickly getting up and taking her hand. "Can you hear it?" I ask. She nods, her eyes growing wider still. Well that's a relief; I thought I was going mad. If D can hear it, maybe that's a good thing. But will it make her black out as well? Actually, I've never shocked her before. I let go of her hand and pick up the velvet bag. Opening it up, I slip the small crystal ball into my hand. She steps closer to me, awed by the sphere as it begins to glow.

"Do you know what it is?" I ask her. She reaches out to touch it, but hesitates. I take her hand and hold it open, placing the ball into her palm. It continues to glow but dims slightly from D's touch.

"I'm not entirely sure," D says as she finds her voice. She moves her hand around so she can have a closer look. "I think it's an orb, although it shouldn't exist here. Not in the real world."

In the real world? But it's here—physically here. Either my face showed my confusion, or she read my thoughts.

"We create them subconsciously. Our mind is what controls our powers." She passes me the orb back and it glows brighter again. "Like what I asked you to do this morning with Jem. We can collect our powers into a ball or orb, and then store them in our minds. It's a bit like having your own personal shopping centre; when you want the power or spell again, you simply find the orb you want and use it."

"That's clever. But if they're made subconsciously, how is it here?" I ask, looking at the glowing ball again. "Unless it's something else . . . Jem did faint when he got close to it." *Oops—blabber-mouth.*

D lets out a long sigh. "Hope, you have to be careful with him." Her tone is nagging. *Like I need a constant reminder of what a monster I am.* "You're not a monster. He's just not as strong as you yet."

I can't help but laugh. "Poor guy," I say with a sigh. "I hope he knows what he's letting himself in for."

D laughs, too. "Poor guy," she says in agreement, and then chuckles again. "He's going to have more than a shock trying to keep up with you."

I hope that he can keep up with me. I put the orb back in its bag and lay it on the bed. "I'll ask the others about this. Maybe they'll know what it is." I reach into the bottom of the trunk and pull out the large, folded paper. Undoing the folds, I lay it out flat on the floor.

It's a map of the world; I recognize the shape of the British Isles, parts of Europe, America, Australia, and the map has a series of symbols all over it. D kneels down next to me, looking over the map with me.

"This was your mother's," she says, running her finger over the hand written initials E.W. "It shows where she had found different populations of species." She points to a symbol—a circle with a shining sun set within it. "That's the fairies," she says, and then points to another circle within which seems to be a simplistic version of an oak tree. "And that's the elves."

The more I look at the different symbols, the more I seem to recognize them. "These symbols are on the coin that Dad gave me," I say out loud, recognizing what I see. "They're on Mum's Box with her book in it, as well." Looking at the map, my instincts tell me that the map is missing some symbols, or maybe it's wrong somehow. I quickly get to my feet and rush downstairs to the kitchen table where I had left the coin. Finding it, I quickly run back upstairs.

"When did you start doing that?" D asks with a large, proud smile across her face.

"Sorry, was I going too fast?" I ask, waiting for the smile to change and her reaction to become the same as Jem's earlier.

"No. Well . . . yes, it was fast as witches go, but for a vampire that's pretty good and controlled." Phew. She knows about vampires and doesn't freak out. Thank god. "Jem saw you move like that?" I nod in response.

"But I didn't know I was doing it. I was just in a hurry. He freaked out," I say, trying to defend myself.

"Hardly surprising," she says with a shrug. "The Sabbath are not fans of vampires."

"That would explain his reaction. He was scared, but more scared that I'd enchanted him."

D laughs a hard and evil laugh, and then suddenly stops and looks at me. "How long have you been doing this?" she asks, her face now quite stern. I sheepishly look down at the floor.

"Dad said that I started showing vampire enchantment soon after I was seventeen. That's why . . ." I was far too ashamed to say aloud that I had been sleeping around.

"Arr, well, that explains that, but how do you feel about Jem?"

I walk over and kneel down next to her. "I don't know. I like him. It's just . . ." Sighing, I look D in the eye. "It's just so fast and I . . . I have to go away and learn all these things."

D leans over and hugs me. "I think you'll be fine."

"Thank you," I say, hugging her back as tears escape from the corners of my eyes.

"It has been an honor to be your guardian," she says, squeezing me tightly.

After a long moment of tears and hugs, we part and look down at the map. "They're the same symbols," I say, feeling proud of myself for remembering them. "Where does this coin come from?"

D shakes her head. "I don't know. The only other one I've seen is Terry's, but his is obviously much older than yours."

"Maybe I should ask Terry what's wrong with this map," I say, voicing my suspicion.

"Why, what's wrong with the map?" Her eyebrows pin together, showing her wrinkles.

"I think someone—or something—is missing."

"Okay," she says, sounding a little disheartened.

I fold up the map and lay it next to the orb, resting the coin on top of it. "Can you help me pack?" I ask D as I start picking up piles of clothes.

"Sure." She looks at me with a questioning eyebrow raised.

"What?" Is it that bad helping me pack?

"It's just that you've really changed since your birthday, even more so when you broke up with Steve."

"Is that a bad thing?" I ask, cringing as I wait for her answer.

"No," she says rubbing my arm with reassurance. "You're just . . ." Hesitating, she looks away from me. "It's just that you've been so nice, and you've let me help you, and the rest of our family. It's like a switch inside you has been turned. I thought it was because you had begun shielding, but it's so much more than that. And seeing you with Jem . . ." She sighs and looks back at me. "You're going to be great at all of this."

I try to swallow against the lump rising in my throat. "I hope so. I don't want to let anyone down."

D pats me on the back. "Come on, let's get this packed." We quickly fill my mother's trunk with all my things. I put the orb in amongst the clothes so it won't break. Finding my mother's rosewood box with her book, I put it with the map, leaving it out to make sure I remember to ask Terry about it. *I suppose I could ask Dad; he did give me the coin, after all. Maybe I should take it with me tonight?* I'm suddenly distracted from my thoughts as D starts folding the top and skirt I had left hanging in the wardrobe.

"Don't pack that," I say abruptly. "I'm going to wear it tonight."

"Tonight?" she asks, that questioning eyebrow raised again.

"Jem and I are going out for dinner . . . if that's alright." I ask, suddenly thinking she's probably going to say "no," even though she aleady knew.

"No, that's fine, so long as you don't do anything out of the ordinary when you're out."

"Now I understand a bit more about the shocks, I think I can control it," I say. It's a bit cocky, I know, but I do feel more confident that I can hold onto the shocks. So long as we don't do anything too close to each other, I'm sure we'll be fine.

"Just be careful with him." I roll my eyes at her. *How many times does she have to say that?* "Just make sure that you are." She's obviously hearing my thoughts.

"Of course." D's smile mirrors mine; I'm feeling a little bit triumphant that we're allowed to go out alone together.

Finally, I close the lid to my mother's trunk. "All set," I pronounce. "I think I'll have a bath before we go out."

"Okay. I'll make sure Jem doesn't come in and disturb you. We don't want a repeat performance of this morning, do we?" She smiles grimly at me.

"Thanks," I say, grateful that she understands my limits with Jem.

17: TABLE FOR TWO

I'm feeling a little nervous as I brush through my hair, and butterflies start to flit around in my stomach. How can I be nervous? I've already kissed him. I've danced with him and seen him pretty much naked. How can going out for dinner make me nervous? I look at the clock; it's seven. I quickly put on my sparkly heeled flip-flops, roll up a pair of shorts and socks, and put them into a beach bag with my trainers. If I'm going to be running later, I'd need appropriate footwear. I fling the beach bag over my shoulder and grab my black clutch bag that has my phone and purse in it. At a rushed human pace I make my way downstairs to the kitchen, finding D stood at the sink, washing up. She turns to look at me and her eyes widen with concern.

"Are you alright?" she asks. Feeling my cheeks burn, I look up at her.

"I think I'm nervous," I say as I rub my stomach, trying to settle the butterflies that seem to be spinning around.

"I'm sure you'll be fine. Just be yourself," she says, smiling at me with encouragement. "He's in the garden with Terry."

"Thanks." I turn on my heel and head out to the garden.

I walk through the living room and out onto the patio. I can see Jem and Terry chatting at the end of the lawn, leaning on the fence. As I stand there watching them, I notice Jem; considering I met him only yesterday, I don't think I really noticed how solid he is. Although he's not a big guy—maybe 5'10"—he's trim; the defined muscles on his chest create a shadow on his fitted t-shirt, and his blond hair is all shades of gold. His skin is glistening under the evening sun, gently bronzed; obviously he is not a sun worshipper, but definitely has been out in it. Why didn't I notice that this morning? Or did I? What happened this morning and last night was electric—completely electric. But now when I look at him, I see a man, not just an object to lust after. Don't get me wrong, he's still very handsome—he'd definitely give Brad Pitt a run for his money—but someone I want to be with for always.

I watch his expression as he talks to Terry. Every time he smiles he flashes his white teeth, his whole face lighting up, and even his eyes start to sparkle. I stand still watching, simply in awe of him. Beautiful is not a word you should use for a man, but he is—simply beautiful.

My stomach makes a loud grumbling sound, breaking me away from my gawking. I clutch hold of my stomach; looking down I can feel my cheeks burn as two sets of eyes look over at me.

"God, I'm hungry. I don't think I've eaten all day." Rubbing my stomach, I hope it can hold on. When I look up again, Jem and Terry are walking toward me.

"Hungry, then?" Terry chuckles. I can feel my cheeks getting hotter.

"We'd best get some dinner before you fade away," Jem says as he offers his hand out to me. I gladly take it, not worrying of any consequences. As our fingers entwine the two hands start to glow. I feel warm and relaxed, like being at home. Jem smiles at me, lifts our hands to his lips, and kisses my fingers. As he does, I can feel the sensation of pinpricks running along my fingers and into my hand. *This is getting easier,* I think to myself.

Terry clears his throat. "Don't do that in public," he says with concern. My face is now roasting with embarrassment; I'd almost forgotten he was there. Jem and I let our hands fall to our sides, and the glow is gone.

"Of course," Jem says, "we'll be careful." Terry's eyebrows pin together, and then he looks back at me.

"Just take it steady, alright?" Terry warns. I roll my eyes. How many times do they have to say that? I'm not exactly a bomb waiting to go off. I can control myself. Well . . . usually, at least. I'm getting better. I walk over to Terry and give him a peck on the cheek.

"Of course we will. Don't worry so much." Stepping away from him, I take Jem's hand again and pull him toward the car. "We'll see you later!" I shout over my shoulder, but he's already gone.

In a very gentlemanly like manner, Jem holds the car door open for me.

"Thank you," I whisper as I sit in the passenger seat. I don't think a guy's ever done that for me before. He shuts the door and jogs 'round to the driver's side. He starts the car and then looks at me.

"Actually . . . where do you want to go?" he asks suddenly, looking out of his element. When I look at him I can't help myself, and I burst out laughing. "What?" Jem asks as he pulls a beautiful smile across his face.

"Sorry," I say as I try to calm my giggles. "What kinds of food do you like?"

"Most things, I guess," he says with a shrug. "What do you fancy?" I can feel a cheeky grin rise on my face and pinch at my cheeks. *I know what I fancy* . . . "*Food*, Hope," he says, his eyes looking stern but his mouth twitching as if to hide a smile.

"Sure," I say as I clear my throat. "Food." I run through different restaurants in my head: ones that will be open on a Sunday night, ones that will let us have some privacy, and ones that have good food. "Do you like Italian food?" I ask him.

"Yes."

"Okay. Let's go to Casanova's in town." And we drive off in the evening sun.

***

"Hope!" Marco calls out to me as we enter the restaurant, his Italian accent soft and welcoming.

"Marco," I say in reply, and we hug as we always do, kissing cheeks. His eyes grow wider as he sees Jem come up behind me.

"Table for two?" Marco asks with a questioning eyebrow raised, his overly bronzed skin wrinkling under his jet-black hair.

"Yes, please," Jem says as he rests his hand on the small of my back. Marco leads us over to the far corner of the restaurant to a candlelit table in a private booth. Helping me with a chair, Marco passes me a menu.

"Thank you," I say, smiling up at him from my seat. He rests his hand on my shoulder.

"You are always welcome, Hope." He then winks at me and then looks over at Jem, his expression narrowing—almost jealous. "I'll give you a minute to go through the menu," and he walks away.

Peeking over his menu, Jem looks at me. "So, do you bring all your boyfriends here?"

"Hardly," I say, as I continue to read the menu. *Don't usually bother with the eating part.* Actually, I don't think Steve and I ever went out for dinner on our own. It was always with Ali and Rob or Nicky and Elliot. For the first time, I wonder why we hadn't had time alone together, like going out for dinner or something. Why on earth did he put up with me for so long? Anyway . . . "You're not exactly a boyfriend," I look up at him, "are you?" His smile drops and his eyes fall back down to the menu. "Jem," I say pleadingly—*I didn't mean it like that.* When he doesn't look up, I reach for his hand but hesitate, my fingertips still inches away from his. "No glowing in public," I quietly mutter to myself. Before I can even risk touching Jem, Marco returns with a pen and a pad ready.

"So, what would you like?" Marco asks. I look at Jem and hesitate, knowing that I could probably eat a whole cow right now. I'm ravenous, but I don't want to look like a glutton for ordering half the menu. Jem clears his throat and looks up at Marco.

"Could we have two Caesar salads for starters, and then a bowl of carbonara for two with extra ham and mushrooms, and a side order of bread?" I watch him order our dinner, my jaw dropping in amazement. I know I was looking at the menu, but I hadn't chosen anything. Jem looks at me and asks, "Hope, what do you want to drink?" Blinking hard and trying to put my mind back into gear, I swallow hard and then look at Marco.

"Can I have a large orange juice and lemonade, please?" I watch Marco writing it all down.

"And I'll have the same," Jem says.

"Okay. I'll be back with your drinks in a minute."

"Thank you," Jem says politely, passing Marco back the menus. "Was that alright?" Jem asks as he turns to look at me. "I didn't want you to starve yourself because you're with me."

Before I can say anything, my tummy growls in reply. I quickly clap my hands over my stomach, trying to quiet the sound. Change the subject before you think about food again and embarrass yourself . . . again. Looking up at Jem, he's smiling, watching me. "Jem, when I said you're not exactly a boyfriend, I didn't mean . . . well . . ." Hesitating, I look out the window. "It's just that . . ." I can't say it. It won't come out. Not through my thoughts or my mouth.

"Here we are," Marco announces as he places the two pint glasses on the table. I look up at Marco, who has a huge grin stretched across his face.

"Cheers Marco."

He turns away and I can hear his thoughts whisper in my head: *It's about time that girl really met someone.* I look back at Jem and he just laughs.

"Well, that answers your question about bringing boyfriends here," I say before taking a sip of my drink. I try to straighten out my thoughts on how I can explain to Jem how he's not a boyfriend.

"Hope," he says, distracting me. He takes my hand; his expression is smooth, but the intense blue of his eyes is serious. "I know what you mean about the 'not exactly boyfriend' part."

"You do?" I ask, feeling my forehead crease with a frown. He nods in reply. "The thing is .." I'm still not entirely sure how to say what I want to. "It's . . . well . . . you're too good to be true." Taking in a deep breath, I continue, "It's like you're a 'Prince Charming' from a fairy tale and you've come in and swept me off my feet."

"I'm no Prince Charming, Hope," he says sternly, letting go of my hand and folding his arms in front of him. He may not be everybody's Prince Charming, but mine? He certainly is. "That's what you find hard to deal with, isn't it?" I nod. "Because it's too good to be true?" We both sigh.

"Exactly. I think I'm still waiting for someone to pinch me and wake me up." I shake my head—that's not right, though. I don't want to be woken up. If staying asleep means I get to stay with Jem, then I'd take it. Even with consequences.

"Two Caesar salads!" Marco's announcement interrupts our silence, and I unfold my napkin and place it on my lap.

"Thanks." He places the salads in front of us and is gone again.

We eat our salads in silence for a long moment until I can't take it anymore, and I drop my fork on my plate, making Jem jump. "I feel like I'm going crazy," I say in a hushed tone. "A piece of me wants you and only you." I see a smile rise across his face. "It's not good! This morning proves how dangerous it can be."

"It wasn't *that* dangerous. I blacked out," Jem says with a shrug.

"And again this afternoon, in the loft," I say, reminding both him and myself. My eyes stinging as they start to water; *I am a monster, a bloody awful monster.* Hearing Jem take a deep breath, I open my eyes and look at him.

"You must think I'm a real wimp," he says as he finishes his salad. I pick up my fork and eat the rest of mine.

After a short pause, I sigh again. "Not a wimp, just a bit dumb for not staying away until I have better control," I say finally.

"But this afternoon . . . you had better control then," Jem says.

"Only some control, and it was different from this morning. We weren't . . . we couldn't . . . go any further."

"Then we'll wait," he says positively.

"For how long?" I ask with frustration. "I don't know that I can hold on much longer, but I know that I have to to keep you safe," my voice croaks toward the end. Definitely a sex-crazed loony; it hurts so much to have something right in front of you that you desperately want but know full well that you can't have.

"As long as it takes, only when you're ready," he says, taking my hand and running his fingers over mine. "I'll wait for you. I don't want anybody else." My tears are now coming thick and fast; he is too good to be true. Every girl dreams of meeting a guy who says things like that—like something out of a romance novel or a chick flick. No real man admits such feelings, and even if what he says is true . . .

"It might take a while." *Could he really wait?*

"It doesn't mean we can't see each other. It just means we need to be careful."

"But that's the other part of me." My breath is now jagged. "The part that needs to keep away from you to keep you safe."

"Hope, I can take care of myself," Jem says defensively.

"It won't be enough. Not until…" I hesitate, my instincts pinching at me. *This is too dangerous.*

"It'll be fine. We'll get through it," Jem says. Taking his hands away from mine, he looks down at the table, obviously understanding where I was going with our conversation. D was right; he can't be with me while I train. It would be too dangerous. "How about for now we talk about something else?" Jem suggests.

"That would be good," I say as I wipe away my tears. "We've got until about quarter to ten, so definitely yes."

Jem raises an eyebrow at me and glances at his watch. "We've got just over two hours. What do you want to talk about?"

Feeling better for the change of subject, I smile at Jem and ask, "What else did Terry tell you about me?"

Placing his elbows on the table and then resting his head in his hands, he answers: "Terry said that you're very clever, passing all your exams with flying colors," he says, sounding like a proud parent. "You enjoy being outdoors, horse riding, running, or going out on a motorbike." He screws up his face at the last bit.

"You don't like motorbikes?" I guess from the sound of his disapproving tone.

"No." He shakes his head. "It's not that I don't like motorbikes, it's that I don't like the idea of *you* on a motorbike," he says, again sounding like a parent.

I roll my eyes at his comment. "Another guy who doesn't like females on motorbikes," I say with a sigh. Steve was exactly the same.

"Not females, just *you*," Jem says clearly.

"That's a bit overprotective, isn't it?" He's as bad as D. If it wasn't for Terry, I'd never been allowed out on a bike.

"Maybe." He shrugs. "It would just worry me seeing you on a bike."

"Can you ride a motorbike?"

"Yes," he says in a grim tone, apparently aware of what's coming next.

"Well then, maybe some time we'll go out together. Then you'll see there's nothing to worry about," I cheekily grin at him. "That is, if you can handle it." He grins back at me.

"Okay. Next time we're at Terry's, we'll take the bikes out. I think I could handle it if you're with me."

I shrug. Whatever—it won't stop me going out on a bike, even if he doesn't like it. "So what else did Terry tell you?"

Pulling himself closer to the table, Jem says, "You like to surf." I nod. It's true, I do like to surf, although it's always been with Terry. "Painting and drawing." True. I do a fair amount of painting and drawing; I find it relaxes me. I've needed to relax a lot in the last year. In fact, I had done so much painting that I gave each of my family a picture for Christmas purely because we didn't have the space left in the house. "He also said that you like to dance. But that . . ." he hesitates as he watches Marco walk toward us.

"Everything alright?" Marco asks curiously as he looks at me, obviously seeing tracks from the tears down my cheeks.

"Yes, lovely, thank you," I say as I pass Marco my plate. Taking Jem's, he walks away again. His thoughts whisper in my head again: *He'd better not be upsetting her; I'll throw him out if he is.* I smile after him fondly.

"You've made quite an impression on the people around here," Jem states as he follows my gaze. "They all adore you like a daughter or a sister." I can feel my cheeks start to burn with embarrassment from Jem's words.

"I'm very fond of them," I sigh, "and I shall miss them while I'm gone." Jem takes my hand, squeezing it gently.

"You're coming back," he says reassuringly. I blink hard, trying to fight back the tears.

"What were you saying before?" I ask, trying to backtrack our conversation to before Marco came over.

"Um . . . you like to dance?" he asks cautiously.

"Yes, and the bit after that. You didn't finish." Letting go of my hand again, he seems to squirm in his seat, uncomfortable about what he was going to say. *But why?*

"Because I'm concerned that you'll be cross with Terry if I tell you," he says, answering my thoughts.

"I promise I won't get cross with Terry for what he's told you," I say as I run a cross over my chest with my fingertip. He sheepishly looks down at the table and fiddles with his napkin.

"Terry said that you like to dance, but would have liked to have a partner like Patrick Swayze to dance with you, like 'Dirty Dancing.'" Now it was my turn to look down. *How embarrassing—I'm such a typical girl.* "Hope, you liked dancing with me, didn't you?" he asks. My mind flashes back to our dance last night—how it felt when he held me, how I didn't want to let go. And then another vision pops into my head, and I can see myself dancing and twirling. My dress is swaying with me, and Jem dips me for our grand finale. How does he keep doing that? Looking up at him, I'm surprised to see him as dumbstruck as I feel. I take his hand, trying to snap him out of his frozen expression. He blinks and then looks back at me.

"Yes, I did like dancing with you—more than I thought possible."

"Me too," he says cheerfully, his answer surprising me. Considering how old he is, he must have danced with thousands of women—women who are much better dancers than me.

"But you knew who I was and what I am to you."

"Yes, but I didn't expect you to react the way you did," Jem confesses, looking away from me.

"Too forward?" I presume. "No wonder I'm single," I mutter to myself.

"That's not why you've been single . . ." He hesitates before he finishes, "Or why you haven't fallen in love."

I cover my face with my hands. I know I haven't fallen in love; I'm single because I'm a sex-crazed loony. I'm single because I can't let anyone see who I really am. It would hurt too much to have someone see the 'real' me and then watch them run away, screaming.

I've been the same. Jem's thoughts interrupt mine. I look up at him, my head still resting in my hands. "It's not the same with you," he says with a deep sigh.

"I'll say." He looks at me with that questioning eyebrow raised. Surely he knows that I'm struggling with being 'with' him—with fighting the temptation of letting the loony within me take control— which, rather than satisfying my cravings, will more than likely render him unconscious. Choosing to be honest with my feelings and knowing that he probably knows more about what I'm feeling than most people would, I add: "With other guys I can control myself and my hormones, but with you . . ." I take a deep breath and look out of the window before admitting my weakness. "I can't." Hearing Jem chuckle, my head snaps back to look at him.

"That's why you got cross last night when we first kissed. You had a moment of weakness and you gave in. Well . . . for a second, you did."

"Yes," I say, remembering how perfect he looked lying out on the grass—how the last remaining pieces of sunlight bounced off his skin.

"And now?" he asks.

"Now . . ." and I think about when I was watching him talking to Terry, and the moment I realized that's where I belonged—with him.

"Hope," Jem says softly, taking my hand. "Even though I knew who you were, I didn't expect to feel like this . . . to want you."

"So it is about sex," I mutter under my breath.

He shakes his head and then lifts my hand and kisses it. "It's so much more than that."

"Carbonara for two!" Marco's Italian accent is loud and intruding as we both look up at him, seeing him carry a large bowl in his hands and a grim smile on his face, as if he's pleased to separate us. Jem lets go of my hand and we both lean back as Marco sets the plates on the table. "Shall I serve?" Marco asks, already stirring the pasta.

"Yes, please," I say, trying to sound cheerful and not resentful that he interrupted us.

So who's this guy that's got our Hope all serious? She's not usually like this. What makes this guy any different? He doesn't look that special to me. I smile up at Marco as he fills my plate, his thoughts actually comforting me.

Am I usually too carefree, or am I just too cold? I clear my throat, trying not to think of the answer to my thoughts. "Sorry, Marco, this is Jeremy Winters. My uncle's assistant."

"Your uncle Terry?" Marco asks, his eye wide with shock. I nod. "That's quite an honor. Terry's usually quite self reliant." I nod again, understanding his analysis. It does seem odd that Terry has got himself an assistant. "So do you come from that way then, Cornwall?" Marco asks Jem.

"Not originally. I've been in Cornwall for about a year now."

"It's a nice place to be," Marco says with a sigh. "I hope to be able to retire there one day." Looking at him, I'd forgotten how old he'd become; even though his hair is still very dark with no signs of greying, his face has definitely aged since I first met him. His eyes, however, have still got that childish twinkle in them.

"Thank you," I say to Marco as he adds the ham, cheese, and mushrooms. He never forgets how I like my pasta, bless him. He turns to Jem, holding the plate of ham.

"Would you like me to do the same for you? Hope's been coming here for so long I don't think to ask her anymore."

"Yes please," Jem says politely. After serving Jem the same as me, he takes the empty bowls.

"I'll leave you to it, then," and he walks away.

Looking down at the bowl of long spaghetti and then looking down at my top, I realize that white was probably not the best decision. Mind you, neither is having spaghetti; *this is going to be interesting.* Jem lets out a loud laugh as I rest the napkin back on my lap.

"What's funny?" I ask as I look at him trying to twist the pasta on his fork.

"Nothing really." He chuckles again.

"Jem," I say in an annoyed tone.

"It's just that . . ." He chuckles some more. "We thought the same thing."

"We did?" I didn't hear anything, did I? No. I'm sure I didn't. But he heard me.

"White top," he says as he points his chest. "White top," and he points to me. He rests his fork on the side of his plate, shakes out his napkin, and tucks it into his neckline.

"Arr . . . you're not safe with long pasta, either." My cheeks

143

pinch as my grin mirrors his. "Fine." And just like him I shake out my napkin and tuck it into my top. "So much for being lady like." I look down at my top; the weight of my napkin is pulling the neckline down, and I can see right down into my cleavage. "Oh dear, this is going to be dangerous," I mutter. A picture pops into my head. It's me, from this morning, in just my underwear. I blank it out quickly, holding my breath. I look at Jem. "That doesn't help," I say as I shake my head.

"Sorry. I didn't mean . . ." he hesitates, swallowing hard on a mouth full of hot pasta.

Feeling confident that the thought has gone, I say, "No. That's fine. I probably would have had a similar thought if you'd exposed your chest." Filling my fork again, I shovel in the food. *God, this pasta's good tonight; I can't believe how hungry I am.* Thinking about the food is definitely a good distraction from my thoughts.

Hope, a teasing whisper sings at the back of my head. Looking up at Jem, I hadn't realized how engrossed I had become in my food. Jem has pulled down the neckline from his t-shirt, exposing his perfectly golden skin.

"Don't do it," I warn him as he stretches the neckline further. "Eat your pasta." I say sternly, only just keeping my thoughts blank. Before long, I've emptied my plate and finished my drink. Glancing up at Jem, I see that he's still eating. I start people watching out the window, still trying to maintain the blankness of my thoughts. When I turn back, Marco is clearing away our plates and Jem has organized his neckline so that it's not exposing his chest.

"Would you like anything else?" Marco asks as he picks up the plates.

"No, thank you. Just the bill, please."

"Of course."

"Thank you," I say, as I pull the napkin out from my top.

"Sorry, I shouldn't have teased you like that." He apologizes.

"I'm sure I did the same," I say as I pull at my neckline so it's not showing the top of my bra.

"Not intentionally, though," Jem says as he gets up from his seat. "I'll settle the bill." As he walks away from me, I watch how his jeans fit so closely to his bum. *How did he keep his towel on so easily this morning? I almost wish he hadn't.* My gaze is so fixed on his bum that I hadn't noticed that it had stopped moving until I feel someone watching me. Jem's looking over his shoulder at me with a grin stretching his face.

"Sorry," I mouth at him. I turn my gaze to back out the window, blanking out my thoughts once again. They're getting easier to manage, but then, if someone witnessed me shock Jem, that could be more of a problem. It's a good motive for when we're in public, I guess—doesn't stop me from thinking about it, though.

I join Jem and Marco at the bar, resting my hand on the small of Jem's back. I sigh as I feel the pins and needles start to run through my fingertips; it's comforting—like the magic in me is happy to be close to Jem. I see Jem look at me out of the corner of his eye, smiling as he signs his name.

"So, are you all packed?" Marco asks. His question startles me so much that I quickly tuck my hands behind my back, hoping the pins and needles don't show anything.

"Yes," I say quickly. "D and I finished the last bits this afternoon."

"Where are you going first?"

"Ali and I are leaving for London in the morning. We were going to have three nights there together at my Uncle Kirk's apartment, but her grandmother has summoned her 'up north' for something, so unfortunately, she'll only be able to stay for one night."

"Oh dear, that's a shame. I know how you girls love your retail therapy."

"Oh, we'll still have therapy," I say with a grin. "There just won't be so much of it."

"Well, London had best watch out if you are going to be there."

"D, Terry, and Jem are coming with us as well now, so I doubt it will be too wild."

"Really?" he grins as he wiggles his eyebrows at me. I shake my head. My wild nights aren't really that bad, I'm sure. Marco takes a quick glance at Jem, who seems to be stalling with signing his name, or simply enjoying listening to our conversation. Marco walks around the end of the bar and gives me a gentle hug, kissing both my cheeks before letting me go. "Make sure you take care of yourself, alright?" I can see Marco's eyes start to water and I peck him on the cheek.

"I'll be home for Christmas, Marco." I say, rubbing his shoulder and trying to sooth him like a child. He smiles and gives me another hug.

"Make sure you pop in when you're home." I smile, hoping that I'll get time when I'm back. I step away from Marco, feeling my own tears now, and Jem takes my hand. "Good night," Marco says as we make our way to the door.

"Thank you," we both call over our shoulders before we step out into the car park.

18: TESTING POWERS

"What time is it?" I ask, realizing that I hadn't put a watch on.

"Half nine," Jem says as he lifts our hands together to look at his watch. The sky is rather dim now; it's dusk. Will it be dark enough when Dad and I run so we can't be seen? We stop a few feet from Jem's car and he turns me to look at him. "I'm glad we did this," he says as he rests his arms around my waist.

"Me too," I say in agreement, placing my hands on his chest and trying desperately not to lose control of myself.

"You look beautiful tonight," he says, pulling me closer to him. I push on his chest so he can't kiss me, feeling whatever self-control I have starting to slip.

"Stop tempting me," I say weakly. My comment obviously amuses him as I watch him grin at me.

"Not even a little bit?" he asks, making his voice sound like a mocking whine. I close my eyes, take in a deep breath, and empty my mind. *Shield, if you could work right now, that would be helpful.* Does talking to your powers actually work? I hope so. Opening my eyes, I'm faced with Jem's expression, which is now blank. *Just one kiss,* I think to myself, *then we'd better go.* Jem still seems dumbstruck as I wrap my arms around his neck, and it's not until our lips meet that he finally blinks. Feeling confidently in control, I pull my hands up into his hair, pulling him closer to me. Jem's hands rise up my back as he kisses me harder. I shut my eyes tight in order to keep control, feeling that any minute my ribs are going to break from my heart pounding; it's like all it wants to do is be with his heart—the heart that pounds against my chest, trying to break through Jem's ribs to get to mine.

I pull away from him, gasping for air, knowing that much longer and the pair of us might end up on the floor and unconscious.

"You shut me out," Jem says sourly.

"It helps me not to hurt you," I say as I run my finger across his forehead, which is creased with a frown. "I'm sorry."

"You can control it, just like that?" he asks, his expression still lined. I shrug. It was sort of like earlier; he couldn't hear me when he fainted near the orb, and then in his room he said it was like interference. Like my mind doesn't want him to know about certain things. *That's pretty cool,* I muse to myself. How could I do that so quickly? Jem said it took years to practice blocking your mind, but I can do it. It's like second nature to me.

"I just asked and it happened," I explain. His forehead smoothes as he smiles at me, pulling me back to him.

He kisses my forehead and whispers, "Definitely amazing."

***

As we take the final turn up the steep hill towards the Gibbet, I pull out my shorts and trainers and awkwardly put my feet through my lyrca shorts.

"Hope, what are you doing?" Jem asks through a chuckle.

"Putting shorts on." *Duh, surely that's obvious.* I pull the lycra over my thighs and up to my hips, then unzip my skirt so I can slip it off. I bring my bare feet up to the seat and put on a pair of thin trainer socks and slip my feet into my trainers.

"Are we running?" he asks as he quickly glances at me tying up my laces.

"I am," I say with excitement. "You're going to keep time."

"Keep time?" he asks. I nod as I tie the other lace. We turn onto the track for the Gibbet. The car's headlights are shining down the long, dirt track as a dark figure walks towards us. Jem stops the car and turns off the lights. "Hope, what's going on?" Jem asks, his voice shaky. I reach over and peck him on the cheek, his gaze still frozen on the figure stood in the dark in front of us.

"Trust me," I whisper, and I get out of the car and rush over to Dad, hugging him like it's been years since I last saw him and not just a couple of hours ago.

"Hello again," he says with a laugh.

"Hi ya, Dad," and we both sigh; it's so good to be able to say that.

"He's not sure, is he?" Dad says as he looks over my shoulder toward the car. I shake my head; Jem looks scared stiff. "Maybe you should get him out of the car before we start flashing past." I nod and walk back over to the car, opening up the driver's side door and kneeling down next to Jem. His hands are still on the steering wheel, his knuckles white in a tight grip.

"Jem." I put my hand on his but he doesn't move—doesn't even blink. "Jem, please. I won't let anything happen to you. You have nothing to fear."

He blinks hard and I hear him take in a jagged breath. "Hope," he says, his voice trembling with fear. I prise his hands off the steering wheel.

"You'll be safe," I promise. Taking hold of my hand, he slowly gets out of his car; I squeeze it gently, trying to reassure him. We stop a few feet from Dad and I can feel Jem's body stiffen. "Jem, I'd like you to meet my father, William."

Dad holds out his hand to Jem. "It's nice to finally meet you, Jeremy." Jem's eyes dart back to me.

"It's alright," I say, still trying to reassure him. Jem holds out his shaking hand, and Dad takes it firmly and shakes it once.

"William Wood?" Jem's question seems to scare him further.

"Yes, that's me," Dad says in a cheery tone.

"When I left this morning . . . after what happened . . ." I look over at Dad for some help.

"I found Hope here and we had a chat. She asked about some of her powers that already have started to *show*."

"That's why we're here," I say, interrupting Dad.

"To see how fast you can run?" Jem says, his angry voice biting at Dad's casual tone.

"Yes," I say in agreement, ignoring his tone. "Dad and I are going to have a race." The tone of my voice rises at the end as I feel my excitement increase.

"No, you're not. I forbid you," Jem says, grabbing my arm and pulling me closer to him.

"Jeremy, I wouldn't do that with her," Dad says, and takes a few slow steps toward us, his hands outstretched.

"You're not having her!" Jem shouts at Dad. I yank my arm away from Jem.

"You forbid me?" I say, stepping away from him. *I knew the perfect man was impossible.* Shaking my head, I step further away from them.

"Hope," they both echo after me.

"Here's a little piece of fact for you, Jeremy Winters. You cannot forbid me to do anything. Not riding motorbikes, and certainly not running with my father. He isn't dangerous to me." Dad lets out a loud burst of laughter, making both Jem and me turn and look at him.

"She's so much like her mum, it's amazing," he says, still laughing. I look back at Jem.

Just trust me, please. I don't want to lose you.

I don't want to lose you either, Jem's thoughts reply to mine in a tone that's no longer angry.

"I don't think you'll win with that one, Jeremy," Dad says, still cheerful. "She's strong and tough and a complete rebel. Just like her old dad." Jem hesitantly looks back at Dad.

"I wouldn't hurt her. I . . . I just don't want her to *get* hurt," Jem stutters, trying to get his words out. He looks back at me with sadness in his eyes.

"Hope's right, Jeremy, I can't hurt her, and of course I wouldn't hurt you because it would upset her." He shrugs almost like he's repeating the obvious.

"I didn't mean . . . I don't want you doing anything dangerous," Jem says. When I look into his eyes, I know that he means it. I walk back over to him, taking his hand. *I'm such a pushover,* I think to myself. "I know that," Jem whispers in my ear. I let out a little giggle. I actually don't think he could hurt me; he faints every time he gets too close. Imagine what would happen if he did try and hit me— he'd probably get zapped before he touched my skin.

"Besides, it's not dangerous, and who better to teach me about some of my powers than my own dad? That's where I got them from, after all." Dad cringes at my statement.

"Are you sure about this?" Jem asks, and I nod with a grin on my face. I know that I can't wait to see how fast I can run. "Fine," he says in a stern tone. "But the moment I think you're in danger, I'm taking you straight home." I roll my eyes at him. *Overprotective fool.* This is who I am. It can't be dangerous for me. Letting go of Jem's hand, I stand up next to Dad.

"So, how are going to do this?" I ask, hearing Jem lean against the bonnet of his car. Dad pats me on the back.

Well done. No one's ruling this little creature. I smile at hearing Dad's thoughts.

I do like Jem, Dad. I just won't be told what to do.

He's just being careful. They don't see me like you do.

They?

The Sabbath. They're a bunch of narrow-minded witches if you ask me.

"Dad," I say in annoyance, but he shakes his head at me, knowing that Jem would be cross about his opinion.

"I think if we stick to the Downs that should be fine." I can hear Jem gasp with air. Maybe he thinks it's too far.

"Can I have a test run first?" I ask, realizing that although I was moving fast in my room, I'm not quite sure how I did it.

"Sure, I'll demonstrate." He darts off and I intently watch him weave off through into the nearby field. I can easily see his movements through the grass and bushes, even though his speed makes him ghost-like.

Feeling a warm pair of hands rest on my shoulders, I suddenly feel irritated that my train of thought is being interrupted. I shrug off the hands, trying desperately to concentrate on the quick steps I can hear in the distance.

"Hope, please," Jem whispers, begging in my ear. I ignore him, still listening to the footsteps. "Hope. I'm sorry. You're not mine to control. I promise to never forbid you anything." I sigh. How does he keep doing this to me? He makes me angry and then—snap—I'm all mush in his hands again. I quickly turn and kiss Jem on the lips.

"It's going to be fine. Don't worry so much." I hear Dad's step slow behind us and I let go of Jem and stand back next to Dad.

"Right then, I think you should be able to follow my scent quite well." I lean toward him and take in a large gulp of air, smelling an earthy, woodsy smell and a hint of sweat. "Let your eyes adjust, and then just follow my trail." I nod and look out along the field, but it doesn't change. I can still see where he went without having to try too hard.

"Dad, it isn't any different," I say, wondering if I should be able to see any more.

"What do you mean?" he asks curiously, watching me concentrate on his trail.

"I mean, I could already see where you had been. I could hear your footsteps as well."

"Really? You didn't have to shift to use those powers?"

"Shift?"

"I have to shift to use speed. The sight and hearing comes with it. When I'm not running, my hearing is only a little stronger than humans."

"Oh."

"Follow my trail as you see fit," he says, rubbing his chin. "Maybe you don't need to shift."

"Okay." I begin to jog out gently. I weave through the gate and I can still clearly see Dad's footprints in the hard ground, and as I sniff the air I recognize his woodsy scent.

Let your instincts guide you. A beautiful, velvet whisper sings through my mind.

Mum? I ask back to the voice.

Yes my sweet, just run. Let yourself go.

Feeling the overwhelming need to run I do as Mum instructs and let go. I push myself to lengthen my stride and lean into the wind, watching the blades of grass and the leaves on the bushes move as I run past. The greens and browns are changing into blues and purples as the night draws in, the moonlight beginning to bounce off the fencing around the field. I can see every beam of light where the moonlight hits the metal. I look down at my feet and the grass seems blurry, but my feet are moving slowly; every step that I take fits exactly into Dad's footprint. I let out a laugh. This is amazing. I'm running really fast, but I don't feel tired or out of breath. There's no strain on my legs—nothing. How cool is that? How far could I run like this? How do I source my energy? If this is a vampire skill, and Dad said I'm not thirsty, how does this work? So many questions. Could Dad answer them?

As the circuit comes to an end, I run back down the dirt track to see Jem and Dad sat on the car bonnet, chatting. I hope they're getting on. I stop just in front of them, but neither of them looks up.

"How was that?" I ask. Jem's expression is smooth and disapproving, and dampens my fun.

Dad gets up from the car bonnet and claps. "Excellent!" he says proudly.

"How do you feel?" Jem asks sourly. I breathe in and out, deeply, normally, evenly. Need air, just not to run? Cool. I shrug, seeing that he's still not happy about me running.

"So where are we going to race?" I ask Dad, his grin mirroring mine as we look out across the Downs.

"We're not going far because you need to get home." I turn back and look at Jem; has he been telling Dad not to let me go too far? I don't sleep that much, why would I need to go home so early? I turn back to Dad.

"I don't need to go home just yet, Dad. We've got plenty of time."

"Hope," he says, his scolding tone sounding like a real dad. Letting out a deep sigh, I give in.

"Okay. How far do you want to go?" I ask.

"Follow the track across Ham Hill onto Rivar. When the track forks, turn left down the edge of the air field and follow the Chasers route through Buttermere back here." I nod, recognizing the trail that Bee and I sometimes take. I turn back to Jem, concerned that we'll leave him alone here in the dark.

"Will you be alright? We won't be long." He shrugs in response, his expression still smooth.

"Jeremy, could you start us off?" Dad says, ignoring my comment and talking over me.

"Fine," Jem says coarsely. He steps away from the car and stands next to us, counting on his watch. Dad and I prepare ourselves, our shoulders brushing as we wait for Jem. "Ready . . . set . . . go!" Jem shouts.

I focus on Dad's directions and push my stride out further. I scan down the track and feel myself automatically shorten my stride as I see a five-bar gate, the first of four that are a few hundred feet away.

"What about the gate?" I call back to Dad, who's now catching up with my stride, but I am slowing down, concerned I'm going to crash into the large metal gate.

"Just jump over it, like doing the hurdles!"

I nod; I'd done the hurdles at school, and in fact I wasn't half bad at them. I got a couple of prizes, as well. But this isn't a hurdle. It's a gate—a large gate. Do I jump harder? Dad sees my concern and takes the lead, and like he said, he simply hurdles over it. I watch him land on the other side and I try to mimic the same movement. Pushing off with my left foot and striding out with my right, I lift high up over the gate and over Dad's head. I start to wobble as I look down at the ground, concerned at how I should land. I fall to the ground on my knees and wince, feeling the gravel of the track break the skin.

"Ow," I moan as I stand up to assess the damage. I can feel the sting of broken skin. I rub down my leg, trying to get the dirt from the cuts. Dad stops right in front of me, apprehension on his face as he sees me breathing deeply. I'm not usually a wimp; I hardly ever hurt myself, but this really hurts—like someone's already pouring antiseptic on the broken skin.

"What is it?"

"I grazed my knees," I say, sounding like a whiny kid. He looks closer at my knees and the stinging starts to dull.

"There's nothing there," Dad says, looking back at me.

"How?" I ask, looking down at my knees. But he's right—there's nothing there. "But it was stinging so bad, I saw I had broken my skin on the gravel," and I look at the ground, "see? That's where I fell—that's my blood." Dad starts to ponder and rubs his chin.

"How do you feel now?" he asks.

I stretch out my legs and shake through my body. "Fine," I say in reply, and I really do—like I'd never fallen over.

"Do you want to carry on?" he asks. I nod several times, still excited about being able to run like this; it's amazing.

"I might need another demo on hurdling gates, though."

"Okay," Dad says as he stands next to me. "I'll show you again at the next gate."

"Okay." I mirror Dad's stance and he chuckles quietly.

"Ready?"

"Go!" I shout, and I sprint off, my stride long and fast. The long track is uneven with gravel patches and deep holes. I can feel the sharp flints through my shoes, but it doesn't hurt. My feet are moving so quickly that the impact isn't enough to break the shoe or my skin.

We cross over onto Ham Hill, still neck and neck. The track narrows, leading through a tunnel of apple trees, their branches filled with young fruit and pink and white blossoms. Dad takes the lead, fallen blossom swirls up in the air as we run through. Out the other side of the tunnel is the entrance to Rivar—an entrance that is shut by another five-bar gate. Dad hurdles over it, again with ease. This time I try not to over think it and just treat the gate like a small hurdle that I've run over before at school. I gently push myself off the ground and stride out before the gate; extending my next stride through the air, I clear the gate and land gracefully on the other side. Automatically, I take my next stride and continue to run. "I did it!" I scream, feeling pleased with myself.

"Well done!" Dad shouts. "Now let's see what you can *really* do." I can feel a grin stretch as I lean deeper into the wind. Lengthening my stride, I pass Dad, running the two-mile track to the end of Rivar in a matter of seconds and clearing the three five-bar gates that separate the fields with ease. I can see where the road forks ahead of me. "Left," I mutter to myself, but I'm travelling quite fast. Can I judge the corner just right to make it onto the air field?

Think about when you're on the motorbike . . . how you lean into the corner. I nod, hearing my mum's voice. Makes sense; motorbikes can travel at speed through corners by 'getting your knee down.' I'd once seen a bunch of guys messing about doing just that on their motorbikes—'getting their knees down' on a large roundabout in Andover. Of course, Terry had never let me lean far enough to get my knee close to the ground like those guys had, but I understood how it could be done. I slowly dip my shoulder to the left and I smoothly turn left without losing speed.

"Excellent!" Dad exclaims from behind me. I run down the edge of the airstrip, focusing on the gap in the hedges that I need to pass through. I can still hear Dad's feet behind me. I risk looking over my shoulder to see how far back he is. As I turn my head, my hair rushes over my face with the speed of my run; *damn, I can't see.* I turn my head forward again, flicking back my head to move the hair from my face. With my view now clear I see Dad overtake me, taking full advantage of my moment of curiosity. He speeds off to the end of the airfield, skipping through a gap in the hedge. I push myself harder, determined not to be beaten. I jump through the gap a second after Dad, and I can see his silhouette running along the track, heading up the hill toward Buttermere. I lengthen my stride, pushing myself again for more speed. My hair is now pulled right back off my face, flowing behind me. I must remember to tie it up next time. I catch up with Dad and with little effort overtake him, leading our way back to the Gibbet. I weave past the old water tower and duck through a tunnel of brambles. My arms and legs are scratched as my skin catches the thorns on the narrow path; the scratches sting like before, but I'm too determined to win to see if they're really bad. I turn right around the tall grasses and I can see Jem sat on the car bonnet. I can hear Dad's footsteps coming up behind me and I push myself one more time, feeling my body almost blur as I take my final steps towards where Jem is sat. I stop abruptly a couple of feet from him. His expression is still smooth as he looks me up and down, and his eyes begin to bulge as he sees me rub my arms where the scratches were. My clothes are now in tatters from where the thorns had caught them, too. As I look at my skin, I smile. "That's better than sticking a plaster on it any day," I say out loud. No cuts, no blood—nothing. Cool.

Dad stops next to me. "Okay, you win," he says as he watches

Jem. He then turns to me and looks at my clothes.

"I think the brambles attacked me," I say with a grin.

"You'll get better at it." Dad shrugs and Jem gets up from the bonnet, checking his watch.

"That was one minute and fifty-seven seconds," he says, checking again.

"Arr... well, we did have a quick stop when Hope fell down." I quickly shoot a glance at Jem and then back to Dad. He shouldn't have mentioned that; Jem's going to freak out now.

"Was that not good, then?" I ask, trying to change the subject. It seemed pretty damned excellent to me considering the distance we just travelled.

"Yes, it was good," Dad says with an encouraging smile. "I think the best I've done that in is about one minute thirty-two, so if you minus the pit stop, we're about right."

"Wahoo! That *is* quick!" I say with amazement. Could we really do it that fast? "Could we try again?" Dad looks over at Jem and then back to me; he steps over and lifts the chain around my neck, pulling the pendent free from under my top. It's black—the same as earlier.

"Not today." Dad's face is now filled with concern. I take the chain from his hand and look at the pendent.

"It went black earlier . . . when we were in the loft." I hear Dad gasp for air, distracting me from looking at the pendent.

"How long did it stay black?" Dad asks in a strained voice. I look up at him; his eyes are closed tight and he's pinching his nose as if to relief stress.

"A couple of minutes," I shrug. "Why? What does black mean?"

After a long moment, Dad finally opens his eyes and takes in another deep breath. "Black means," and he glances over to Jem, "a dead motion, or a black motion. Like your heart stopped."

"But it didn't stop!" I shriek, my voice pitching with fear. I push my hand on my chest, checking that I can still feel a heartbeat. "I'm still here. I'm still alive."

"You can't do this often, or for too long," Dad says in a stern tone. "It would be very dangerous."

Terry's words from last night run through my head. *If your father remained a vampire for too long he'd become thirsty, just like a normal vampire.* I look up at Dad and glance at Jem.

"Because I'm your daughter," I whisper, feeling my eyes begin to sting. I found something that I enjoy and now I can't use it—well, not often. It's just the same with Jem; I like him, and yet I have to be careful how I touch him.

"Yes," Dad says, confirming my thoughts. He wraps his arm around my shoulder, rubbing my arm. I thought of how the pendent changed when we were in the loft. One end white and the other black—balance and death? But the pendent wasn't always black when I was strong, and I'm sure it wasn't when I was in my room. Maybe the orb has something to do with the dead motion? Black or not, it didn't change me. The powers were still there. Maybe my heart motions have nothing to do with my powers. I look back at Jem, who's frowning, and then I remembered something else that Terry said: *That's where your Mum comes in. She gave him a reason to shift back to his normal self.* Jem's my incentive—incentive to be good. I take a step toward Jem. "Dad, were you able to shift back easily when Mum was about?" I ask, edging closer to Jem.

"Yes, but . . ." Dad grabs my arm, turning me back to face him. "Hope, you must do this on your own."

"But you and Mum . . ." He squeezes my arm tighter. "Dad, you said Jem and I are a pair. Doesn't it make sense that he . . ."

"You have to do this on your own," he shouts at me. "A black motion is dangerous . . . for both of you." Panicked, I look at Jem and then back to Dad. This is getting worse; too often would make me thirsty, and after too long I'd hurt Jem. Dad watches the pendent hanging from the chain as it turns a shade of grey.

"What happened before? When you used your powers?" he asks curiously.

"Nothing really," I shrug, trying to think how I worked with my powers in the loft. "We found Mum's trunk in the loft and I carried it downstairs, and then . . ." My eyes are wide as I look at Jem. "I carried Jem—he fainted. The orb in Mum's trunk . . . it glowed, and when Jem was close I gave him a little shock. I couldn't catch it quickly enough, and he fainted." My words get higher and quicker as I tell Dad what happened, tears now rolling off my cheeks. "But the pendent changed when I carried Jem," I mumble through a sob.

"You could still carry him even though it wasn't black?" He sounds amazed. I nod.

"It was half white and half black," I say.

"What did you do to stop?"

I shrug again; I don't think I did anything. I still felt strong when I carried him to his room, but I didn't when I left. Feeling my cheeks begin to burn, I remember kissing Jem and how I suddenly felt so weak. "I kissed Jem." Dad turns his head in Jem's direction.

"Did she hurt you?" Dad's voice is now furious. I gasp, clamping my hands over my mouth. I couldn't have, could I? He fainted. He said he was embarrassed. Jem shrugs and walks toward us.

"The shock was nothing compared to this morning. Hope stopped it . . . pulled it back to her." He runs his hand through his hair and I see his cheeks redden. "I think I fainted because of the enclosed space. I can get a bit claustrophobic," Jem confesses, and Dad lets out laugh.

"That's a first. A wizard who doesn't like enclosed spaces. Couldn't you just *blink* out?"

Blink out? What's that?

Jem shakes his head. "No, I couldn't." He looks at me. "When I came to, Hope had created a psychic field on her thoughts. We couldn't hear each other; actually, she's still a bit fuzzy even now. Or not fuzzy, but pieces are muted out." Dad smiles at me proudly.

"Psychic shield and controlling the connection," he states. I smile up at him, realizing from this angle how much I'm like him. My emotions change so quickly; one moment I'm the nasty monster, and the next I'm as soft as a little puppy.

"I thought it had something to do with the orb . . . because it glowed brighter when we were together." I ponder for a moment. "But it glowed when D touched it, too, just not as bright when it was just me. She said it shouldn't exist here—that orbs were created subconsciously."

"Yes. Did you say it was in your mother's trunk?" I nod. "In a purple velvet bag, a little bit smaller than a tennis ball?"

"That's it. Do you know what it is?"

He shakes his head. "You'd have to ask your mum. I don't think it's what caused the shock, though. I think it's because you were out of balance . . . or maybe you felt safe and Jem didn't." He starts pacing back and forth, preoccupied. He mutters quizzically: "Could it be possible? She was born with it. I've never seen that before."

Jem stands next to me, taking my hand.

Dad stops and looks at us. "Could you pick Jem up now?" he asks.

"But you just said . . ."

"Just humour me," Dad says, intensely watching Jem and me.

Letting go of Jem's hand, I turn and stand in front of him. "I'm sorry if I hurt you," I whisper to him. He smiles and lifts my pendent. It's white. "Let's hope I can still carry you then," I say with little confidence. I take Jem's hand and wrap his arm around my neck. "Just hold on to me," I say, and he brings his other arm around my neck.

"You can do this," he whispers in my ear. I take a deep breath, and the same as before, I try to clear my mind of 'wrong' or 'rude' thoughts and concentrate on keeping Jem safe. Crouching down with his arms still around my neck, I place my arm behind the back of his knees and take a firm grip around his back. I swiftly lift up his legs, taking on the rest of his weight and cradling him in my arms.

"Good," Dad says, still watching with intensity. "Could you run with him?" I look down at Jem; I can feel his weight, but it isn't a burden. I guess my powers are working. Jem smiles at me encouragingly. I nod back at Dad and run down the track a couple hundred feet and then back to where Dad is stood. His jaw is dropped as I gently set Jem back down on his feet. Jem lifts the pendent again and shows me the color change, a large grin across his face.

"It was black just a second ago, when Hope first picked me up," Jem says to Dad, showing him the pendent. "But when she was running and when she put me down it changed from black to red." I look over to Dad, waiting for his answer, but he's grinning as much as Jem is.

"What?" I say, feeling paranoid. "What does red mean?"

Dad raises an eyebrow at me and then says through a chuckle, "Holding back some thoughts, Hope?"

I can feel my cheeks burn again. "Yes," I say, realizing what they're grinning about. "When we were in the restaurant, and when I had to carry Jem. I have to blank out *some* thoughts otherwise I can't hold onto the shocks or the pins and needles."

"Open up your mind and let those thoughts come through," Dad says excitedly. I close my eyes and let my thoughts come flooding through, all of them of Jem. The first time we met, dancing, kissing, smiling, and ending with Jem standing in the garden talking to Terry, the moment I felt home. Opening my eyes, I watch my pendent as the burgundy red begins to swirl, the red getting brighter as it moves and then mixing in with a shocking pink. The two colors swirl and swirl until the centre begins to twinkle; the whiteness takes over, bleeding over the other colors until the whole pendent is white again.

"That's impressive," Dad says, that excited and amazed tone still clear in his voice.

"Really?" I ask, not feeling completely convinced.

"Definitely. You didn't need to touch him to balance out."

"But I was holding him when it changed."

"Yes. What were you thinking about?" Dad asks, my cheeks now roasting hot with embarrassment as I answer.

"Jem," I say keeping my eyes toward the ground. Jem walks over to me and takes my hand, and the two hands together start to glow. Jem lifts them up and kisses the top of my hand.

"Arr," Dad says, and my grip stiffens around Jem's hand.

"Is there something wrong?" Jem asks Dad.

"Not wrong." I loosen my grip, feeling a bit relaxed.

"Your connection is strong even without a union. I don't think I've ever seen anything like it before."

"A connection?" Jem asks, his face now creased with concern as he looks at me.

"I showed Dad what happened this morning. He thinks we

made a connection." I then suddenly think about when I got back home after seeing Dad this morning. 'Soul recognition.' "Dad, you said that hearts glow when they find their 'soul twin,' or parents. The soul recognizes its sibling and the soul that it's born from, yes?"

"Yes, that's right. But you're not Jeremy's 'soul twin,'" he says, his expression creased.

"Yes, I know that. But 'soul recognition,' does that happen amongst witches?"

Dad's jaw drops again as he looks at the pair of us. "No. Not with witches and wizards."

"Anybody else?" I ask. Maybe vampires or shape-shifters do. I would have a piece of all of them, wouldn't I? I watch Dad as he shakes his head and looks back at me, his expression now smooth.

"No. I don't think so," Dad says, unsure. I shrug; I'm pretty sure it's something like that. It's going to drive me nuts now trying to figure out where I've heard that—it just seems to fit. I'm not sure that I love Jem, but to belong to him does seem right. Does he feel like he belongs to me? Dad walks over to us with a serious expression on his face.

"You need to be confident with all your powers before this union happens." Jem and I both nod, understanding the dangers if we are too hasty with a union. I'm still not sure how that works, though. Is it some sort of ritual, or what? "Hope, you need to make sure that you don't hold a black motion for too long."

"Why, what would happen?" I ask, getting seriously concerned about this black motion.

"If your heart stops through a black motion, you wouldn't be able to change it back. Your heart would forget why it wants to." I look back at Jem, my eyes stinging with tears again. If my heart stops when it's black, it will forget Jem. "You're going to have to be careful . . . keep a balance." Dad reaches over to me and cups my cheek. "You can do it. You're stronger than me, cleverer than your Mum . . . you'll find a way, I'm sure."

Jem squeezes my hand. "We'll find a way, together. We'll be fine. I promise." Glancing at the pair of them I force a smile, not sure that it's possible. I'd have to die someday. Until then, I'll have to find a way for Jem to be safe without me.

Letting go of Jem's hand I walk back to the car, needing a change of subject as well as a change of shoes; I hate wearing trainers. They're practical, but uncomfortable. I open up my bag and then sigh, finding the change of subject but disappointed in myself for not remembering it sooner. "Dad, could you come back to the house? I found a map in Mum's trunk, and, well . . . it seems wrong to me—like it's missing something." I shout from the passenger seat.

"Of course," he shouts back. "I'll meet you there. I need to get something before I come over." I nod back at him and Jem makes his way back to the car.

Excellent. If Dad comes to the house, Terry can see him, and D can see how he's not as dangerous as she remembers.

19: POWER SIGNATURES & MAPS

Back at the house, the interior is dimly lit, and I can hear Terry and D chatting out on the patio. I'm just about to step through into the living room to say that we're home and safe when Jem pulls me back into the dark kitchen.

"Get changed before D sees you like that . . . she'll freak out." I look down at my clothes; there are tears all over my shorts and top, exposing my bare skin. I smile down at my exposed skin; even in this light I can see that there isn't a scratch on me. Okay, it stings when it heals, but it's pretty neat that it does heal so quickly.

"Good idea," I say back to Jem. D would definitely freak out if she saw this.

"I'll tell them that we're here, and that your Dad's on his way."

"Cheers," I shout as I run up the stairs to my room.

I dig through my nearly empty drawers and find another top and an old pair of shorts. I pull off my lycra shorts with ease now that they are in tatters. I tug at the zip on my top but it won't budge; the frayed fabric is caught in its teeth, and it's stuck. I tug again, but it's no good. "Oh hell," I say out loud. "I need help."

"Is it safe to come in?" Jem asks.

"Sure," I call back, not really considering that I'm stood in my knickers and a seriously torn up top. I hear Jem come into my room while I still tug at the zip on my top.

"Can I help?" he asks as he comes toward me. I look up from the zip and see him grinning at my frustration.

"I think I need some scissors; the zip's stuck." I yank again at the zipper and the fabric breaks, and the top falls away from my body.

"Damn it," I curse as I hold the remnants of fabric in my hands. I screw the pieces up together in a ball and throw them in the bin. There's no way anyone would salvage that now. "I guess that's a side effect of these powers." I pull on the shorts and top, pulling the pendent out from under my clothes. It's red. "What does red mean exactly?" I ask as I brush through my hair, but Jem doesn't reply. I turn around and look at him; he's frozen-still like a statue. "Jem?" but he doesn't even blink. Oh god, please don't say I've done something else to him. This really has been a tough day with him. "Jem?" I ask again. Walking over to him, I gently run my fingers across his face. He blinks, and I watch as his eyes unfreeze and his mind comes back to the room.

"Hope, your whole body just glowed. Did you feel it?" he asks, his eyes still wide.

I look down at my body and rub over my arms. "No. I didn't feel anything. Did you?" Jem screws up his face and then looks at me.

"It was weird. It was like I was looking at you for the first time . . . seeing every detail." I cringe away from him. I think of all my flaws; it's no wonder he was frozen with shock or pure fear at my ugliness. "No, Hope." He holds my shoulders, making me face him. "You're more beautiful to me than you could ever imagine. But I wasn't looking at that. Well . . . actually, I wasn't looking. I just felt . . . well, I felt that's where I belonged. With you . . . always." I close my eyes and let Jem see what I saw and felt when I was watching him in the garden this evening, knowing that's where I belonged—where I wanted to be. Jem interrupts my visions with a hard, urgent kiss. "That's it," he says, kissing me again. "This is where I belong."

"Me too," I whisper, resting my head on his chest.

***

I rummage through the fridge, knowing exactly what I'm searching for. That's odd; Terry always brings some of the Cornish pear cider with him. He knows I like it and it doesn't make me puke.

"Looking for this?" I hear Jem ask. Peeking around the fridge door, I can see him holding out two bottles of pear cider. I smile back at him; at least the thoughts he does hear are helpful, even if they're not essential.

165

"Do you like The Cornish Cider, too?" I ask as I take one of the bottles from him. He takes a swig and shrugs.

"I'm alright with this one. It doesn't make me puke." I let out a loud laugh and wrap my free arm around his waist.

"I think we're going to get along just fine." I give him a peck on the cheek.

We make our way out to the patio where we heard Dad with D and Terry.

"Do you have any idea how much danger you have put her in by showing up now?" D shouts at Dad. I wonder if she'll ever see it my way—not dangerous.

"I've been here all along, Dion. There's no reason to suspect that they'd be out in force already. Plus, she shields, so I doubt they could see her anyway."

"She'll be continuously moving, D. There's no need to worry, our family will protect her. We have done all these years and now that she's showing, I'm sure she'd do a pretty good job at protecting herself and the others." Terry says, trying to calm D down, but it's not working.

"But what about Jeremy? What happened this morning is bound to have caused a signature." D shouts out at the pair of them. Jem and I stand at the edge of the living room, listening to the shouting. Jem squeezes my hand, breaking me from my frozen stance. A signature—a power signature—someone would see that? But who would be looking for that signature? I gasp for air, realizing who they're talking about.

"The Masters, the others—they'd see you." I feel my knees weaken, and Jem catches me before I crumble to the ground. He guides me out onto the patio and sits me on the bench. "It's going to be fine. I'll keep you safe," Jem says, pulling me into his chest.

"But you shouldn't have to," I say as I sob into his shoulder. I feel the shadow of three silent adults now standing around us. "Is there any way to see what they see?" I ask, thinking that if they've been hiding for so many years, they must have found a way to protect themselves . . . or maybe prepare themselves.

"I'll ring Sara," Terry says in a confident tone, and he walks back into the house.

"You'll be fine, Hope," D says as she rubs my arm, trying to soothe me.

"But what about the rest of you?" I ask. It's one thing if I'm in danger, but what about them?

"Honestly, Hope, we've been doing this for a while; everything will be fine in the end. Once you're announced peacekeeper, they won't be able to touch you." Dad's tone is just as confident as Terry's. I shake my head, still cuddled up in Jem's lap. I don't think I can be a peacekeeper, and certainly not like Mum; I'm not brave enough and not nice enough to find peace. Wars would break out again and then we'd all be dead.

"For goodness sake," Jem says with irritation toward Dad. "You're frightening her." Terry comes bursting back through from the living room. His fast steps make me jump, and I sit bolt upright with Jem's arm still around my shoulders.

"It's alright; Sara said she can't see anything. No signature and no tracker, so we're safe for now. I've given her your mobile number, Hope, just so if there is a change she can contact you immediately, alright? So, no worries," Terry says cheerfully. My whole body slumps as I sigh with relief.

"Excellent," Dad says with a triumphant smile on his face. D turns to him and gives him a deadly stare worse than I've ever seen before, almost like she's ready to slap him. "It's alright, Dion, I'll keep my distance, just as I always have," Dad says, finishing his sentence with a sigh.

"No, Dad, please. You can't. How am I going to figure out these powers if you're not here to help?" I get up from the bench with force, anger at D coursing through my veins. How could she even think it? He can't go away; I've only just got him back.

"We'll figure something out," he says, carefully avoiding eye contact with D. "Although I don't know that we need to. Today when I found you, I knew you needed me. I'm not sure what sort of distance that would still work at. But I think if you need me, I'll find you."

I reach out and hug him. "You promise?" I ask, feeling my tears again.

"I promise. And your mum will help with your powers, as well. Just ask her."

K. M. Buckland

"She did tonight when I did my test run," I say, happily remembering hearing Mum's voice.

"Really? What did she say?" Dad asks, his tone happy, but it seems to carry a hint of envy as well.

"Follow my instincts and just let go," I say, repeating the words she had said to me.

"And you did. You out did me on your first run; that's definitely impressive."

"Thanks, Dad," I say, and hug him again; it's nice to have him here—to be proud of me—to enjoy this with me. It makes up for Jem being so protective and the fact that he 'forbid' me to run. Dad gave me the chance to test myself and show Jem the vampire skills I have.

"So, this map you found in your mother's trunk . . . you said it seemed wrong?"

I nod. Taking his hand, I lead him into the kitchen where I left the map and the coin. Unfolding the map, I lay it out flat on the table. Terry, D, Dad, and Jem all stare at the map, silently looking over the different symbols.

"Why do you think it's wrong?" Terry asks, looking up at me.

"I think it's missing something or someone . . . maybe both?"

"Like what?" he continues. I feel my forehead crease as I try to muddle through in my mind what's missing, but all I keep envisaging is something that looks like a dragon. Not a fierce creature, but a powerful one. Its eyes are green with shots of red, like how I imagine a ruby would look if it were trapped inside an emerald. The dragon's scaly body is different shades of blue, purple, and green; the coloring continues to its wings, but the very tips are sparkling white, glistening as if they're made of the coldest ice.

"Maybe a dragon," I say, looking at Terry, whose face is creased with concern. "I'm not sure."

"Where do you think it is?" Terry asks, but I shake my head.

"I'm not sure, but it has something to do with what else is missing . . . like they connect, or require each other."

"There hasn't been a dragon here for a very long time," D says. "Maybe you're thinking of an old map."

168

"But I've never seen a map like this before, have I?" I ask, but they all shrug and look at me.

"What do you think the other thing is?" Dad asks as he runs his hand over the map.

"It's a bit weird, but also seems simplistic in its symbol." I run my hand over the map and point at the symbol for vampire—a crescent moon set inside a circle. I then move my hand over to the symbol for witches—two small 'stick people' set inside another circle, and then move my hand again, finally resting on the symbol for shape-shifters—a bird in flight, again set in a circle. "It has something to do with those three. I keep seeing a piece of rope that has three knots in it." When I think about it, I've known about this piece of rope for a long time; the knots represent something, but that the rope had fallen apart into a piece with one knot and another piece with two knots. I look up and see them all looking at me with wide eyes. Suddenly feeling defensive of my thoughts I say, "I'm sure it's nothing to worry about; I expect my imagination is just in over drive."

I pick up the coin and take a closer look at it. The side that has the series of circles on it has a large circle that surrounds all of them, and for the first time I notice that the large circle has three knots in it—just as I had imagined. I turn it over to see if there is a reference to the dragon, but the only thing I see is what looks like the texture of the creature's scales on the background for the pair of hands.

"I'm not sure that it's your imagination," Dad says as he starts pacing in the kitchen. "Leave it with me. I'll look into it." I nod back at him, relief embracing me; it hasn't overly concerned me, but it was bothering me, like something had been lost and can't be found. I fold up the map and rest the coin back on top of it.

"Well, I guess if there's no worry about someone after us tonight and we don't know about the map, I think I'm going to have another drink and sit out in the garden." They all smile at me and I shrug. I can't stay mad at anyone for too long, so D's in the clear. Dad's said he'll be here if I need him, which helps. So will Mum, which is good too. Maybe I've developed multiple personalities—cry one minute, angry the next, then relaxed and calm the other. What a weirdo I am.

20: REINCARNATION

The five of us sit in the garden and chat for a while, discussing my journey. Dad agrees with D that Jem should be away while I train. Actually, D and Dad agree on quite a few things: safety, training, who I'm seeing first, and what they'll be teaching me. I don't partake in much of the discussion as I begin to feel unusually tired.

"I'm going to go to bed," I announce as I get up. I kiss D and Terry goodnight. Dad gets up and gives me a big hug and kisses me on the top of my head, and as he looks around he pulls a thick envelope from his pocket.

"This is for you," he says as he hands it to me. I open the envelope and pull out a black debit card and a pin number slip.

"What's this for, Dad?" I ask, feeling a bit confused by the bankcard.

"It's your money," he says, mater-of-factly. "Well, some of it."

"My money?" I ask, still feeling confused.

"Yes, your mother organized some things when she was pregnant with you. You'll receive a wage packet each month."

"Wage packet? I'm not working, Dad, I'm going travelling."

"Travelling *and* working. And although our family will be supplying food and a bed, I know how much you like to shop, so this will give you a chance to go back to reality every now and then."

"Thanks, Dad."

"I wouldn't let you go with nothing," he says, giving me another squeeze. He lets go and then shakes Jem's hand.

"Night, kids," he shouts after us as we walk back into the house and up the stairs to my room.

Automatically, I go into the bathroom and wash my face, brush my teeth, and change into some pajamas. I walk back into my room and brush through my hair again. In the reflection of the mirror I can see Jem hovering near the door, looking nervous.

"Are you alright?" I ask; he isn't usually nervous. He looks at me and then looks away again. "Jem?" I ask, but he still doesn't answer. "I can't mind read all the time, could you just tell me what's wrong?" I ask, finishing with a yawn. I am seriously tired.

"I was just going to say goodnight," he says, not once making eye contact with me.

"No you weren't. Liar," I say, my voice mocking him as I start to laugh. "Why don't you just ask me? I don't think I'd be shocked with what you have to say after how today has been." Yawning again, I walk over to the bed and pull back the covers. Leaning up against the pillows, I turn and look at Jem still at the door, my tiredness starting to make me a bit irritated by his hovering. "Jem, if you're going to get changed, could you hurry up about it? I'm really tired." He stops hovering and starts staring at me. "Fine. If you're staying up, that's up to you, but I'm sleeping. Could you turn the light out please?" And I turn away from him and snuggle down under the covers, closing my eyes.

After a moment of quiet the lights go out, and then I feel the bed covers pulled back and a warm body lie down next to me. I roll over and cuddle myself up under Jem's arm and rest my head on his chest. The odd thing is it doesn't bother me; I purely want to sleep. But to have him here next to me seems like we've been doing this for years. I feel Jem's chest rise as he takes in a deep breath and then lets out a long sigh. A sigh of relief? But if it is relief, his pulse shouldn't be so fast.

"Didn't you stay with me last night?" I was pretty sure he did. Not all of the night, but he stayed with me when he brought me to bed.

"Yes, I did, for a bit," he says as he starts running his fingers up and down my arm. "But you were already a sleep then."

"I'm nearly a sleep now, if that helps," and we both laugh. Not the usual thing for either of us to just be lying in bed with another person—what a pair of sex-crazed loons we are.

"No, you being awake is much better."

"Even if I'm really sleepy?" I ask through another yawn.

"Even if you're really sleepy," Jem says through a chuckle, and starts running his fingers through my hair, making me sink deeper into the comfort of his arms.

"Can I ask a really random question before I fall asleep?"

"Of course. Anything."

"Do witches or vampires or even shape-shifters believe in reincarnation?"

"Blimey, that is really random."

"Sorry, it was just something I thought about earlier. I was just remembering it." *What if it's another lifetime before I truly love him?* This is comfortable—like we've been here before. Maybe our hearts glow because our souls have been here before?

"What were you thinking?" Jem asks. Oops; I don't know that I want to talk about the 'L' word with him—not yet, anyway. Maybe I could just say only half of what I thought? That could work, couldn't it?

"I was wondering if I get more than one lifetime of this," I say as I snuggle in deeper to his chest.

"Really? You believe in reincarnation?" he asks, a hint of shock in his voice.

"Yes, I think so. Do others? Do you?" I ask. I didn't want to say that I get déjà vu at funny things—weird, funny things, and quite graphic things as well, sometimes. I've a definite sense that I've been somewhere before.

"Not reincarnation. But then, I guess that witches live for so long that they simply wish to pass on."

"Like heaven and hell?"

"Yes."

"What about shape-shifters?"

"They do sort of reincarnate. A piece of the father carries onto the son, so a shifter would have generations of knowledge passed to them. The presence of that knowledge always guides them."

"Like Mum does," I say, and I feel his head nod. "You talk about them as though they're all male. How do they procreate?"

"Yes, they're all male. They pair with humans, which would

probably explain why they're life expectancy isn't as long as ours."

"Yours," I say, correcting him; I really don't think my life expectancy would be as long as his.

"Why not ours?" he asks, his voice sounding sad. *Well done, Hope, you're totally ruining the moment. You might as well get it off your chest.*

"I don't think that my life expectancy is as long as yours. Sorry."

"Why not?" he asks, his voice starting to sound a little angry.

"I don't know exactly, I just feel that I won't," I say, almost whispering now. I'm angry at myself for correcting him. *Stupid girl; keep your mouth shut, or even better, change the subject quickly.* My thoughts feel like they're slapping me around on the inside of my head.

"So, what about the vampires? What do they believe in?"

"I don't think they'd believe in anything like that. They're immortal, so I guess not," he says with a shrug. *Phew, he doesn't sound angry anymore.*

For a long time, we lie in silence. My eyelids are beginning to feel really heavy when Jem suddenly sits up and turns on the bedside lamp. I squeeze my eyes shut, the sudden light hurting my eyes.

"Why do you feel that you won't?" Jem asks in an angry voice again.

"What?" I ask, lifting my head from the pillow with my eyes still shut.

"Why do you think that you won't live as long as me?" he demands, his voice so angry it's actually scaring me. I roll away from him, opening my eyes away from the light.

I knew I shouldn't have said anything. *Hope, you're a bloody idiot.* "It doesn't matter, Jem. Could you please turn the light out? I'm tired." He forcefully takes my shoulder and rolls me back to face him.

"It matters to me," he says, his voice a little softer than before. Shutting my eyes tightly, I shake my head; I don't even want to think about it. The nightmares I've had and the pain that I feel each time I'm killed; I'm always left in darkness, always left alone, without love and without a place to go, watching my death over and over again. My tears start to run down my cheeks as pieces of the nightmares come back to me: my blood falling from my body to the ground and watching as the pool of red grows deeper and my life falls away.

"You've seen yourself die, haven't you?" Jem asks, his voice now a soft whisper as he wipes the tears from my cheeks. I nod my head, feeling almost relieved to have admitted it to someone. D always knew I had nightmares, but I never told her the details, I just always said it was just a bad dream. "Is that why you believe in reincarnation?" I nod, hoping that if it is possible, that maybe one night I'll dream of dying as an old woman rather than someone not much older than what I am now.

"Hope my love, it's alright; you're with me now. I won't let anything happen to you." He lies back next to me and wraps his arms around my body. "We belong together, my love. It's going to be you and me, together forever." Feeling the comfort of relief in his secure arms, I fall soundly asleep.

***

I'm back in the woods, and the dappled light touches the leaves and branches that glisten in the morning dew. A cloaked figure is stood in front of me with its back turned. The figure starts to walk away; I want to follow, but something's holding me back. A warm hand squeezes mine and I turn to see who the hand belongs to. It's Jem. His expression is sad as I pull my hand away. Why would he hold me back? I turn back to the cloaked figure still walking away from me. "Wait!" I cry as I rush after it. The figure stops and then turns to me, and the white velvet hood falls from its head, revealing long, brown hair with blond, sun-kissed streaks, and soft, brown eyes shadowed by long, beautiful lashes.

"Mum?" She nods and holds out her hand for me to take. When our hands touch, our bodies begin to glow, growing brighter and brighter until I can only see the brightness of the light. My body feels strong and wise; my heart is beating hard and each beat is meaningful; the flow of my blood, hot and thick, heals me in its movement. I can hear and see nothing except for the beat of my heart. I close my eyes, embracing the sensation. Never before have I felt so safe and secure in my dreams.

Mum's hand lets go of mine and I open my eyes to see where she has gone. I'm still in the woods, but it's darker. Little, twinkling lights scatter around the edge of the trees. The clearing that I'm standing in is smaller than before. I turn and turn, surrounded by hundreds of cloaked figures all facing me. They all have their hoods up and their cloaks are different shades of blue, green, and purple. I can't see faces, only the cloaked figures. I stop turning, clapping my hands over my face. This isn't a nice dream; they've come to kill me, haven't they? They don't want me here.

A warm pair of hands takes hold of mine and pulls them from my face. Mum's smile is soft and loving. "They're not here to hurt you."

"Then what do they want?" I ask as I turn around in a full circle again; there's so many of them.

"There has been no balance for so long. They wish for you to return that balance."

"But how . . . why me?" I ask.

"You are the piece that ties us together. Being a piece of all of us, your blood binds us to one another." Mum's hand waves over the crowd and they all bow.

"How did this become unbalanced?" I ask, concerned with how I'm supposed to help.

"The ties were broken," she says in a solemn voice. "A greed for power broke the ties, creating an imbalance in our world." She takes my shoulders and speaks to me square in the eye. "You must find the balance and make those ties strong again."

I shake my head. "I'm not a peace keeper, Mum. I'm not like you."

"No, you're not a peace keeper." I look up at her, shocked. Finally . . . someone who agrees with me.

"You're here to return the balance. Peace will follow when the hearts are restored."

"But how do I find balance?" I ask. If I'm not a peace keeper, then what am I?

"Your love of the spirit will help you. The ancients are sending the elements; their path will lead to you, and you must protect them. They are the power that will join these ties." She softly kisses my forehead, and then disappears.

21: BECAUSE IT IS LOVED

Carefully, I try to open my eyes. I glance over at the clock—6:30 a.m. Well, at least I got some sleep. Five hours isn't bad for me. Weird dream, though—at least there was no dying or fighting. Mum was there, and that was cool. I didn't get to speak to her much, though; I have to remember to ask her some questions next time. But who were all those cloaked figures? And if I'm not a peace-keeper, then what am I? I'm here to return the balance. Seems an odd thing to do . . . isn't there always a balance? Where there is life there is death, where there is light there is dark, and where there is goodness, there will always be a piece of evil. Even the light from the rising sun cannot carry everywhere, a shadow will always be found. But goodness cannot take over; it's not possible. Mistakes are always made. Without them, we cannot learn and cannot grow.

Well, that piece of mental babbling was far too wise for me. I have no idea where that came from. Maybe Mum has been teaching me after all, and it's just the first time I've really listened. Spooky.

Stretching out my arms and legs, I realize for the first time that Jem is lying next to me fast asleep with a cute grin across his face. Resisting the temptation of kissing him, I pull myself out of bed. I'll have a shower while he's still asleep.

Peeling off my pajamas, I get the shower going so it can warm up. I peer into the mirror, looking closely at the color of my eyes. They seem darker—browner, even. Where's the purple? The purple that outlines the brown—the part that makes them the same as Mum's. That's odd. Maybe it's because I'm still tired. I shrug off the thought and get into the shower, hoping it's just my imagination playing tricks on me.

Thinking only of retail therapy and my girly day with Ali, I don't notice the bathroom fill with steam—a screen of foggy steam that's so thick I can't see the other side of the bathroom. Stumbling around the bathroom, I dry myself off and wrap my hair up in a towel, finding my way to the window and flinging it open to let the steam out. I can't believe how thick it is; I don't think I had the shower that hot, it felt just right to me. Odd.

Looking down at my pendent, I can see the I-stone is white with specks of purple in it. I have no idea what purple means. Maybe D can write down what these colors mean so I can figure some stuff out when it changes. I know the white is balance—it's Jem. Jem, who I'm still going to have to leave behind while I travel. My tears start to flow down my cheeks and onto my bare chest. Now that I've found him, I don't want to let go. I don't want to be without him— ever. But I have to. Mum's words ring through my mind: "You're here to return the balance. Peace will follow when the hearts are restored."

I need to learn about my powers—to find the balance that has been lost.

Knowledge and love can walk hand in hand, but they must balance. I listen as Mum's sweet, whispering words continue to sing through my mind. So I still have to leave him; to gain knowledge, I would have to be away from him. A sharp, piercing pain bursts in my chest. My heart aches against my ribs and I crumble to the floor, wrapping my arms around my legs. No matter how insane this is—how irrational this could be—my heart aches for the distance that must come between us. When this is over, will I have the time with him that I want? To wake up next to him every morning until we're old and grey.

My heartbeats become harder and painful; I shut my eyes tightly and push my lips together, holding on to the scream that wants to escape. *I can't do it. I can't do it. I won't. I want him with me. Please.*

Pushing my head further into my knees, I sob against the pain of my heart. *Our* heart, beating together, for each other. If we can't have a union, what can we have?

"Love, Hope. We'll have our love." I open my eyes and wrap my arms around Jem, not caring that I'm naked and still a bit wet. "Don't worry, my love. It will be alright." As he whispers in my ear and smoothes down my hair, I look up at him and see his eyes glistening with tears. My vision blurs as I start to cry again. I rest my hand on his chest over his heart.

"I'm sorry to have caused you pain," I say, expecting his tears to be from the same pain that I'm feeling. Jem takes my hand from his chest and kisses it.

"The pain isn't from being hurt," he says. *I've done worse than just hurt him, haven't I?* "It's in pain because it's loved," he says, pulling me back to him. Swallowing hard, I fight the lump rising in my throat, knowing that I want to say something in return but I'm too scared. The coward that I am can't speak the feelings that I have; I'm too scared that my feelings aren't the same as his. Jem lifts my chin and softly kisses my lips. "Because it is loved, Hope," he says again, smiling at me triumphantly as he rests his head on my shoulder and wraps his arms tighter around me.

"Because it is loved," I repeat in a barely audible whisper. Without our hands, our heart begins to glow. Jem's chest shimmers with a beautifully warm light. "This is where I belong," I say confidently, as I kiss Jem's glowing chest. "I will always find my heart."

"And I promise it will always be your heart to find," he says. My heart beats faster, somehow knowing his words to be true. With that, I'm melted—ice maiden no more. I kiss him gently and lovingly, wishing to never have to stop. I need to remember everything about this moment: his touch, his smell, how his bottom lips tastes against my tongue, how warm his skin feels against mine. No distance can break this—this heart that is now loved.

22: PROTECTION & GOOD-BYES

All four of us sit at the kitchen table, eating eggs and bacon in silence. The sudden sound of the phone ringing breaks the quiet of cutlery against crockery, and D rushes off to answer it. As she talks quietly in the living room, I can hear her pacing—an excited pace. Terry clears away the plates and stacks up the dishwasher. He's such a good guy; he knows exactly how D is and how much of a tidy "neat freak" she is.

"I guess when we're ready, we'll make a move," Terry says through a long breath as he rubs over his now-full tummy.

"Okay," I say as I get up from my chair. "I'll just be in the garden a minute." Jem gets up from his chair as if to follow me. I raise my hand, gesturing him not to follow. "Can I be alone for just a minute? Let me say goodbye," I say, needing just a moment alone before we leave.

"Sure. I'll bring the bags down," he says, smiling at me.

"Thanks."

I stroll down to the end of the garden and lean on the fence, my favorite place to 'lean' and think—to straighten things out.

How am I going to explain this to Ali? We've never let a man come between us; Rob has always been so good about mine and Ali's friendship. I just hope that Jem can be the same. Could he have the same relationship with Ali that I have with Rob? Will he understand how me and Ali are—how we're so different and still very much alike? Will he get that, or will he run away screaming? Although, I guess he might runaway screaming once him and Ali have spent some time together, because no doubt Ali will give him the low down on me, the infamous Hope. Joy! Chuckling to myself, I shake my head. Poor guy is gonna have a shock of a lifetime when he's spent some time with Ali. I hope that he can cope with it. I expect Ali will be rather intense.

"Hope," I hear D shout, interrupting my mental babble.

"Down here," I shout back, waving in her direction. Seeing me in the garden, she jogs down to where I'm standing.

"Hope, do you mind if we have a little change of plans?"

I cringe at the idea of change of plans; am I really not going to get any time with Ali? "That depends."

"Well," she says, catching her breath. "That was some old friends of ours on the phone."

"Oh . . . right," I say, still suspicious of what she's getting at.

"They're on their way to London. Well . . . sort of; they're having a pit stop on the way and invited me and Terry to join them."

"Join them?" I ask, concerned about what she's saying.

"Yeah, they're looking at a house near . . ." she hesitates and screws up her face. "Actually, I'm not too sure where it is. North of London, I think. Terry knows where to go."

"Oh, okay." I say, still not sure of what she means.

"Kirk and Louise are going to join us as well. So if it's all right with you. I'll give you the keys for Kirk's apartment and we'll meet you there later."

"Really? You're going to trust me to be alone with Jem and Ali?" I ask, excited, scared and maybe a little relieved to not need a full entourage.

"Terry said that I should, so I'm hoping that he's right. But if you have any problems or anything happens, you ring me straight away, alright?" she says sternly. I pull her to me and hug her tight.

"I promise," I whisper as my eyes start to water again.

"You're going to be great; just be careful, that's all I ask."

"I promise," I say again, my tears falling faster, and D pulls a tissue from her pocket and wipes around my eyes, looking at me like I'm still a little girl and not an adult.

"Come on," she says as she takes my hand and leads me back to the house. "Let's get the car loaded and be on our way."

***

My trunk is loaded in the back of the Land Rover and mine and Jem's suitcases are packed in the boot of his car. Terry and D bounce down the steps from the front door like a pair of kids about to go on holiday.

"Okay, all the windows and doors are closed. I'll just lock the door and we're all set," D calls from the car door as she puts her bag on the back seat.

"I just need to get my bag," I say and run over to D, taking the front door key from her. "I'll lock up." And I jog back into the house.

I pick up my bag from the kitchen table and slowly look round the downstairs rooms. It's mesmerizing how the house looks today— the day I leave to go on my adventure. The sunlight beams through the windows, making everything look golden and precious; my priceless pieces of childhood and fun are lit up with love. "I'll be back for Christmas," I whisper to the house. "Keep D safe until then," and I walk back out through the door and close the large, oak door with a loud slam. "Keep them safe and keep them well. Shelter and protect," my mother's words whisper through my lips as I kiss the tips of my fingers and press them to the door, then turn the key to locked. I turn around and stop short to see three pairs of wide, shocked eyes watching me. "Now what did I do?" I say, feeling a bit irritated by their gawking at me. Terry's the first to blink himself out of the gawking and smiles up at me.

"What did you do?" D asks quietly, uncertainty in her tone. I shrug at her question; it didn't seem like much. I, or rather Mum, asked the house to protect D and Terry and keep them safe and well.

"A protection spell," Jem says with a proud smile across his face. Smiling back, I nod.

"Yes, a protection spell. Did it work?" I ask, and Jem's smile grows as he looks up at the house.

I walk down the steps and look up to the house alongside Jem. It looks like it's surrounded in a golden bubble—shimmering in the sunlight. *I've never seen a shield before; is that what they look like?* Jem wraps his arm around my waist and whispers in my ear.

"No, a shield you can't really see, but a protection spell you can, or we can . . . not humans, at least, or vampires, which helps." I frown at his comment about the vampires. I am still part vampire, but I can see it. Does that mean I can't go back in the house? Jem kisses my cheek. "You're part witch as well," he says reassuringly. D walks over to us and wraps her arm around my waist as well.

"Thank you, Hope, that truly is a magnificent gift you have given us."

Pulling away from Jem, I give D a warm squeeze and say, "It's from Mum as well, and you're very welcome." Terry clears his throat, interrupting the moment of awe, and then jumps in the Land Rover and starts the engine.

"Right then," D says as she lets go of me. A small tear escapes the corner of her eye and runs down her cheek. "Let's go!" And she gets in the passenger side of the Land Rover. "We'll see you later on. Please make sure you behave," she says, the softness of her tone now changed to her usual stern and motherly one. Both Jem and I turn and salute at the same time, and shout

"Yes Ma'am!" and we both giggle as we see her tut and finally shut the car door.

***

Jem turns the car up the drive to Ali's house and parks up next to Claudia's BMW. He turns off the engine and starts to get out; I grab his arm and pull him back in the driver's seat.

"Can you just give me a minute with Ali?"

He smiles and kisses me on the forehead. "Of course. Don't worry; you and Ali will have some time together, alone. I promise I won't get between you two." I see him cringe in response to my frown.

"Eavesdropping, were you?" I ask suspiciously. *Wasn't I thinking that earlier when I was in the garden?*

"Not intentionally . . . you seem a lot clearer today," he says, running the tip of his finger across my forehead.

"My thoughts aren't always going to be a nice thing to know, are you sure you want to be hearing them?" I ask, smiling at him. Jem kisses my lips, gently holding up my chin with one finger. He looks me in the eye and as I stare back at him, I feel like my soul is falling into the pools of deep blue in his eyes. Cool and clear, but soft and warm—a place to get lost and not want to ever be found.

It's not until Jem blinks that I realize that he's not looking at me the same way. He seems to be studying my eyes, checking and re-checking.

"Your eyes have changed color, slightly," he says in a confused voice.

"Yes, I noticed that this morning. The purple seems to have gone." I shrug because although it is a bit odd, it doesn't hurt; my eyes seem fine. I can still see clearly, in fact maybe even a bit better. I look out over Ali's front lawn and focus on a tall ash tree. I look once and I can see the tree standing still, holding strong against the breeze, and when I look again I can see the detail of the brown and green bark on the tree trunk; the tree is actually moving ever so slightly in the breeze. The branches sway in rhythm with the leaves, creating the most restful rustling sound that travels to me on the wind. "That's pretty cool. My eyes are focusing in further detail. I can see everything . . . every detail." I blink hard again and find my sight has returned to a normal vision. "And now it's back to normal, just like that. Easy-peasy," I say, a bit cocky.

"Are you sure?" Jem says, sounding troubled. Again I shrug; Dad said last night about being able to focus for using vampire speed, and now I can understand why. The speed at which we travelled needs better vision. Although I didn't have it last night, I could still run. Thankfully my vision has always been good, day or night. I wonder why someone would need such detailed vision. I think I'm going to have to start writing these questions down, although I don't really know who is going to be the best person to ask. Terry? Or is Dad better? I don't know; either way, it will have to wait for now. So long as I can control it and it doesn't mess me up too much, I think I'd rather concentrate on being with Ali at the moment.

"What are you thinking?" Jem asks. I turn back to him, feeling a bit shocked by his question.

"That if it's under control I'd rather be concentrating on being with Ali. I'd rather she wasn't affected by what's going on," I say, and give his knee a gentle squeeze to reassure him. Then, I get out of the car.

***

I knock on the front door and then walk in, even though there's no reply from my knock. Mind you, I've been doing that for years—

just walking into Ali's house like I live there—but then, I guess that Ali does the same at our house.

"Ali?" I call out from the bottom of the stairs. I can hear her rushing about, her crazy pixie footsteps tapping about up-stairs between her bedroom and her dressing room. I know; she has a dressing room. It's probably a good thing though, considering how many clothes she has. Ali's house is a fair size, the same as Eastwick (where D and I live), but Ali's room is like the princess suite. She has a dressing room and en-suite bathroom with a whirlpool tub and one seriously huge bedroom with the most amazing fairy tale four poster bed. My room, of course, is quite different—not so princess like. It's true that I have my own bathroom with a grand roll-top bath and shower and whatnot, but no dressing room. My bedroom is nearly twice the size of Ali's, but I have a 'snug' area with a comfy sofa and flat screen TV. It's not a fairy tale room in a castle like Ali's, but it's me—practical and comfortable. Ali always laughs about my organized shelves and drawers. Even my knickers drawer has sections in it. I don't know what the problem is—I just like being tidy. It helps me think—to see things clearly. But even though our houses are big and financially we're comfortable, I'm grateful that Claudia and D have brought us up to appreciate money and how hard it is to earn. We both work, even if it's not for a lot. Our wages pay for our "therapy," as Ali calls it: shopping, going out, and all the other stuff. We do quite well really, compared to a lot of people we know. Ali's been working in a bar in town to earn money for while she's at university, saving up so that she doesn't have to work while she's away and can still have fun going out and shopping. I can understand that, and Claudia has agreed to give her some money each month for food and supplies. Again, I'm very grateful for the situation that we have; I know a lot of our friends from school are struggling to find enough money to feed themselves and get the equipment they need to go to school.

I walk up the stairs and make my way along the landing. Claudia bursts out of her room, her hair pulled back and her face creased with stress lines.

"Hope. Sorry, Ali's in her room. She's changing what she's taking, as apparently it's going to rain the next couple of days." I reach out and gently rub her arm, trying to release the stress she seems to be under. Ali can be a nightmare. She always leaves things until the last minute and then gets in a tizzy because she can't sort things out. It's quite funny sometimes, although it can be quite dangerous, too.

"It's alright Claudia. I'll help her." I smile, trying to make her feel a little bit better, but her face is still wrinkled into a frown and when she looks at me her eyes are sad.

"She's going to be no good about being ready for anything when you're not here." She opens up her arms and gives me a tight hug. "You will be sorely missed in this house." My eyes start to water. I hear Claudia sniff as if she's doing the same, and I pull back to look at her.

"I'll be back at Christmas, I promise. You won't have to miss me for too long, and you can always ring me." She hugs me again, squeezing me tighter this time.

"I'm sorry Ali has to leave London earlier than you had planned. My mother insists that Ali must come with me."

"That's alright. I'm sure we'll have fun with the time that we have," I say, and she looks at me with that long, Cheshire cat grin that Ali does.

"I bet you will. Ali said that you've met quite a catch of a man," she says teasingly. Feeling my cheeks go pink with my embarrassment, I nod my head. I can't exactly say I've fallen head over heels for the guy, especially since I only met him Saturday night. "So, what've you done with him? Ali said he's driving you girls to London, to your Uncle's apartment." I still can't speak, so I just nod toward the window. Letting go of me, she walks over to the low window on the landing and looks out onto the drive. "Goodness me! He's rather handsome, isn't he?" I nod again; now I'm not feeling so embarrassed, but maybe a little possessive.

Released from Claudia's grip, I turn on my heel and walk into Ali's room. My mouth pops open as I see the large four-poster bed covered in what looks like Ali's entire wardrobe.

"Err . . . wow! You look amazing," Ali says from behind me. Turning around, I see her smiling, cradling a mountain of shoes in her arms.

"Thanks," I say as I look down at my outfit. I guess it is a bit different from my usual ensemble. Must have felt quite feminine this morning. I've pulled my hair back into a high ponytail, pulling down a couple of pieces of hair to soften my face. I found I didn't need so much makeup this morning, as I'd actually slept quite well, so I'd only used a small bit of shimmer around my eyes and framed them with soft brown eyeliner and mascara. In keeping with the summer weather, I'd put on my white tube top with my favorite, amazing strapless bra. I've married it up with a red cotton A-line skirt and my favorite red ballerina pumps. My little denim jacket I had been left off with my bag in the car.

She even looks like she slept. Maybe the date didn't go so well last night. I sigh, hearing Ali's thoughts; it had been a while since I'd heard anyone's. I just wish sometimes I didn't have to hear them.

"I actually slept really well last night, amazingly enough."

"What?" she asks with a shocked frown. "Are you saying you went out on a date and didn't sleep with him?" *Bloody hell! There's something wrong with her. She doesn't usually sleep after a date. She's usually . . .*

"No, I didn't have sex with Jem," I say, interrupting Ali's trail of thoughts and feeling even more ashamed of my previous behavior. "We definitely did the sleeping, but there wasn't any sex, alright?" I walk over to Ali's bed and start folding and hanging up clothes.

"Really?" she asks, and I nod, continuing to fold away the mountain of clothes.

"Can I ask you something?" I ask, still not making eye contact with her.

"Sure," she says, and out of the corner of my eye I see her shrug and walk over next to me, dropping her mass of shoes onto the bed. Ali turns my shoulder so I'm looking at her. Letting out a long sigh, I look her in the eye. "Am I really a tart?" I ask. She smiles and then starts filling her designer suitcase some more.

"Before you were with Steve, you were a nightmare," she says teasingly. I turn 'round and sit on the bed.

"And now?" I ask, slumping down amongst the clothes and hating that this vampire enchantment thing has made me do some nasty things. Ali stops and looks at me, a deep frown wrinkling her forehead.

Just be honest with her. I close my eyes, sensing that what Ali's

186

going to say next is going to hurt, but I guess I'd rather she was honest with me. "When you finished with Steve, I was expecting you to go back to how you were before." Gathering up more clothes, her thoughts continue. *I was contemplating not being friends with you anymore.* My eyes start to water, my sadness making a lump grow in my throat. Did Ali really not like me? "But you didn't. You stopped drinking so much. You stopped sleeping around. In fact, I'd bet that you haven't had sex since you were with Steve." I nod; I've sworn off men for a while. Well, until now. "And since you split up with Steve, you've been my friend again. You even get along with Rob, which I think still surprises him." I wipe the tears from my eyes and look at her.

"I'm sorry, I didn't realize I was so bad," I apologize, wiping away another tear.

"You're a lot better now. It was like you were an animal before, on some kind of continuous heat . . . like you needed to get it out of your system." That's exactly how it felt to me—like an animal that wasn't happy until it'd had an orgasm. It didn't matter with whom, I just needed that feeling of intense pleasure—warm-blooded contact. Crap. Vampires' needs. "Saturday night though, seeing you with Jem, it was like you were completely a different person. Melted even, and the way you kissed him after the race around the house. Well . . ." My cheeks start to burn with embarrassment. Ali sighs and sits down next to where I'm folding her clothes. "I can see that you like him, and that you want to be with him. I'm just amazed that you haven't." She pulls my hand away from the clothes so that I look at her again.

"It's not without difficulty," I say, my voice barely a whisper.

She's waiting. That's a first. But why is she waiting?

With a deep sigh, I answer her thoughts. "I promised myself that after Steve, the next time I have sex, I'd make love—that it would mean something."

"I can understand that. I think that's why Rob and I waited . . . well, at least a month," she says with a cheeky grin and a giggle.

"When you two finally had sex, what was it like?" Ali's eyes widen at my question. "Sorry, sorry." I say hastily. "I didn't mean to pry."

"No. It's not that. It's just . . . that's the first time that you've asked."

"I think I was too jealous to ask before," I say, knowing deep inside what I longed for was what Ali has with Rob.

"But you're not jealous now?" she asks, a singular eyebrow raised.

"No, I'm so happy for you I could burst. I like Rob, he's great, and he puts up with me, so he can't be bad."

"I feel the same about you with Jem. I know it's not been long, but I guess I expected that for you. When you found the right guy you'd melt, and I think you have."

"But Ali," I groan, feeling my tears come again. "I'm so out of my league. I don't know what to do, and now he's driving us to London." Ali gets up and closes her suitcase and puts it down by the door.

"What if I didn't like him? What if I said I only want *us* to go to London, what would you do then?" she asks, standing at the door with her hand on her hip. Her thoughts question me some more. *Would she send him away? Would she risk losing him just to spend time with me? Even though she seems completely melted by the guy.*

"I guess I'd ask him to give us our space . . . let us be girls."

Her stiffened posture softens, and I can see her eyes start to glisten with tears. "You would do that for me?" she asks, watching me with surprise.

"Of course I would," I say confidently, and I walk over and hug her. "You're my best friend. There isn't a man alive that could replace you."

"No man could replace you either," she says through the tears.

Wiping our faces, I pick up Ali's suitcase. "Come on, time for retail therapy," I say, and Ali nods as she checks herself in the mirror. "Actually Ali, one other question." She looks over at me while she puts on more lip gloss. "When we go shopping, why don't we go together?"

Ali just laughs and comes over to me. "I guess because I'm not very good at that bit of shopping . . . too selfish, maybe? Two great things can't always be together. They have to go their separate ways every now and then." I nod, understanding that it's not a bad thing that we don't exactly shop together. We just know what we like.

***

We stop at the open front door, watching Ali's mum chatting to Jem.

"So, you and Terry are going to London as well, then?"

"Yes. Terry is in the midst of opening a new club there. We'll be doing some final preparations this week."

"So, Terry's assistant . . . that's quite an honor. Looks like he pays well." Claudia nods towards Jem's car.

"Oh, it's just a rental. My car is in Scotland at my mother's place."

"Really, where in Scotland? My mother lives not far from Edinburgh—a place called Fife."

"Not far from Loch Ness." *Wow. Sara and Peter live just by Loch Ness in a really pretty cottage. I wonder if I get to meet Jem's mum while I'm there.*

"Mum, have you finished quizzing Jem now? We're wasting valuable shopping time." I quickly stand up straight, trying not to look like the eavesdropper that I am.

"Good Morning, Ali," Jem says as I step through the door and see Jem give Ali one of his amazing smiles.

Wow. He really is hot. I can't believe she hasn't slept with him. I bet he looks great naked. I quickly grab Ali's arm, pulling her out of her gawking.

"Err, yes. Good morning, Jem," Ali says, and looks at me a bit guiltily. Jem walks over next to me with a cheeky smile on his face.

"I'll put that in the boot with ours," he says, and his hand runs over mine as he takes Ali's suitcase from me. Hmm . . . he's hot, alright, I muse to myself, embracing the feel of his touch.

You're pretty hot yourself. Jem's thoughts whisper to me, making my smile grow even wider. Our hips quickly bump together and I suddenly remember we're not on our own.

"Thanks," I say, trying to act normal; Jem lets out a little chuckle and walks back over to the car.

I turn and face Claudia and Ali, who are staring at me. Oh my god, is it really that bad? Maybe I should have slept with him, then I wouldn't have all this staring.

"Well, Claudia, I guess this is goodbye for now," I say and give her a big hug.

"You take care of yourself and we'll see you at Christmas," she says, her eyes glistening with tears again. I make myself blink hard, trying desperately not to cry yet again.

"See you at Christmas," I say through the lump that's rising again in my throat. I let go and turn and head to the car. Jem holds the front passenger side door open for me and I shake my head.

"Let Ali sit in the front, she gets a bit travel sick in the back." He nods and runs around the other side and opens the driver's side door. I follow him 'round, wiping my face as tears start to escape.

"Are you going to be alright?" he asks as he passes me a tissue.

"Sure. I'm just not very good at goodbyes," I say, taking the tissue and dabbing around my eyes.

"It's not forever, Hope," he says, and he kisses me sweetly on the cheek.

"No. Not forever," I say with a sigh, and I slide myself into the back seat.

"Okay, Mum. I'll see you tomorrow," Ali shouts over her shoulder as she jogs to where Jem is standing holding the door open for her.

"Err, Ali, you might want to put your hair up," I say as I tap on the collapsed soft top of the car. "You don't want to do a Bridget Jones, do you?"

She looks between the collapsed roof and me. "Ah. Hell no," she says as she digs through her bag to find a hair band, and to both our surprise, Jem chuckles. "You've watched Bridget Jones?" Ali asks in a shriek of a voice. Jem nods, covering his mouth to stop from laughing again. *Oooh, he gets better by the minute. She'll definitely keep him if he likes movies; Hope watches a ton of them.*

We make our way through the village and up to the motorway. I sit and watch the familiar trees and houses whip by us in a blur. My eyes begin to sting as more tears form and I say goodbye to my old life.

It's not forever. You'll be back for Christmas. Jem's thoughts whisper into my mind.

Not forever, I reply, *but it feels like it. When I come back it will be different—I'll be different, even more so than what I am now.*

Ali sits and chats away to Jem like they've known each other for years, asking questions mainly about me, school, friends, and hobbies—everything. I shut my eyes and rest back into the seat; at least they're getting on, even if the topic of conversation is me. I slowly nod off, comforted by their friendly chatter.

***

I'm back in the Brail, at the edge of the wood—a place I haven't been to in years. I'm standing at the wooden gate that leads to a tiny cottage. I can feel myself frown as I look at the thatched roof and tiny windows. They're new and unbroken. The cottage I remember seeing in The Brail is abandoned and unloved; the roof is nearly all gone and the windows have all been smashed. It certainly doesn't look like this in reality, but for a dream, it's beautiful. It's delicate in its surroundings; it's almost magical how the flowers grow so happily in its little garden, making a colorful wave up to its wooden door.

The door opens as I step through the gate, and standing in the doorway is a beautiful woman. Her copper brown hair is tied up into a bun, and her skin is so gently bronzed that it glows in the sunlight. But her eyes . . . wow. They're green, but not a normal green that looks mossy; they're emerald green, bright and sparkling. She smiles as I walk toward her, stretching out her arms to embrace me. I gladly step into them, feeling the warmth and love of home.

"Are you ready to meet him?" the woman asks, her voice musical as she speaks.

"Lizzie, you know I am. I just wish I could have been here for the birth." I feel my lips move, but the voice that I hear isn't mine. It's softer than mine, and musical—the same as the woman's. She squeezes me tightly and then pulls back, studying me.

"You've been away for so long. I wondered if you could still sense me." My hand cups her face and I can feel a tear escape from my eye.

"I can always feel your presence, even when I must be away from you." Lizzie wipes the tear from my cheek.

"We won't always have to hide. One day, the elements will work together again, and our world will be in harmony once more."

"I fear it may be some time before that day comes."

"Until then, we shall keep them safe." Lizzie takes my hand and leads me into the little cottage.

An open fire is burning away in the wall of the open space; two wooden chairs sit on either side of it with a small crib between them. Inside the crib, a small bundle of blankets wriggles and releases an arm from the binds of the cloth; the arm stretches out toward me. The tuft of hair on his head is copper and bronze toned—the same as Lizzie's—and his eyes are green, although they're not as bright as his mother's.

"He's been waiting for you," she says as she stands next to me, watching adoringly into the crib. "We've named him Robert." The "we" in her sentence startles me and I look around the space and glance out the window. "He's still in the North, fighting alongside the Sabbath." The father is a soldier and is fighting alongside the witches. My heart sinks to my stomach; a clutching pain tells me that the father won't return. "It's alright, Eleanor. Robert and I will meet again in the afterlife. That's why he brought me here and built this house. To keep us safe from the war, so that our son could live in peace." She's talking to Mum. Is Lizzie her twin?

As if to answer my question, Lizzie takes my hand and the two hands together glow warmly, the comfort of home running through into my soul. Little Robert laughs from his crib, and his hands reach to catch the glow. Instinctively, I reach down into the crib and pick him up. He nestles into my long hair as if he had been doing so since he was born; cradling him comfortably in one arm, Lizzie and I join hands again and let Robert join his touch to our glow. He watches, mesmerized by its brightness, and then looks back at me. His eyes glisten with tears as he lets go of our hands and places his hand over my heart.

"Not yet, Robert," Mum says softly to him. I take my hand from Lizzie and let Robert grasp a single finger in this chubby, creased hand. His hand glows, but only slightly. "Only your twin will glow as bright as your mum, but you will have to be patient." The baby in my arms nods. Can he really understand? He looks no more than a couple months old. But yet for his size, he carries his head and understands what we say. Is this how "witchy" children are? Advanced in intelligence compared to their age? I don't think I was like that. Dad said Mum had been teaching me.

"He has his father's gift already," Lizzie says, her voice a little afraid.

"Already?" Mum asks, her voice just as afraid as Lizzie's. Lizzie nods and turns to the table, lifting up the blackened kettle. Inside, the water is clear.

"I haven't filled the kettle since he was born; it's always full. Always ready to boil." I shut my eyes tightly, letting the heavy tears flood from my eyes. When I open them again, the cottage is different—brighter. The crib by the fire is gone.

"Auntie E! Auntie E!" a little voice cries from the garden, and then little footsteps thunder to the door. The door is flung open as a little boy runs and jumps into my arms. "Auntie E," his little arms hold tightly around my neck, "I've missed you."

"And I have missed you, little Robert." Holding the child close to me, I stroke his cropped, curly copper hair and breathe in his scent. It's not woodsy or flowery, but clean, like clear spring water—refreshing. I close my eyes again, memorizing the smell of the refreshing water.

When I open them again, I'm standing at the gate. The cottage is no longer looking so new with its greying thatched roof and peeling window frames.

"Auntie E, come and see," the little boy older than before shouts, his eyes now as sparkling emerald green as his mother's. His hair is cut short again, and the waves of bronze and copper shimmer in the sunlight. His figure is now slim but healthy, and his cheeks are glowing red as he waves breathlessly at me, encouraging me to follow him. I run after him, intrigued by what he has to show me.

Robert runs around the back of the house and along the pathway between the pens for the pigs and chickens. He runs past the fences where the wood begins to thicken, and then he stops, looking down over a large hole. I stop next to him, holding onto his shoulder and stopping him from falling into the hole.

"The water is coming to me. I could hear it running toward the house. When it stopped, I dug this hole." He looks up at me, his eyes wide with excitement and fear.

"Robert, you must be careful what you draw to you. It might not always be safe." He bows his head, saddened by Mum's words. My hand rubs his back as Mum tries to reassure him. "It is very clever of you to do this. The power within you is very strong." I feel my body sigh. "Just promise that you will always be careful." Robert's head nods as he wraps his small arm around my waist.

"Yes, Auntie E, I promise." I bend down and kiss the top of his bronzed curls, gently closing my eyes as a tear escapes from my closed lids.

When I open my eyes, again the scene has changed. Robert is not near me. I can't hear him or see him. I'm standing at the gate, hesitating to move towards the door. Fear runs through me as I look up at the cottage; the garden is deadly brown. The once-colorful wave of flowers lies limp and dull. The windows are covered in mud and dust, and the thatch is now so beyond grey that it's black. The sky above is dark in charcoal greys and heavy purples. Although I sense it is not night, the sky is preparing for a storm—a heavy storm. I clap my hands over my face, my fear shaking me so strongly that I crumble to the ground.

TEASER:
Finding Hope – London, England

We push through the door, hastily trying to escape the heavy downpour. An old bell rings as the door slams shut. I take in a deep breath of one of my favourite smells—old bookshops. Not a WHSmith or a Borders, but an old bookshop. The smell of paper and ink is the smell that makes me think of endless knowledge—where dreams are made and places are found--where the subconscious can roam freely. Out of the corner of my eye, I see Jem screw up his face. To each their own, I guess.

"Good afternoon." The greying gentleman behind the counter greets us. His soft smile wrinkles his entire face. "Are you looking for something in particular?"

"Yes. I wanted to get some books on France, site seeing and such like, and I was wondering what Jane Austen novels you have." The gentleman steps out from around the counter and I follow him into the far corner of the shop, leaving Jem near the front door to look at some books on sale.

"This section here is 'France,'" he says as he runs his finger along the middle shelf. "And the Jane Austen books are over there." He points to a row of shelves on the other side of the shop.

"Thank you," I say with a smile, and he smiles back and then turns, making his way back to his counter.

Finding several interesting books on France, and more specifically, the south of France, I decide on taking only two. Kirk and Louise don't have any books on where we're staying, but they live there most of the time, so I wouldn't expect them to. Tucking the two books under my arm, I follow the shelves along to where the man had directed me for the Jane Austen books. I was hoping to get a copy of *Pride and Prejudice*; I've seen several versions of it in movies

195

or on the telly, but I'd never read it, and thought it would be a good book to take with me while I'm travelling.

I hear the old bell ring as the door slams shut again. Focusing on the titles on the spines of the books, I don't notice a long, white finger running along the shelf from the other way.

"Ar, *Pride and Prejudice*," says the most musical, charming voice I think I have ever heard. The white hand rests on mine—a cold, hard hand. I look into the eyes of its owner. They're the darkest brown eyes I think I have ever seen. The boy (he looks about the same age as me) is deadly pale, but somehow glorious with his hair roughly cropped, the copper and bronze tones shimmering amongst the brown waves. His smile is crooked as he looks back at me. "Sorry, cold hands," he says, and he takes his hand away from mine. An intense rush of warmth runs back into my hand and I stretch out my fingers, the bones cracking from the sudden coldness.

"You must have a warm heart." His smile quickly fades as I rub my hands together. His expressions is now so sad; I wish I could reassure him—take his hand and share the warmth of mine—but he tucks them behind his back. He is trying to force a smile, but is struggling.

"Did you find it?" says a girl from behind him. I feel my mouth pop open; her voice is just as charming as his, only maybe sweeter— like the sound of a wind chime. Her complexion, which is nearly as pale as his, has a subtle pink that sits in her cheeks, and her hair is long and wavy and chocolate brown with the same bronze streaks as the boy. She smiles at me in a friendly manner, and I notice her eyes are the strangest color I have ever seen. Like mine, they are brown, but where mine used to have hints of purple, hers have what looks like shards of a ruby—fiery, almost.

"Yes," the boy answers as he takes the book from the shelf.

"Excellent," she says, taking the book from his hands. They both smile and nod. Then, turning around, they walk back to the front of the shop.

Blinking hard, I pull my mind out of its stunned trance. *Wow. That felt really weird.* I turn back to the shelf, looking at the gap where the copy of *Pride and Prejudice* once was. I let out a long sigh; they've taken the only copy. I'll have to get a copy another time. And with that, I walk back to the front of the shop where I had left Jem.